Blood on the Bayou

A Miranda Marquette Mystery

J.T. Kunkel

Published by Taylor and Seale Publishing, LLC
3408 South Atlantic Avenue
Unit 139
Daytona Beach Shores, FL 32118

Cover design and layout by WhiteRabbitGraphix.com

Publisher's Note: This is a work of fiction. Names, characters, places, and incidents are a product of the author's imagination or used fictitiously. Locales and public names are sometimes used fictitiously for atmospheric purposes. With the exception of public figures or specific historical references, any resemblance to actual people, living or dead, or to businesses, companies, events, institutions, or locales is completely coincidental. Any historical personages or actual events depicted are completely fictionalized and used only for inspiration. Any opinions expressed are completely those of fictionalized characters and not a reflection of the views of public figures, author, or publisher.

Dedication

I dedicate this work to Susan, the Love of my life. You have worked for years to make one family out of two. While it hasn't always been easy, you have been the glue that has held all of us together. I will never forget all the selfless efforts you made through the years, seeking no reward, just to make others happy. I will Love You forever.

Blood on the Bayou

Chapter 1

Spring 2007

I finished typing my latest blog entry as my blackberry rang. I didn't recognize the number flashing across the screen. I said a prayer and pressed the answer button, bracing myself for another complaint call from a provider that I rejected or an angry patient whose surgery didn't go as planned. Who knew that a blog about my plastic surgery journey would turn into a booming business in just three years? Soon, my recommendation of a plastic surgeon was akin to an author getting on the Oprah Book Club. After six months, I had so many daily hits on my site that I decided to try selling advertising to generate income. As it turned out, physicians had no problem paying me a percentage of their fee to increase their market share. I'd like to take all the credit, but in some ways, I was just in the right place at the right time.

When I started my plastic surgery journey, I never would have anticipated such drastic changes in my life. After being shot in the face while on duty with the State Police in North Carolina several years ago, I needed multiple surgeries. The circumstances of the shooting left questions about the orders that had sent me into harm's way without backup. In the end, a sharp old attorney settled for a nice bundle on my behalf and I walked away from police work forever.

"Hello? Is anyone there?"

Startled, I realized I hadn't yet spoken into my Blackberry, so in a forced professional tone, I said, "Miranda Marquette speaking, how may I help you?" I cringed at the feedback of my voice echoing back at me; it always came out higher when I spoke on the phone. Sometimes I worried that the person on the other end thought I was fourteen rather than thirty-three.

A woman with a vaguely familiar accent asked, "Miranda? Is that you?"

My heart lurched. The voice took me back to a safer place and time, but I still couldn't place it. My mouth went dry. "Yes, it is, and who am I speaking to?" I knew I sounded distracted, and I was. My shrink told me I needed to work on staying in the moment.

The woman sounded taken aback by my dismissive tone. "Wow . . . I knew you had stepped up in the world, but I didn't think you would have forgotten me, *mon amie*."

The realization clicked, and I exclaimed, "Sabine!" My eyes widened, and so did my grin. "It's been so long.*"*

She laughed and clicked her tongue with pretend disapproval. "Remember, for every day I didn't visit you, there's a day you didn't visit me."

I chuckled. "I get it. The road goes both ways." Then I sobered. "Hey, is everything okay? I haven't heard from you in a while."

"Does something have to be a matter for me to call my favorite cousin?" She forced a laugh.

"Well, the last time you called it was because hurricane Katrina came through, and the two times before that were to tell me about Grandpapa Marquette's dementia and then to invite me to his funeral." I tapped my nails against the desk in apprehension.

She sighed. "Which you didn't attend."

"Did you call me to rehash the reasons I couldn't be there?"

"No, no. I'm sorry. I understand you had your own problems."

I drew a deep breath. I loved my cousin, but sometimes . . . "So how are you, and where are you?"

"Things have been better, but I can get into it later." Her voice took on a more hopeful tone, and she said, "I'm actually in town, and I'd love to get together."

Her revelation floored me. "No Way! Miss 'I will never step foot on the West Coast' is here? How did that happen?"

I could tell she was scowling the way she did when we were kids. "Well, smarty pants . . ."

Ha! She only called me that before begrudgingly complimenting me.

"You know how you have always told me I needed to get in touch with the fishing community if I ever wanted to expand the business?" Her voice sounded smaller and less confident than usual.

"Yeah?" I said, pressing my blackberry to my ear with my shoulder so I could type in the tags and publish the post before something happened and I had to rewrite everything.

"Well, I listened to you." She laughed but sounded serious. I held my 'I told you so' and let her continue uninterrupted. "I've become part of an online community of shrimp fishermen worldwide, and their annual convention is in L. A. this year, so I wanted to see if you had time to get together."

Sabine took over our grandfather's shrimping business after his diagnosis and moved downriver from Meraux to Venice, Louisiana to be closer to the shrimp in the Gulf. That was a smart move, but she still had a lot to learn. I was glad to hear she took my advice about expanding her knowledge base. It was the least I could do to repay her for her guidance during my formative years.

"I can't wait. Do you want to drive up to Malibu, or do you want me to meet you down there somewhere?" I was thrilled she'd be visiting; I saw her as the big sister I never had. "Of course, I'd love for you to see the house, but I don't want you to get too jealous." I made a face before remembering she couldn't see me.

"I thought you'd never ask, *mon amour!*" I could hear the excitement in her voice as she said, "I'd love to see it, and I can't wait to see *you.*"

"I can't wait to see you either." I was practically jumping with excitement myself. "When do you think you'll be coming by?"

In typical Sabine fashion, she said, "I would hope so, my dear! How does tonight work for you? Around seven?"

"How about six? I'll cook dinner," I suggested. "I hope my cooking skills can still impress your delicate French palate." I laughed at my joke, thinking about all the intense spices they used back home.

"I'll be the judge of that," she threw back at me laughing. Then she said, "Yeah, that sounds great!" Her voice took on a sour note of disapproval. "The food at this conference leaves a bit to be desired. See you at six!" I heard a click, and then she was gone.

I set the phone on my desk, closed my brick of a laptop, swiveled in my desk chair to survey my living room, and gasped at the mess. To the untrained eye, it wouldn't look like much of a mess at all. However, I knew the books were out of place, blankets and pillows were askew, and I swore I could see a few crumbs strewn across the carpet. All I cared about was making everything completely spotless, regardless of whatever magazine on my end table that got caught in the crossfire.

When I finished vacuuming the russet brown carpet, I flopped on the couch and exhaled deeply, trying to settle my racing heart. Speed cleaning should be an Olympic sport—it was utterly exhausting. The calming breaths I took didn't help much; I was going crazy with anticipation. I hadn't seen Sabine in five years and that I barely remember. I was still in the hospital, my head and face wrapped in bandages. Another lifetime ago. Suddenly, I felt guilty for not going back home much. The last couple of times I went back, I blew in and out of town after a quick dinner with my mom and stepdad. As far as my dad went, I hadn't seen him since my parents got divorced when I was thirteen.

I mulled over what I would make for Sabine and tried to remember what I had in my kitchen, groaning when I realized that I was severely lacking anything remotely resembling a full meal, except perhaps for the several bottles of Cabernet Sauvignon in my wine cellar. If my housekeeper were around, I'd have asked her to pick something up for me, but her husband was ill, so I told her to take the week off. I snatched my keys off the coffee table and then scrambled around for a few minutes looking for my purse, not realizing I'd hung it up while cleaning. Eventually, I found stashed it in the downstairs closet, after wasting precious time lifting the same three pillows over and over.

With my purse slung over my arm, I sped out the door and climbed into the red convertible waiting in my garage. A few minutes later, I pulled into the Pavilions. I parked as close to the entrance as I could. Luckily at 2:30, I was only competing with retirees and stay-at-home moms for a parking spot. I started a mental shopping list while I speed-walked toward the door.

"What do you cook for someone who grew up in France? It's like the cooking capital of the world," I muttered. "I bet she's tired of shrimp by now, so that's out . . . what's left?"

Suddenly, the only recipes I could think of involved shrimp as the main ingredient. As I passed through the sliding doors, the fans, meant to keep bugs out, hit me with a blast of air, and I had to run a hand through my hair to make it lay flat again.

As I scanned the signs atop each of the aisles, my eyes landed on the produce section and inspiration hit me in the face.

"Where are we? California." I clapped my hands and laughed to myself. "What do Californians eat? California Cuisine!"

A woman passing by gave me a strange look as if she'd never seen someone talking to herself. I smiled at her and pushed my cart over to the leafy greens and scooped up plenty of salad makings—romaine, butter lettuce, fresh spinach, and some kale for good measure. Before leaving the section, I picked up avocados and a bag of chopped walnuts. I also grabbed the ingredients for a spicy dressing. Growing up in the Big Easy meant food wasn't food unless it had some spice.

Before going to the checkout, I stopped at the meat counter for some fresh organic ocean-caught salmon. I carried the groceries out to the car, leaving the cart near the front door. After sliding into the front seat, I took a moment to lower the roof.

I headed up the Pacific Coast Highway, or PCH as the locals call it, which was my favorite way to go home. I loved it because if I looked to the left, I could see crystal waters glistening in the sun, tiny sailboats on the horizon, and crying gulls circling the beaches in search of an unsuspecting beach-goer's lunch. If I looked to the right, I saw gorgeous homes sitting on the hilltop. I'm still not used to it, and I hope I never am. The ocean views, the smell of the air, the laid-back feeling—even though it's not that far from bustling LA, it was like night and day.

I pulled into my gated driveway and raised the roof again as I pulled up to the garage doors. I gathered my groceries and took a moment to admire the exterior of my home, with its light orange stucco walls and the delicate white accents. I adored my house; it had everything I ever dreamed of in a home, including a gourmet kitchen with French doors opening to a large deck that ran the whole width of the house, overlooking the Pacific. The view spoke to me when I first walked into the house—but the high vaulted ceilings sealed the deal.

I could have been happy in my kitchen all day, chopping veggies, and marinating salmon, but I didn't have all day. By the time I finished the preparations, it was already 4:30 and I had yet to shower and figure out what to do with my hair, put on some semblance of makeup, and get dressed. I set down the paring knife and looked down at my clothes. My everyday wear of jeans and a t-shirt wouldn't do. I guessed Sabine wouldn't dress to the nines to see me, but since she was there for a conference, I wasn't entirely sure, and I didn't want to feel underdressed in my own home.

I ran up the stairs to my bedroom ever aware that time was ticking by and opened the closet. A dress was an easy way to look put together without much effort on my part. However, it was usually windy in the evenings, and I was hoping to hang out with Sabine on the deck that served as my backyard. I decided to go with an in-between look by wearing light jeans and a dark blue blouse paired with gold gladiator sandals. I laid out my clothes on the bed and headed to the bathroom.

After letting the water warm up for a minute or two, I climbed into the glass shower, letting the water run on my hair before lathering it with shampoo.

I glanced at my alarm clock when I got out and had been in the shower for ten minutes which was five minutes longer than I could afford, but at least I didn't have anything on the stove yet. Luckily my flat iron worked on wet hair, so I didn't have to eat up a lot of time by blow-drying my long hair.

After I finished doing my hair, I moved on to getting my makeup done. As I did that, always self-conscious of the fine scar lines, I thought about Sabine and how she *always* looked great no matter what she wore. I struggled for years trying to compete with her. It didn't help that she always seemed far more mature than I was, despite the three-year difference. Everything just seemed so effortless for her, while I barely managed to look half as good as she did. I wondered what she would think of the new me.

When we were in high school, because we were in different grades and never in the same classes, it was easy to avoid being around my drop-dead gorgeous cousin. When I was a gawky freshman and she a prom queen junior, I chose to go Goth. I didn't feel pretty, so I preferred having a look that put people off. I didn't get asked out much except by scary-looking guys and geeks and when I said no, it seemed to add to my mystique. People weren't sure if I was a snob or just had particular tastes. What they didn't know was that I was scared to death. On the other hand, Sabine wore mini-skirts and mixed with the cool crowd. Boys and girls, everyone loved her.

As soon as boys started looking at me like that, I made sure it wouldn't happen again. That was what drew me to the law enforcement field. Since it was a career that traditionally attracted males, I figured I would be one of the guys. That didn't quite work out; I didn't realize most male/female partners end up either dating, hating each other, or both. I ended up living with mine even though he was twenty years my senior. But, eventually the age difference and the stress of a law enforcement lifestyle was too much for me to handle. My shrink always said it was because of unresolved issues with my dad. She was probably right.

I carefully pulled my shirt over my head to avoid messing up my hair and makeup. I ended up facing my nightstand and I let out a gasp as I caught sight of my alarm clock. It was already 5:45 and I hadn't even started the salmon. My sandals slapped on the kitchen tiles as I raced in to finish up. Knowing Sabine, I figured she'd be early, but with any luck, LA traffic would be on my side for once. I quickly got out a pan and threw in some oil, placed the salmon skin-side down and allowed it to crisp.

Once that was done, I stepped into the hall to look at myself in my floor-length mirror and to double check that I wasn't going overboard. I decided I looked good but not too good, which was what I was aiming at because the last thing I wanted was to turn things into a competition; I knew I'd lose. Ever since the reconstructive surgery, I'd been self-conscious about my appearance. That was something my therapist and I had been working on. That and my distinct lack of interest in having a relationship with a man. I'd have my fun when I did the two-year criminal justice program at college in North Carolina. After that, I was recruited by the police and there I stayed for six years until . . .

The doorbell rang and brought me out of my thoughts. I quickly ran into the kitchen to flip the fish and then raced down the stairs two at a time, wishing at that moment the house was just a bit smaller. I made it to the door as the bell rang a second time.

I opened the door and managed to puff out, "Sabine!"

She chuckled as I worked to catch my breath. "I knew you would be excited to see me, *mon amour,* but I don't want you having a coronary."

"Come in, come in! You look *fab*ulous!" I laughed and took a few breaths before saying it. I was secretly hoping that she'd begun to look older than me by now, but no. Quite the opposite; at thirty-six, she looked younger than me. "Oh, speaking of having a coronary, my salmon is about to burn!" I turned and dashed back up the stairs.

"Do you want me to lock the door?" she asked.

"Yeah, thanks," I called over my shoulder. "And then you can make yourself at home in the living room."

I heard the click of Sabine's heels as she followed me and her impressed whistle as she reached the top of the stairs. I grinned, but then picked up speed as the smell of smoke began to waft out at me from the kitchen. I made it to the stove just as ugly black smoke was starting to billow up from the pan. I quickly grabbed a spatula and put the salmon on my cutting board before the fire could ruin the filet.

Sabine called, "Did you make it?"

"Yeah, it's fine. It just gives new meaning to the phrase 'crisped salmon,'" I called back as I dropped the blackened pan into the sink.

"I'm not surprised; you always were a firecracker!" I heard her chuckling.

I playfully tossed back, "It takes one to know one!" Then I left the salmon to cool and walked into the living room to join her. "Do you want to eat out on the deck or in the dining room?"

Her jaw dropped as I came around the corner and she finally got a good look at me, "Who the heck *are* you and what have you done with Miranda?"

Before I could say anything, she added, "I wasn't sure what to expect after everything you went through. That must have been horrible."

"I'm still working through it. My shrink says it's post-traumatic stress disorder. But, most days I'm just happy to be alive."

She paused for a moment, looking a little uncomfortable, then said, "Anyway, you look wonderful!"

"You saw me when I answered the door," I chuckled, trying to lighten up the moment, and reached for a hug.

"Barely, before you flew up the steps to rescue dinner." She hugged me for a moment and then stepped back to inspect me. I spun around, and she continued to gape to the point of leaning close to examine my face. "When I last saw you all wrapped in bandages, I had no idea how amazing the outcome would be. Who would have thought you could turn into such a beauty queen!"

I'd never sent photos to my family, afraid of how they'd react to the changes. I pulled her close again and said, "Thanks." I pushed back the tears momentarily reliving the scariest days of my life. She held me at arm's length. The look on her face told me she noticed my tears, but she didn't comment. She kept it light. "Nice digs by the way. You've done good, kid!"

Someday I would tell Sabine about everything, but this wasn't the time. I replied with another heartfelt, "thanks," and then changed the subject. "Do you want anything to drink?"

"How about some of that famous California wine everyone is always raving about?" She asked, setting her purse on the couch. "I sure could use some."

"How does red sound?" I offered, hoping she'd jump on the Cabernet Sauvignon train with me.

"Sounds great!" She grinned, and I did a mental arm pump of victory.

"Come to the kitchen with me and I'll get you a glass." I beckoned. "We can catch up a little while we're waiting for the salmon to cool since I'm planning to put it on salad."

I picked two large wine glasses and filled them with my favorite cabernet. Then I led Sabine onto the deck.

"Wow, what a view," she said with a sigh as she sat down in one of my wicker chairs gazing out on the Pacific. "I could use a view like this when I get up in the morning."

"Sometimes I miss the sight of the mist drifting and the fireflies dancing across the muddy river water back home," I replied, taking the seat opposite her and wrapping my cardigan around my body to keep out the marine wind.

She took a sip from her glass. "I guess you heard I moved down to Venice, so my commute wouldn't be so long. I was spending all my time on the road after I moved the operation. Granted, there's not much going on down there, but I don't really have a social life anyway." She set her glass down on the table between us. "Shrimping is my life now, for better or for worse."

I laughed. "I'll bet you still have those shrimpers coming after you like they always did. You certainly always did know how to put them in their places, though." I took a deep sip as well.

We sat in silence for a while, staring at the ocean and watching the sun make its final descent below the horizon. I could tell she was working up the nerve to tell me something, but I wasn't in a rush; the ocean always made me feel peaceful and grounded. I was also subconsciously avoiding the conversation for as long as I could; I didn't want to ruin the moment.

My cousin tried to make her voice sound deep and impressive like a CEO in the Board Room. "You're probably wondering why I called you all here." She started laughing halfway through; typical Sabine, always trying to lighten the mood by making terrible jokes.

I laughed too. "I was, but I figured you'd get to it eventually."

She closed her eyes as if she was trying to think of the right place to start. After a few moments, she asked, "Do you remember when the doctors diagnosed Grandpapa with dementia?"

I nodded, trying to hold back a new set of guilt-riddled tears. By the time I got down to see him, Grandpapa had no idea who I was. "It must have been horrible to watch him going downhill like that."

She looked down at her hands. "He was well on the way to killing the business and I couldn't bear for him to sell it to someone outside the family." She sighed. "He got plenty of offers, but they were all too low to even consider. When he made me an offer three years ago, I bought him out. Well, he pretty much gave it to me, but I needed to invest my own capital in the business almost immediately because I figured out pretty quickly that I needed to expand or I'd be bankrupt within a year."

She paused briefly, and then continued. "Grandpapa believed in the more traditional method of shrimping in the riverbeds." She turned to me. "I'm not sure how much you remember about how it all works, but river shrimping is a seasonal activity governed by the locals along the river. It only occurs during the summer months."

She paused to take a sip of cabernet, and then continued, "However, shrimping in the Gulf is a year-round activity, and the Federal Government only loosely governs it. They don't have a lot of time to pay attention to us because they have other problems. They mostly monitor how we're protecting sea turtles."

The more Sabine drank, the grander her gestures became. "We don't want to get in trouble with the Feds and, quite honestly, never bother the turtles!" She thumped on my glass table so hard, I cringed, hoping it wouldn't break. I considered taking the glass away from her; if she was that worked up about turtles, who knew what she'd do by the time she got to the point. But I kept my concerns to myself.

"Anyway, with the three boats we have, we have been doing pretty well." She struggled to regain her laid-back demeanor. "I'm not sure if you knew, but we bought out two smaller shrimping companies. The owners got older, and their children decided not to continue operations."

"Wow, that's great." I was impressed.

She smiled, but there was still a small furrow between her brows. "Anyway, things have been going pretty well. We've had the typical issues: turnover, bad employees, petty theft and of course, Katrina."

"I was glad you called after Katrina pushed through," I said. "I was worried sick that something happened to you."

She nodded. "We were really fortunate. The boats were all in dry dock out in Hackberry, just east of the Texas border, getting overhauled for the fall season. Luckily, they didn't take a direct hit. I was renting a house and dock-space at the time, so I had no financial loss, and I was the first one ready to do business when there were docks rebuilt to tie up to." She looked out at the ocean, but I could tell that her mind was in another time. She whispered, "Yes, I was lucky."

I felt terrible how out of touch that I had been with everyone. All I could say was, "You've always been the lucky one."

"Yeah, me and your parents." She paused and retracted at her gaff. "I mean your Mom and stepdad . . . theirs was like one of five houses in Meraux that wasn't obliterated. It was eerie walking around the old neighborhood with all that destruction and rebuilding going on with their house looking as if the storm had never hit." She shook her head and shuddered, then asked, "How are your parents doing anyway? I haven't seen them since I moved."

I bit my lip. "Um, I haven't seen them in a while."

"You had better get out there, Miranda" she scolded. "Have you even been back since Katrina?"

The only thing I'd done was call them as soon as I'd heard. I felt guilty about not going to help, but I told myself that my own recovery was still too recent and I couldn't face more pain by seeing the destruction of the places where I grew up.

I looked at the floor feeling like the ten-year-old I was when Sabine and I first met. "Um, nope."

She gasped and muttered, "*L'enfant est gâté.*"

Frowning, I said, "I am not a child, and I am certainly not spoiled!"

She gestured around, and I sighed in resignation. She pushed her dark brown mane behind her right ear and crossed her legs. "I know you are busy, *ma chère,* but you need to get back there." I nodded absently and she continued, "Well if I have my way, maybe you can kill two birds with one stone." She smiled and winked, then continued, "Okay, let's get to the point."

Finally! I thought but didn't say it aloud.

"I'm in trouble," then she added, "well, I'm not in trouble yet, but I'm going to be if I don't get this figured out."

I leaned forward in my chair. "I thought you said things were going pretty well?"

She nodded. "Things have been going great—until now, that is."

"What changed?" I asked, intrigued.

She placed her glass on the table and leaned forward. "I recently secured a contract with Costco to buy all the shrimp I can catch at a premium rate."

"That's great," I commended her.

"Yes, except almost immediately after getting that contract, my volume started to dive. "Two months ago, we were averaging over a thousand pounds per day per boat. Some days we would take as much as twenty-five hundred, so I was conservative when I guaranteed Costco at least twenty-two hundred and fifty pounds per week in my contract. That's only seven-hundred and fifty per boat per week."

"That doesn't sound too bad," I said, trying to cover up that I'd wiped most of the information about the shrimping industry from my memory.

"Yeah well," she continued. "Since I signed the contract, my take has been less than five hundred pounds per boat, some days less than two-hundred!" She threw up her hands with a groan and leaned back in her chair again. Then she gripped the edge of the chair and slid herself forward. "I'm technically not in trouble with them yet because my contractual obligation is based on a three-month average, but if this continues, they will drop me." Her voice took on a frustrated tone. "Miranda, this contract was a game-changer for me! At twelve hundred per day, I'd be grossing close to three million dollars a year. That's ten times what I grossed my first year in the business. What's worse, is my business can't survive at this volume even selling locally at wholesale *or* retail. It just isn't enough volume to be profitable."

I could tell her rant was winding down, and I got increasingly anxious the closer she seemed to get to her point.

She paused. "This is where you come in."

I would have liked it if Sabine had come solely for a social visit, but my gut told me she needed something. But after all she had done for me over the years, it was only fair.

"Okay," I said, intrigued.

"I believe there is foul play going on." She crossed her arms.

"Can't it just be a coincidence?" I asked. "Something to do with global warming?"

"Right when I got the Costco contract?" She glowered and shook her head. "It's fairly predictable how long it'll take to get the greatest amount of shrimp out of a bed before we move on to the next one. Lately, we're depleting the beds in about half the time that we would expect."

She stood up and looked out at the Pacific. For a moment, everything was silent, and all we could hear was the ebb and flow of the waves down on the beach.

She turned to me and said, "I believe that someone is informing a competitor where we are finding the shrimp, allowing my competitor to fish them in the off-hours, thereby depleting the potential catch quickly. They may also be selling shrimp out the back door to a competitor after catching them."

I frowned. "Can't you just go back out to where you fished, after hours, to see if someone else is fishing there?"

She gave me a look that told me she'd already thought about it. "It's not illegal or even a bad business practice to shrimp where someone else has recently been. Law enforcement couldn't do a thing, even if I did find a competitor out there. It's also very dangerous; bad things happen out there at night, especially when someone doesn't want to be discovered. That's why I need you. I don't have the money or the inclination to hire a private investigator, and I'm losing more every day." She sat back down and looked me in the eye. "I need you to be my eyes and ears for a while in Venice. I know you worked undercover back when you were a cop, so you've got experience. No one knows you down there especially the '*new*' you."

"Why me, Sabine?" I leaned back and crossed my arms and legs. "I'm sure you know plenty of people in the area who could help."

"I don't." She shrugged and said, "You are my last resort."

"Thanks for the vote of confidence," I exclaimed.

She looked a little more relaxed now that she'd finished her pitch.

My cousin rolled her eyes. "You know what I mean, *mon amour*."

"You think you can just speak French and I will fold just like when I was little." I crossed my arms. "Well, let me tell you, I've got responsibilities here, and I just don't know if I can drop everything." I protested too much.

"Miranda, the little I know about your business is that you can operate it from anywhere, isn't that true?" She grinned, and I knew she'd caught me. She could sell gator-skinned boots to a gator. "Come on, sweetheart, don't make me beg!"

"Well, I suppose . . ." I paused and took a deep breath, "Okay, all right, I'll do it."

She squealed with excitement. "I knew you'd help!" Louisiana was the last place on earth that I wanted to be. As she jumped up and kissed me on both cheeks, I had a sinking feeling that I'd made a deal with the devil in high heels.

Chapter 2

The doorbell rang, and I glared at my alarm clock. *"Oh my gosh, it's nine o'clock already!"* I rubbed my eyes, stretched, and hopped out of bed all in one motion.

"Coming!" I threw on some running shorts and a t-shirt, dragged a brush through my hair, and ran for the door.

There stood Heather, my assistant, all five foot two and one hundred pounds of her. She looked me up and down and laughed. "Did you oversleep again?"

I turned and leaped up the stairs two at a time. Over my shoulder, I yelled, "Guilty as charged! Make some coffee; there's some of that cinnamon swirl bread you love so much in the bread drawer."

I gasped as I reached my room--suitcases and clothes were strewn everywhere. Sabine hadn't given me any indication how long I'd be gone, so I figured I'd better pack heavy. I took a deep breath as I meandered back to my bed and sat down, collecting my thoughts. First things first, I needed to shower and make myself presentable. While I adored Heather, I was still her boss, so I wanted to maintain a little more dignity than I had shown when I answered the door.

After surviving the obstacle course from the bed to my bedroom door, I ran back to the second-floor landing so Heather could hear me when I yelled down. "I'm gonna hop in the shower. Are you okay for a few minutes?" The house needed an intercom.

Heather laughed from the kitchen. "Believe me, I have lots to do, and I'll have plenty of questions for you when you come down."

The hot water running over my head and down my body was ecstasy. As my therapist had suggested for combatting my occasional bouts with anxiety, I focused on making my mind go blank and enjoying the sensation. Since accepting Sabine's challenge to investigate her business issue, I broke out in a cold sweat every time I started to formulate a plan. It was no coincidence that the last time I headed up an investigation, I was shot three times and nearly died.

With that thought, I shivered while I dried myself off, my hot shower just a memory. *Note to self: Turn down the air conditioning.* There was no time to blow-dry my hair, so I tied it back and hoped for the best. I slapped a little makeup on, and I was good to go. After all, I hadn't seen Sabine in years and I saw Heather yesterday, so I wasn't quite as particular. I searched through my walk-in closet for something suitable to wear. I decided on a pink and white flowered sundress. I stood back and looked at the full-length mirror. Even after all these years since the surgery, I was still getting used to my face. "Stop over-thinking, Miranda," I said out loud as I headed downstairs.

Heather, looking like a college student in cutoffs and a Bon Jovi t-short, sat at the kitchen island on one of my leather stools, concentrating on the screen of her laptop. "Can you believe this? I just got an email from a woman who got a nose job through one of our referral plastic surgeons. She wants to sue us for pain and suffering." I groaned and rolled my eyes as she continued. "Her husband left her for a younger woman with a bigger nose. Now she blames *us* because her nose is too small."

I went to the fridge for some fresh-squeezed orange juice. "Thank God for attorneys. They wrote a nifty waiver that absolves us from any risk related to the use of our services. This one's obviously outrageous, but we've had people sue us for malpractice along with the doctor when a procedure went wrong.

While I certainly feel bad for them, we can't be held responsible for individual doctor performance." I strolled over to the wall of windows overlooking the Pacific, sighed and slid open the door to the deck. "I'm gonna miss this view."

Heather grimaced as she breathed in the rush of salt-sea air. "I'm going to miss *you*, boss."

I patted her arm, hoping my touch would give her some confidence even if I wasn't feeling that way. "You'll do fine without me," I struggled to sound positive.

Heather went back to her screen, and I poured myself some coffee. "Want some more?" I asked her, holding up the pot.

Heather jumped up with her cup. "I'd *love* some! Thanks."

I leaned over the opposite side of the island, resting on my elbows as she sat back down. "So, what other questions did you have?"

"Do you have the house stuff written down anywhere? When the housekeeper comes in, your vet's number in case the cats or horses get sick, stuff like that."

I snickered. "Oh, you mean the kind of stuff that you already take care of for me?"

She nervously twisted her hair in a ring around her finger. "Well, yeah, kind of, but you're usually here to help me find what I need. Now you're going to be gone, like uh, forever. So, I'll need a source other than you, so I'm not emailing or messaging you every five minutes."

I thought for a second. "Well, no, it's not all in one place, but I'll get it to you before I leave. I *promise.*"

Heather chuckled. "You'd better, or I'll be out in New Orleans hunting you down." She looked thoughtful. "Okay, now that we have that out of the way, when do you want me to move in?"

I hesitated.

She looked inquisitively at me, and then after a few seconds, mumbled, "I guess I'll wait until you go." She broke eye contact with me, and I immediately regretted, inadvertently giving her the message that I wasn't sure about her moving in. I desperately wanted the company. But I was also secretly afraid I would lose her as a friend and employee. The last time I tried to live with someone, it didn't end well.

"Any time is fine." I regained my composure and brightened at the thought of her moving in sooner rather than later. "In fact, why don't you move in tomorrow and we can do a trial run. You can pretend I'm not here and see how everything goes without me."

Heather started packing up her laptop. "That sounds great! I thought you were having second thoughts." She grinned sheepishly, regaining eye contact. "Hey, do you mind if I take the rest of the day off to get my stuff together if I'm going to move in tomorrow? I mean I don't have a ton of stuff, but it's gonna take some time to get organized."

I should have thought of that. "Of course," I responded

She gave me a quick hug and headed out.

I watched her run down to her VW Bug. "See you tomorrow," I said more to myself than to her.

I walked into my living room and plopped down on the overstuffed leather couch. Suddenly, I felt overwhelmed and oddly exhausted. "You'd better get your act in gear, girl!" I spoke aloud hoping it would motivate me. I had so much to do and so little time. At least my anxiety didn't have a chokehold on my willingness to move forward at the moment.

First, there was the matter of figuring out what I was going to do when I got out there. I had made the mistake of texting my mom that I had agreed to help Sabine, which forced me to promise to spend a couple of days in Meraux with her and Tom before moving on to Sabine's. At least I'd be able to take some time to breathe before tackling Sabine's problem. Thankfully, Venice was nearly two hours from where I grew up, so I had a legitimate reason not to stay in my childhood home for the duration of the visit. Sabine was right about one thing. I avoided going home like the plague. It was awkward, and unrewarding, except seeing my mom, but even that had become a chore. My shrink said I had to face these family issues sooner or later.

On top of that, my brother Michael and I had never been super close. He was four years younger and when we were growing up, I saw him as more of a pain than anything. By the time we started to get to an age where we might have more in common, I had moved to North Carolina. I had a bad habit of biting my thumbnail when I was thinking. My shrink said it was my adult version of sucking my thumb to comfort myself. I wasn't sure about that, but it was hard to quit.

I wondered if there was a chance for Mike and me to start over now that we were adults. I needed to make that a priority since he was my only sibling. Then there was my stepdad, Tom, who was pleasant enough, but I didn't know him well since I had already moved out by the time he and Mom got together. So, I avoided going home because I didn't feel like I was part of the family. On the other hand, this trip offered me the chance to bury my resentment and move on. I decided to stay optimistic, at least for now.

Staying in the house I grew up in would be a double-edged sword. I felt very much at home in my old bedroom, especially since my mom hadn't changed a thing since I moved out at eighteen. So, if I just hibernated in my bedroom upstairs, I'd be okay if I didn't regress. On the other hand, because I never dealt with my parent's divorce, it seemed like when I spent time with my mom, I got sucked back into that emotional rabbit hole. It seemed like my years of business success were helping with my self-confidence, though, because the thought of going home didn't make me want to throw up anymore.

I was up until two a.m. packing and repacking. I finally settled on two suitcases and an overstuffed carry-on. I figured I could buy whatever I forgot to pack. By the time that I finally crawled into bed and passed out, rejected clothes covered the floor of my room. It made yesterday's mess seem like a walk in the park. When the doorbell rang at 9 a.m., I felt like I was living *Groundhog Day.*

"Coming!" I yelled, even though there was no way she could hear me outside. I nearly tripped as I hopscotched across my bedroom in my jammies, my feet skipping between rejected sundresses and open suitcases.

I ran to the door and skidded to a stop on the throw rug in front of the door. *I need to get a rubber mat under that rug before I kill myself.*

Heather sat on the top step surrounded by boxes and bags, so my mad dash to the door must have taken longer than I thought.

As soon as I opened the door, she turned around and looked me up and down at my PJs. "Girl, what if I was a salesman or a terrorist or something? We're not that far from LA! There's plenty of strange people out there. You should really get dressed before you answer the door." She clicked her tongue like a schoolteacher.

"I saw your car out the window!" I lied.

She pushed past me on a beeline to the kitchen, carrying a box of pots and pans. "You'd better put some clothes on." She scolded. "I'll make coffee then I'll bring in the rest of my stuff.

Where should I put these?" she asked, pointing to the overfilled box of kitchenware.

I thought for a second. I had cabinets I'd never fill by myself. "How about the lower cabinet just to the left of the cooktop in the island?" She started unpacking the box as I padded upstairs, counting my lucky stars for finding Heather. By the time I showered, dried my hair, put on my makeup, a jean skirt, and a light sweater, Heather was lugging up her last box and playfully collapsed face-down at the top of the stairs. She flung her arms behind her in the direction of the steps. "The first ten times, the stairs weren't so bad, but the eleventh put me over the edge." She had a flair for the dramatic, and I smiled to myself, thrilled that she'd accepted my invitation to move in.

We raced downstairs giggling like schoolgirls to the kitchen, where her laptop sat open on the marble counter-topped island. She sat on a stool at the counter, looking perplexed, confused and finally, cross-eyed, clearly just for my benefit. "This is the kind of thing I worry about when you're gone. We just got an urgent email from a woman who says she's on the verge of divorce because her husband said, after she got a facelift and a tummy tuck, that she wasn't the woman he married."

I put my hand on her shoulder. "C'mon Heather, I've seen you handle tougher ones than that. I think you're just getting nervous because I'm leaving. Send her that list of family therapists. Change is hard for some people."

Heather nodded tentatively. "I guess you're right. But what if I mess something up and you're not here to fix it?"

I wasn't worried about it, but since she was, I needed to allay her fears. "I'll be just a phone call or a message away."

Heather didn't look convinced. "And if you're out wrestling some alligator and I can't get hold of you for hours during a crisis?"

I thought for a minute how to get her past this out-of-character panic. Finally, I had it. *"Bernie!"* I said, more to myself than to Heather.

She looked puzzled.

"Bernie is the publicist I told you about a couple of weeks ago. I worked with him when I was first getting started." Now it was her turn to watch me flit aimlessly around the kitchen, high-fiving sconces on either side of the double oven. I loved having a great idea.

"I remember now, but what does that do for us?" I tried to read her expression but couldn't tell whether she was confused or annoyed.

"He helped set all this up, so in the unlikely situation that all hell breaks loose, and you can't get hold of me, call Bernie. I'll give him a call to let him know to expect your call should you need anything. I'm sure he'd be happy to do it. I'll be generating a lot of business for him soon, so he has a vested interest in helping," I explained with an encouraging smile.

Heather finally relaxed. She exhaled loudly and finished her third cup of coffee with a flourish. "That should work. Thanks, Miranda."

The rest of the day flew by. Heather relaxed more as the day went on and was even joking around by the time we went to bed. I had an early flight, so I didn't see her in the morning, which was just as well—I hate goodbyes of all kinds. My shrink traces it back to losing my partner after we moved to Vegas from North Carolina. But I still can't think about that without severe depression kicking in.

I dressed in a blue, lightweight pants suit. Though I loved my sundresses, I always had visions of having to deplane down one of those slides in an emergency, so always wore slacks on flights. Though I put on dark blue heels to match my purse, I also carried a pair of flip-flops to wear on the plane. Anything to make the flight more comfortable. Last thing was to stuff cash in a pocket for tips so I wouldn't have to fuss with finding it in my purse or carry-on.

Luckily, I'd managed to book a non-stop flight, so I didn't have to spend several hours in Denver or Dallas buying overpriced designer clothes just for something to do. Shopping was better in airports than it used to be, but there's only so much Gucci and Victoria's Secret you can stand. No layover also meant that I only had three and a half hours to turn my emotional clock back fifteen years.

The limo I had arranged arrived just in time. I took a deep breath and dragged my carry-on behind the Cadillac for the driver to load into the trunk. Before he could get back in the car, I smiled sweetly and pointed the exasperated driver to the rest of my luggage, which was just outside my front door, ten steps from the ground. I climbed in the back seat and ignored his groans after lifting the bags into the trunk. I slipped him a hundred-dollar-bill when he got in. It looked like I'd be paying an overweight bag fee again.

By the time I got to LAX, it was as crazy as usual. I was glad that I'd invested in getting a ride rather than fighting for a precious Long-Term Parking space. I tipped my driver another hundred, and he parked illegally, helping me lug my heavy bags inside. There, I found the long line at the check-in counter and an even longer security line. Thank goodness I checked in online or else I might have died of old age waiting to get my bags checked and my tickets printed. Either way, I was still way behind their recommended early arrival time, although I didn't care. The security lines are so long that they let people move ahead if their flight is about to take off—a policy that effectively removes all incentives to arrive early. I took a few steps forward as the line moved up.

A TSA agent called from his podium, "Flight 2256 is boarding now. Is anyone here for Flight 2256?"

I checked my ticket. "Nope . . ." I muttered to no one in particular. Mine was Flight 429.

As I contemplated raising my hand anyway, I was jostled aside by a tall thin man in a suit. He pushed his way up to the beckoning security guard while crying, "Me! That's me, okay, excuse me!"

I briefly flashed his receding form an amused look and then returned to my musings. As much as I had apprehension about going back home and reliving the same old family issues, I also couldn't wait to get back to the Big Easy. The food, the music, the strange and fabulous personalities that you invariably met on the streets or in the bars made it a magical place for me.

I made it through security with just a couple minutes to spare, wary of the full-body scans I'd recently read so much about. Shaking off my paranoia, I grabbed a salad at one of the side kiosks and walked over to my gate. Unfortunately, all the seats in the waiting area were full, so I had to drag my carry-on to the window and perch on it while I gulped down my impromptu lunch. All manner of foreign planes from Australia to Japan cluttered the runway. It was mesmerizing to watch the jets landing, taking off, and docking with the gates. As impressive as it was, I suspected that the heavy traffic meant we'd end up with a late takeoff.

A few moments after that thought crossed my mind, the flight attendant announced, "Our departure has been pushed back until 1 p.m. Boarding will begin at 12:30."

I sighed, pulled out my cell phone, and dialed my mother's home phone; she insisted on picking me up from the airport, despite my protests.

Mom and Tom's voices came through at the same time. "Sorry, but we're not home at the moment. Leave a message!"

After the beep, I said, "Hey, Mom, my flight is delayed so I probably won't be in until 5:30 now. I'll meet you at the baggage claim. If you want to check my progress on the board in the airport, it's Flight 429. Love you. Bye."

I disconnected and tucked the phone away again, hoping that she would get the message before inadvertently spending an extra hour waiting around for me to show up. I made a quick dash for the trash can while trying to keep my bag in view. All of those announcements about not leaving your luggage unattended made me worried someone would plant a bomb in my carry-on as soon as I looked away.

When I finally made my way onto the plane, I snagged a window seat, thanks to shelling out a little extra for early boarding. After changing my shoes and putting my leather ones in my carry-on, and that into the overhead bin, I crossed my fingers as the other groups began to board, wishing for an empty middle seat as a buffer between me and whoever else was in my row. My hopes were dashed when a flight attendant announced that the flight was full.

A teenage girl snagged the aisle seat, so I reset my goal in the hope that she'd be traveling with a friend. I wanted to avoid the inevitable middle-aged overweight, carpet salesman from Chicago who would try to talk to me for the whole flight. Eventually, in answer to my prayers, the middle seat was filled by a teenage boy. He was far more interested in speaking with the girl on the aisle than with me.

Suddenly I heard a voice buzzing over the intercom. "We are on our final descent to the Louis Armstrong New Orleans International Airport, and we want to thank you for flying Southwest. We know there are other airlines . . ."

I must have dozed off. Of course, that was an understatement—the plane ride was a full three hours.

I stopped listening to the loudspeaker and instead texted as we taxied toward the gate. *"Hey Mom, I'm here!"*

I was surprised when she texted back quickly. *"I'm just finishing up some errands honey. I'll be there to pick you up soon!"*

As usual, she was running late. I shouldn't have bothered telling her that my flight was late—maybe then she'd have been on time. I figured I had at least forty-five minutes before she got to the airport since she had a thirty-minute drive and still had to fight her way through airport traffic.

I sighed. "That'll give me time to visit the restroom and get my bags from the carousel."

We reached the gate, and the lights in the cabin rose; the few people who hadn't been jostled awake by the bounce of the plane hitting the tarmac began to stir, and a flight attendant spoke over the intercom again. *"Be careful opening overhead compartments, as items may have shifted during flight."*

I sprang up in anticipation, forgetting how long it takes to deplane. The teenagers were still chatting away, oblivious to the activity around them. The aisle filled up quickly with people as anxious to stretch their legs as I was, and the air was suddenly filled with the sound of overhead compartments clicking open and bags sliding around. The whole process took about half an hour and the moment I walked off the gangplank and into the airport I took a deep breath; it felt good to breathe air that hadn't been inhaled and exhales thousands of times by my co-

passengers. I still had fifteen or so minutes to spare and had things to check off my list. After I 'powdered my nose', washed my hands, and bought a Venti Café Americano at Starbucks, I headed toward the luggage area. Halfway there, I realized I still wore my flip-flops. What the heck, they were comfortable.

I tried to remember what carousel they'd said when I left the plane. I scanned the baggage claim for carousels with my airline attached to it. There were three belonging to Southwest, and one of the LED screens had my flight number flashing. Gathered around carousel C were hordes of people getting ready to fight anyone to the death to make sure their bag didn't have to go around on that thing again. I pushed my way to the front as I caught sight of one of my bags through the gaps in the crowd. As I reached for it, another hand did too—one far meatier than my own. We both lifted it up and glared at each other from either end of it.

The red-faced fifty-something man in a beige suit was panting furiously, no doubt because his weight made movement difficult. "Give me my bag!"

I scoffed and pulled at the bag. "Excuse me?" I swatted at his hand, but he refused to let go.

"I'll report you!" he growled, pulling back, but I refused to lose the tug-of-war.

This man did not seem the type to own a mauve suitcase with a yellow Livestrong bracelet on the handle; he was either colorblind or trying to steal my luggage. Either way, I was losing patience.

Rolling my eyes, I used one hand to reveal the luggage tag while gripping the handle tightly with the other. "Miranda Marquette! See!" I said, following it with an emphatic 'hmph.'

He dropped the suitcase with an apologetic look, and it fell toward my legs. I jumped back to avoid it and bumped into another woman who was reaching for her luggage. I quickly apologized and returned to searching for my other bag. A few moments later the remaining bag arrived, and I reached for it, glaring at a priest in full garb, and practically daring him to take it from me. Then, I loaded my bags onto a cart that cost me two dollars and headed outside to wait for my mom.

"I'm at the Southwest terminal. Are you here yet?" I texted her. She better be. I'd given her plenty of time.

She texted back, *"Southwest of what?"*

I let out an audible groan and then cleared my throat as people started looking at me. *"No, Mom, the name of the airline is Southwest."*

Ten minutes later a strange Jeep pulled up in front of me, and my mother jumped out. "Miranda!" She ran over to hug me and said, "Let me look at you. Oh dear, you're so skinny." She stepped back and grimaced, "What happened to your lips? Did someone hit you?"

I wanted to scream, feeling like she had forgotten that I took multiple bullets in the face, but I said out loud, "No, Mom, the surgeon had to do a lot of reconstruction. He said he could make my lips fuller while he was at it and I agreed."

"Well, it worked," she frowned and then looked me over again. "Really, Sweetheart, that's not the face that God blessed you with."

I glared at her in disbelief. "I was shot in the face. It wasn't my choice."

She patted me on the arm. "I know, dear. That must have been horrible." Clearly, she didn't understand what I had been through, and I doubted she ever would.

Changing the subject, I said, forcing the most cheerful voice I could muster, "Let's get my suitcases in the car and head home."

She shrugged and squeezed me again, "What matters is that you are home." I started inching my way to the car pushing the baggage cart and she followed behind me, chattering away excitedly—so much so that I couldn't get a comment in edgewise. "How long has it been? I have missed you so much! It figures I would have a boy that I can't get rid of and a girl who lives all the way across the country." She laughed and put a hand on my shoulder. "Well, thank goodness you don't have children for me not to be able to know."

"Oh, Mom." I smiled at her through gritted teeth. "You always know just what to say . . ." I shoved my suitcases into the back and slammed the rear hatch shut.

She seemed oblivious to my growing anger. "Thank you, dear. I like to think so."

As we drove out of the airport, she caught me up on what *everyone* was up to. I didn't remember half the people that she was talking about, but I smiled, nodded, and looked interested.

Suddenly, evidenced by the sour look on her face and her closed body language, her mood and subject changed. "I can't believe it took a visit from your *cousin* Sabine to get you to come home. I'm trying not to take that as an insult." I had been hoping that she and Sabine had buried the hatchet, but evidently not.

"Really, Mom?" I sighed in exasperation. "I thought you loved Sabine as if she were your own. That's what you always used to say."

"Well, Sabine has done some things that haven't made the folks around here or me very happy." She gripped her steering wheel tighter.

"What do you mean?" I asked, curious.

I regretted asking almost immediately; she always drove more erratically when she was agitated. "First, she practically stole your grandfather's business after he went completely senile. Then she took advantage of several other neighbors who had their life savings sunk into their shrimping businesses after the storm cost them everything."

Interesting—at least, now I had some idea of a possible motive behind her so-called saboteur. "That's not exactly how she described it. But it sounds like she hasn't made any friends while building up the business." Casually, I asked, "Do you know anyone who might want to take her down?"

"Everyone." She laughed sarcastically. "You know that she moved down to Venice because she was practically chased out of town. What people can't figure out is why you would come back here to help her."

"You know how people are down here." I tried to turn the conversation away from me. "They hate anyone who has any success. I'd bet it's not so much Sabine but what she represents to people. Besides, she is our flesh and blood." Then I crossed my arms. "And, no offense, but she practically raised me when you and Dad had your issues. You didn't have much time to pay attention to me with all the fighting you were doing. By the time you divorced and straightened out your lives, I was already grown. You're lucky Sabine took an interest in me, or I'd be like any one of those 'pink collar girls' who never left the neighborhood." I wanted to have a peaceful visit, but she made me angry with the Sabine-bashing.

"Now, young lady, don't you look down your nose at those girls. Granted they aren't as successful as you are—" She wagged her finger at me, and we swerved.

"Mom—the road!" I grabbed the handle just above the door for dear life.

She turned back to face the windshield and gripped her steering wheel with both hands. "Those young women have stayed and helped to support their families during the

35

devastation that was the devil, Katrina. I didn't see you around here helping to rebuild."

She had me there. "You're right, Mom. I should have come back after Katrina." I sighed. "I regret not doing something, but I was at a critical time in building my business, and I was terrified that if I came home, I would lose it all." I stared out my window and added, admittedly with some sass, "What I don't regret is adopting the values that Sabine drilled into me about making myself a success no matter what."

She sat quietly watching the road for a few minutes. At first, I was glad that my words seemed to affect her, but I got worried the longer she stayed silent. Finally, she spoke in a very soft tone. "I am sorry for being emotionally absent for all those years. I am thankful that you turned out so wonderfully, even if I can't take all the credit. I love you, Miranda. Let's not fight. Maybe this trip is a chance for us to start over."

Chapter 3

It wasn't until Mom and I rode silently for a while that I became painfully aware of the mass destruction caused by Katrina. It had been nearly two years since the hurricane, and I felt like we were in an entirely different world. The result of the storm and the rebuilding surrounded us wherever we drove. I knew the damage in Katrina's path was devastating, but I couldn't fathom the idea that entire neighborhoods were gone completely.

Tears streamed down my cheeks, and for a moment, I closed my eyes, and the new world order wasn't visible. It broke my heart and made me feel even guiltier for putting my business ahead of these peoples' lives. The houses in my old neighborhood were in three categories: rubble, homes in the process of being rebuilt, and my parent's house. It was just as Sabine had described it—not a single scratch on it. I couldn't quite explain the feeling. It was eerie to see it standing alone on the street where I played all those years. Quite honestly, I wished that the structure had perished with the rest of the neighborhood. It would have provided me with the closure that I needed to move on from that chapter of my life, and yet, for some cruel reason, I was deprived of that chance.

I realized I had been staring out the window with my mouth open. "I didn't know. I didn't understand."

Mom said quietly, "You should have been here when it happened, Miranda. It was worse than you will ever know."

"Is Tom home?" I asked, changing the subject as we pulled up to the house.

"He was working in the kitchen when I left. Knowing him, he hasn't moved." My mom snickered with a touch of sarcasm.

True to her description, he was sitting at the kitchen table with a laptop when we walked into the house. I rocked on my heels. "Hey, Tom, how's it going?"

He stood, and we briefly hugged; my mom looked pleased.

"Hey, the kitchen looks great!" I said, looking around at the unfamiliar cabinets. "When did you have it redone?"

Tom puffed out his chest. "I did it myself. It saved us a bundle but took forever."

My mom rolled her eyes, "Yes, it did. If we had to cook on the grill outside for one more meal, my head was going to explode!"

After the trip and the tense ride from the airport, I was ready for some 'me' time. I'd gotten used to not sharing that time with anyone if I didn't want to, so coming home was going to be a challenge. I hadn't decided how long I was going to stay with them, but I knew even a couple of days would test my patience.

As if she read my thoughts, my mom asked, "How long are you planning on staying?"

It all depends on how long the investigation is going to take. If I'm going to be in the area longer than a couple of days, I'm going to need to stay with Sabine so I can get her take on what's going on down there. Besides, it's too far to commute to Venice daily.

"Are you all right, honey?" I looked up to see my mom staring at me.

I realized that conversation had been in my head. "Yeah, I'm fine. I'll probably just stay overnight right now and head down to Venice in the morning, but I'd like to come back before I leave if that's okay."

She seemed thrilled. "That's great, Sweetheart! It's so great to see you. I hope you know you can stay here anytime."

My head was starting to ache. "I think I'm gonna head upstairs and maybe rest a while." I juggled my suitcases and left my carry-on at the base of the stairs for my next trip up.

"Okay, honey," my mother said, "We'll just be doing what we do, so don't feel like you have to entertain us and we'll do the same." Thankfully, she seemed to have moved past our earlier difference of opinion.

"Sounds good, Mom." I gave them both a wave and headed up the stairs, my suitcases thumping as I climbed.

I pushed open my bedroom door with a creak of its hinges. As I'd been imagining, nothing had been disturbed, although it was clear my mother had dusted it periodically over the years. My posters were still up and my curtains and bedspread matched. I cringed at the number of lighthouses decorating the fabrics in my room. As I stood staring at them, I could hear my old life echoing in my ears.

My father banged on my door and shouted, "Turn that music down, Miranda!"

"No!" I screamed back, crossing my arms, and turning away from the door. "I'd rather hear my music than the sound of you two fighting!"

He pounded again. "Turn it down, or I'll throw that stereo out the window!"

I didn't want to think about any of that, so I opened my carry-on and retrieved my iPad to check on the website and the business; I needed to clear my head before going back downstairs for round two. As I climbed onto my bed, I wished that I could go back to when I was ten, and everything was fine; it was everything that happened after that that made me who I am today. It was so strange to be sitting on my old twin-sized bed with my back propped against the wall. I suddenly pictured myself at sixteen doing my homework with my B-52s and

Depeche Mode blaring, wishing that I was anywhere else, although not because of the comfort of the mattress.

"Maybe I'll rest just for a few minutes . . ." I thought, sliding down the bed and laying my head on the pillow.

It felt like only a few seconds before I heard a knock on the bedroom door. "Sweetheart," my mother asked, "Can I come in?"

"Sure," I said, my voice coming out hoarse.

She opened the door and peeked in. "I was beginning to wonder if you were going to wake up at all before morning."

"Why?" I asked, still groggy, "What time is it?"

"Almost seven." My mother stepped inside and closed the door behind her.

"Wow, I must have been tired," I said. "You didn't hold dinner for me, did you?"

"We ate, but I wanted to see if you were hungry." My mother was always trying to feed people. "I wanted to talk first though . . ."

"Uh-oh. That's never good," I said, sitting up and pulling my legs in close to my chest so that my mother would have somewhere to sit.

She sat on the bed and looked at the floor, her hands, my posters, anywhere and everywhere but at me. She started slowly, "Okay, Miranda. There's something I haven't told you about me, about our family . . ." she trailed off.

"Okay," A feeling of dread began to spread through me; no good conversation ever started that way.

She continued, "You were so young when you left home and then the few times you've been here, the timing just wasn't right."

I couldn't even begin to imagine what she was trying to say. "Yes? So?"

"So, now that you're here and you're truly all grown up and before you take off for Sabine's, it just seemed like the right time to explain some things."

"Geez, Mom. Can you get to it?"

She took a deep breath and looked at the wall instead of me. "You remember when Sabine moved here to Louisiana from France to stay with your Grandmama and Grandpapa, right?"

"Of course, I do," I said.

How could I forget? Once Sabine arrived, she became my 'parent,' and she came to the right place at the right time; I needed her. By her early teens, she had learned that no one was going to protect her from bad men if she didn't protect herself. She saw me as someone to teach, to protect, and to nurture. The best thing was that she didn't just talk about it; she led by example. My older cousin and idol had learned how to say 'no' without sounding like it was an absolute no. She knew how to get what she wanted by keeping guys interested, but never really giving them what they wanted. You could say that Sabine saved my life or, at least, my innocence. Without her, who knows where I would have ended up.

From her first day in this country, Sabine taught me how to lead the horse to water, but never let it drink. Sure, let it nuzzle you and give it a piece of sugar every now and then, but never more than that. My social life has been lived with that thought in mind.

My mother speaking again drew me back to the present conversation. "We never really talked about why she came from France without her parents." She hesitated, took another deep breath, glanced at me briefly before turning back to the wall, and then continued. "You probably also remember that your father and I started fighting pretty regularly around that same time."

"Yes, I remember that too. What's your point?" I wished she'd just tell me.

Now, she turned to face me, and her expression struck me as one who is facing the gallows or the electric chair. My anxiety level revved up ten notches. When she spoke again, her voice was low and quiet. "Sabine is not your cousin. She's your sister . . ."

I let out a breath I didn't realize I'd been holding. "What are you talking about? Wait, you mean . . ." then my voice grew shrill, as I asked, "Dad is her father?"

"No. Let me explain," she continued, her focus now back on the wall. "Jean Claude and Marie are her real parents."

"Then what . . ." I started to ask.

She cut me off, "Your father is not your biological father."

"What are you talking about?" I was too tired to make sense of things.

She paused and closed her eyes, then spoke in an almost monotone voice as if she'd practiced this speech a thousand times. "Jean Claude and Marie were married four years before you were born. A year later, Sabine was born. A year or two later, Louis—your father—his parents, Jean Claude, and Marie had a plan to move to America. They planned for a year to make the move. During that time, Marie became less and less sure that she wanted to leave France."

I said nothing, anxious to find out the relevance of this information.

She continued. "Jean Claude was dead-set that he, Marie, and Sabine would be leaving France for America with the rest of the family. They started to fight more and more, and finally, Marie told Jean Claude that she was not going, and if he went, she would divorce him. Well, to make a long story short, they divorced and he came to America with his brother's parents."

That confused me. "But Jean Claude and Marie are married now," I protested.

My mom nodded. "I'll get to that. Anyway, I was in my second year of college at Tulane. In my history class, there was a new boy, Jean Claude. He was so handsome and French and a little older than me. I knew a little French and he knew a little English and we immediately hit it off. We spent as much time as we could while still going to classes. In a few short months, he asked me to marry him and I said yes. He wasn't the school type and had left Tulane within a couple of months, so he found a job on a shrimping boat and we eloped."

I stared at her, stunned by this news. "You and Dad's brother were married?"

She flapped a hand to shush me, focused on finishing her story. "For a short time, it was like a fairy-tale and I got pregnant almost immediately after we married. But a couple of months into my pregnancy, Jean Claude became very depressed. America was not everything he imagined. He was working himself to death and making very little money. One night, he came to me with tears in his eyes. He told me that he had made a huge mistake, that he still loved Marie and wanted to go back to France to raise Sabine."

Tears welled up in her eyes and mine. I could almost feel the anguish that she must have felt. She attempted a smile and continued. "I was devastated. I was three months pregnant and my husband was leaving the country to rejoin his first family."

She wiped her eyes and blew her nose and attempted to compose herself. "Louis, your father, lived with his parents just around the corner. He and I had become friends while Jean Claude and I were falling in love. We started talking every day.

I told him everything I was feeling, and he was a strong shoulder to cry on and helped me survive a very trying time. Once it was clear Jean Claude wasn't coming back, he helped me to get my marriage annulled. He was so sweet and kind to me. Somehow, by the time I was seven months pregnant with you, he proposed to me. I told him yes. I, frankly, didn't have another plan. Were we head over heels in love? No. But he was there for me when his brother wasn't. I'll always admire him for that. When you were born, we decided together that you never needed to know, and that's why we never told you."

"No wonder I've never known who I am." My whisper was barely audible.

She reached out to touch my arm, but my mind was racing too fast to be rational.

I couldn't believe what I was hearing. "No wonder Daddy never loved me."

"I realize now that we should have told you long ago." She backtracked, but it didn't make much of a difference to me; I wasn't listening. She touched my arm, trying to comfort me, but I pushed her away and ran out of the room.

I could barely see through my tears, but I still managed to make it out the front door and started running away from the house, my flip-flops slapping my heels with every step. I would have jumped on my motorcycle to try to clear my head, but it was back home in California. I honestly didn't care where I was going as long as it wasn't that house. I had no idea what to think. I just felt so confused and angry for having been lied to my whole life. After probably a half-mile, I slowed to a walk, clutching my stomach in pain. I hadn't run in a while.

My mind still raced. Would my relationship have been better or worse with my dad had I known he wasn't my biological father? I had no idea, but it *would* have been better had they let me find out. My mother didn't expound on her and my dad, Louis', divorce except for saying they were never really in love. No wonder they hadn't stayed together. And it finally made sense why I never really felt like my dad loved me.

I continued walking north toward the city. My cousin Sabine was my sister. That information wasn't nearly as shocking or disturbing, probably because I had already thought of Sabine that way, but still, I hated to be lied to. I wondered if she knew.

About halfway to The Big Easy, I sat down on a park bench to collect myself. My first thought was to run away—that's what I've always done, why I live in California, why I left home when I was eighteen, and why I didn't come home to help when Katrina hit.

I didn't get it. "Why tell me now? Why tell me at all?" I muttered to myself and kicked at stray debris in the street.

I felt emptiness burning inside of me. But I also felt sane. I had always been so sure I was crazy. Now, I realized that I was the sane one. I kept my distance from people so I didn't get hurt and it was no wonder. My whole life had been built on a foundation of shifting sands.

I walked and walked, and my legs carried me through Chalmette and Arabi, upriver all the way to the Quarter. "Perfect. Here's a place I can blend in," I muttered, looking around at all the tourists who seemed to be having a ball.

My tension and anger fell away as I smelled the creole in the air and heard the moan of a trumpet escaping from a bar a few doors down. My mouth was so dry that my tongue was starting to stick to my teeth and the roof of my mouth. I was dehydrated and needed water.

I checked my watch and was taken aback—I'd been walking for three and a half hours. I wanted loud, and I wanted music to drown out my thoughts. Since it was already eleven-thirty and the nightlife was in full swing, that wasn't too hard to find at all. I didn't know or care the name of the place that I walked into; all I knew was that there was a seat at the bar. A scruffy guy who looked old enough to have built this place stood behind the counter and grunted at me as I plopped down in front of him, which I guessed was his way of asking what I wanted.

I reflexively said, "Cab?"

"Huh?" he grunted.

"Oh yeah," I forgot where I was. "You have any red wine?"

"No wine. You want wine, go to one of those snooty wine bars up the street. They're ruinin' this town, I tell ya. Beer or the hard stuff?" He slammed a glass down in front of me and snapped, "C'mon lady. I got other customers here."

God help me. "A Tanqueray Gin and tonic and an ice water."

"Gin and tonic we have." He served it up in fifteen seconds. "$7.50."

I threw a ten on the bar and he scooped it up and was gone. It didn't look like there was any ice water in my future.

I was staring into my drink when a nearby voice said, "The name's Mark. Nice to meet you."

I looked over to see a good-looking guy, nice hair, cool smile, nursing a beer and flirting with a girl standing between us at the bar, or trying to. She picked up her drinks, flashed him a quick smile that said, "Sorry, I'm busy," and then went back to her friends. He didn't look at me, but from the side of his face, I felt like I knew him.

I must have stared a little too long because he turned to face me. My face felt hot and I could only imagine it was a striking shade of red. I was hoping he would just go back to his beer. I didn't get my wish.

"Hey, aren't you . . .?" He looked more closely. "No, I guess not." He returned to his beer.

46

Still looking straight ahead at the wall mirror behind the bar, I interrupted before he embarrassed himself with some pick-up line. "No, I'm pretty sure I'm not."

He turned to stare at me again. "I guess you're right. But there's something familiar about you."

I wiped up the ring my drink was making on the bar with a napkin. Cleaning was my 'go-to' when I didn't know what else to do. I stared at my glass when I muttered under my breath, "I don't even recognize myself anymore so I'm pretty sure you don't."

He smiled and continued to stare. "Say that again."

I peered over at this guy. He was starting to annoy me. "Say what again?" I said with a touch of sarcasm.

He was getting more excited by the second. "Anything! Say anything!"

I instinctively moved my bar stool away from his. "Okay, I don't know what your game is, but please leave me out of it."

"Miranda Marquette! You're Miranda Marquette. I can hear it in your voice." He nearly jumped up from his barstool.

That caused me to turn and give him another look. I *knew* he looked familiar, but I still couldn't place him. The look on my face must have given me away.

He continued, "You really don't know who I am, do you?"

I hated it when this happened. "You look kind of familiar, I guess."

"It's Mark . . ." I shook my head, and he tried again. "Mark Peterson. Wow, I haven't changed *that* much, I can't believe you don't remember me. I sat behind you in science class. I must have asked you out ten times. Granted, you always said 'No.'"

"Mark? Mark from science class?" My synapses were finally starting to connect. Mark was a real nerd with thick glasses when

I was going through my Goth phase. "Wait a minute. You dated my friend Danielle."

"Yes, that's me. I settled for Danielle after you turned me down all those times." He gave me a funny look, like what else did I expect?

"What's she up to these days?" I asked. "We lost touch after I left."

"I married her." He looked down with a slightly twisted smile. "We got divorced a few years back. It was pretty messy."

"Oh, sorry. Any kids?" I said the only thing that popped into my head.

"No, we couldn't have children. That may have contributed to our demise." He gave a small shrug. "We still run into each other sometimes. She's a Facebook friend." He'd lost steam since his enthusiastic entrance, and I felt terrible.

He looked good. Well dressed, like he had money. I imagined contact lenses replaced the glasses. We transitioned into an awkward silence, thus reminding me why I left town after high school. I didn't have to make small talk with people I never had much in common with in the first place. I never liked high school, so reliving those years didn't make me long for the *glory days*. My Goth girl phase made most ordinary people steer clear, which was fine with me, but for some reason, Mark never got the memo. He was constantly asking me out. He was either clueless, or he saw something in me that most people didn't. Either way, I wasn't ready to date at the time. Maybe Sabine's dire warnings scared me off boys.

I looked up after being lost in thought to see him staring at me in anticipation. My eyelids were getting heavy after the flight, the fight with my mom, and my three-and-a-half-hour walk. "Hey Mark, I hate to ask you this. I'd like to catch up, but I flew halfway across the country and had a less than stellar first couple of hours visiting with my mom and I'm exhausted. You think you could give me a ride home?"

He smiled. "Sure, on one condition."

My heart dropped to my toes. "What condition?" I asked with my best cop-intimidating glare.

He laughed. "It's not going to be that painful. I was just going to ask you to continue this conversation tomorrow. I'd like to hear what you've been up to."

Okay, that was nice; I couldn't refuse him, and I still needed a ride. Too bad for him he hadn't had this down in high school. "Deal," I said, as I attempted an awkward high five that he hardly noticed.

We stood and walked out with his hand on the small of my back. I can't say that it was an unpleasant sensation. His Porsche convertible was parked less than a block away, and he opened the passenger door for me.

If he bought it to impress the girls, it worked. "Nice."

He smiled as he settled into the driver's seat. "I figured I might as well enjoy some of the benefits of my success, even if I had to do it alone."

I felt a little sorry for him even though my social life wasn't much better. "I'm sure things will improve."

He nodded but didn't look convinced as he pulled out of the parking spot and headed back toward Meraux.

I closed my eyes and must have nodded off because in no time we were sitting in my parent's driveway. "Wow, that was fast." I tried to pretend I had been awake the whole time.

He laughed. "So, I'll pick you up in the morning?"

I felt like I had missed something. "The morning . . .?"

He patted my arm. "You remember our deal, right?"

I protested. "Well, I didn't know . . ."

He interrupted, "Early bird gets the worm."

I was too tired to argue; besides, maybe it would be fun to catch up. I hadn't even taken the time to ask him what he did for a living. "Okay, how about ten? Early enough?"

He grinned, "Perfect."

I smiled a weary smile. "See ya."

He sat in the driveway until I was inside. Always the gentleman.

Chapter 4

I woke up to the sun streaming down on my face through a space between the lighthouse print curtains. I squinted at the alarm clock on my bedside table. *Darn. 8:30.* I wasn't planning on waking up for at least an hour so I wouldn't have to socialize while I waited for Mark. I heard someone making breakfast downstairs, but I refused to show myself. Since there was no way I was getting back to sleep now, I decided to get on my laptop and do a little business.

At 9:30, I took a nice long shower. By the time I dried my hair and made an attempt at putting my makeup on, I felt almost human. Not bad considering I only had four hours' sleep after flying halfway across the country and walking ten miles. Mentally, I was feeling better. I still wasn't thrilled about the news or my mom's timing, but I could either deal with it or be miserable the whole time I was here. I decided to clear the air when I went downstairs so that we could all move on. Whether I could get there emotionally would be a stretch, but I had come to learn if you acted okay, you would be okay most of the time. That was another valuable lesson I'd picked up in therapy somewhere over the years. Sometimes I felt older and wiser that than my thirty-three years.

I reflected on the strangeness of life as I shimmied into a pair of shorts and a conservative blouse I didn't love, but one that I knew my mom would like. I mused to myself, "Sometimes bad things do turn out good." I bolted down the stairs with a new lightness in my heart. Mom and Tom were sitting at the kitchen table and stopped talking the moment I walked in, giving one another a 'Shhh, here she comes,' look.

"Before anyone says anything, I want to speak," I announced. "I was upset last night, and I believe I had a right to be. However, in the interest of keeping the peace, I am going to try to accept that you and Dad did what you thought was best under the circumstances. It's possible I will never come to terms with the fact that Dad is not, in fact, my real father. On the other hand, considering our relationship, it may help me to put the emotional pieces together."

A warm and relieved smile spread across my mom's face, and she walked over and hugged me so tight and warm that I flashed back to my life as a delighted baby burrito gurgling incoherently at the world. *I don't want to cry.* She started crying too while Tom made an awkward effort to look at anything but us.

She sniffed. "I love you, Sweetheart, and I never wanted to hurt you. I just didn't know what to do, and the more time that passed, the more it just seemed to be okay to do and say nothing. I realize now that probably wasn't the best way to go and I'm sorry."

I didn't want to rehash everything, so I just said, "I'll probably have more questions later about our family history so that I can understand it better, but for now, let's let it be. Okay?"

She seemed satisfied with that, and Tom looked relieved not to be stuck in the middle of a fight. She then shifted back into entertainer-mode, "Well, what do you want for breakfast? We have eggs, pancakes, waffles, bacon, crepes, oatmeal, cold cereal and anything else you might want."

I thought I might gain twenty pounds just thinking about the considerable spread I knew she wanted to put out for me. "I'll just have coffee. Thanks. With cream would be great."

She looked at me like I was an alien but didn't push her luck. "So, Miranda," she beamed at the fact that we had gotten past our fight, "are you seeing anyone in California?" She was under the impression that I was going to die an old maid but was still holding onto her hope that I'd go in another direction.

"Not at the moment. I was seeing a guy for a little while named Paul, but it fizzled." I smiled weakly.

"That's a shame." She sounded like she could tell what he was like by his name alone. "What did he do for a living?"

I just wanted to get through the inquisition. "He was a very successful real estate developer, and he was writing a novel, last I heard."

"Has he ever been married, dear?" She scurried around the kitchen, pulling out half-and-half from the fridge, and then pouring a cup of coffee for me.

"Nope, he never had time for relationships while he was building his office-building empire," I mumbled.

Tom finally piped in, "So, you're saying he's a real estate novelist who never had time for a wife?"

My mom interrupted without missing a beat, "Oh, Miranda, did I tell you that your Cousin Davey re-enlisted in the Navy?"

Tom started to snicker. There was an inside joke in there somewhere, but I didn't have a clue, so I nodded, grabbed my coffee, and headed out the front door to get some air. It was warm out for March, but down here it could be hot and humid any day of the year. I felt restless and tired. I sat on the front porch as Mark's Porsche convertible with the top down inched slowly into sight. It wasn't quite ten, so I guessed that he was trying to buy some time by driving like he was eighty.

I ran over to his car. "Wanna go get a bite to eat?"

He smiled broadly. "Sure! Sounds like a plan."

"Okay. I'll go get my purse." I ran back to the house.

Mom and Tom were still at the kitchen table, engaged in a private conversation. I decided to come clean so that my mom wouldn't give me the third degree. "Hey, Mom, you remember Mark Peterson from school? We're gonna go catch up."

"Mark? How did you reconnect with him so soon?" she said with a frown, then as if she realized that expressing her concern about my activities was being too motherly to a daughter in her thirties, she added, "Well, have fun. I hear he's is an attorney now, so if you need any free legal advice, this is your chance."

"All right, Mom. Whatever." I rolled my eyes and gave a curt wave. "I'll see you guys later."

Mark was checking out his hair in the rearview mirror when I got back outside. "Ready to roll, handsome?" As soon as I said it, I regretted my slightly sarcastic tone. *You're never going to make any friends with that attitude, Miranda.*

We rode in silence for a few minutes while I tried to think of something more positive to say. "So, I hear you're a lawyer." I asked, "What kind of law do you practice?"

He grinned from ear to ear with the realization that I knew something about him, "I practice criminal law."

I laughed. "Oh, really now? Hey, it's always a good thing to have a friend who's a lawyer."

He smiled. "I'm pretty sure you'll never need one. But believe me, there's enough crime in these parts to keep me plenty busy. It's usually not that exciting, petty theft, assault. You know, you were a cop. I'm just the next step up the food chain."

I touched his arm and smiled. "Better a step up the food chain than down."

He jerked the steering wheel, and we swerved sharply into the left lane. He barely managed to pull the wheel to the right in time to miss an oncoming truck. He said sheepishly, "Sorry, I wasn't expecting that."

Note to self: *Don't touch Mark while he's driving unless you want to die.* We rode the rest of the way in silence with my right hand glued to the handle in the car door; there's nothing like a near-death experience to get your blood flowing in the morning. Luckily, it didn't take long to get to the Quarter. We were fortunate to find a parking spot within walking distance of the Déjà Vu, a twenty-four-hour eating establishment that I hadn't stepped foot in since I moved away. But I knew I'd always feel at home here. Nestled on Dauphine Street between Preservation Hall and the Museum of Death, it attracted an eclectic crowd.

We made our way to the door through the debris left, no doubt, from a parade. Whether it was a funeral, a holiday or for no reason at all, they loved their parades. "Wow, this place hasn't changed at all," I said, looking down at my feet. "Looks like they haven't washed the floor since I was here last," I whispered to myself and added, "Welcome to New Orleans."

As we settled in at a table near the front window, I felt relaxed for the first time since I hit town. A waitress with a for-real beehive hairdo and a name tag that read 'Josephine' chomped on a wad of gum and tapped her foot impatiently. I scanned the menu searching for anything that wouldn't add five pounds to my hips. Seeing that I was struggling, Mark jumped in. "Two Crawfish Po-boys and two coffees."

I muttered under my breath. "Thanks, it's been a while."

He smiled as Josephine turned on her heal and headed for the kitchen. "Hey, Miranda, I hear that you are here to visit Sabine."

I was surprised the word was out on that. That wasn't good if I wanted to work undercover. "Where'd you hear that?" I did my best to keep my annoyance under wraps by sounding inquisitive instead.

"People talk. Meraux is a small town." He gave me a smile that seemed sincere. "You know, it's somewhat of an event having you back here. Besides, I have some personal interest in the matter." I looked at him, uncomprehending. "I guess you hadn't heard that I was seeing Sabine for a while."

She had never been one to talk about her love life, but you could have knocked me over with a feather. "Wow, Mark. I didn't know you were her type. She's older and, well, you know . . .." I gestured at him.

"I know I'm no John Stamos, but I do okay." He grinned. "And I know she's, well, difficult. But, I'm one of the few men around here who doesn't either smell like fish or smoke. And she's a successful businesswoman. Besides, she's not *that* much older. Just because you left town doesn't mean we all stopped aging when you left."

"I know that," I lied. Coming home made me feel trapped in high school all over again. "So, what happened between you two?"

He hesitated for a moment, and I wondered what I dragged myself into this time.

He plunged in, "We dated for a while, but it was platonic. I was not looking for anything serious and neither was she. Well, one night I was dropping her off after dinner and a movie, and I kissed her good night. It seemed like the right thing to do."

I agreed. "But still scary if you don't know her intentions."

He nodded. "Anyway, we were booked to go away for the weekend together, separate rooms of course. We were going to a bed and breakfast in Kemah, Texas, right on the Gulf. Granted we pretty much live on the Gulf already, but we wanted to get out of town, so it seemed like a fun idea. Anyway, everything seemed fine right up until the day before, and then she broke up with me. By *text*!"

I grimaced. "Ouch! That had to hurt."

"Well, it wasn't like we were head over heels in love, but I thought it was going somewhere. It was weird. I haven't heard from her since." He looked away, but I saw more pain than he was admitting.

We sat in silence for a few moments. "Sabine and I haven't been in touch at all, so I have no idea what she's been up to." I was looking at Mark, but my mind was elsewhere. "Of course, she was never really one to talk about her love life." He shifted nervously in his chair. I took that as a signed that he was through with the Sabine part of the conversation, so I asked, "So are you seeing anyone now?"

"I've had a couple of dates with women from Match.com, but nothing serious. I'm not getting any younger, so I'm still hoping for luck in that department." He shrugged.

"You and me both. Well, let's toast to staying as young as we can for as long as we can." We clinked our coffee mugs. "There's always cosmetic surgery, ya know, to help you stay looking young," I said, putting in a shameless plug—I couldn't help myself, work first, socialization later.

"Yeah, I guess you are the poster girl." He smiled, "Did I mention that you look fantastic. Not that you weren't great before. But you've managed to get the wholesome look without looking too innocent. You're perfect."

I cringed internally but punched him playfully on the arm, hesitant to remind him why I had all the surgeries. "I'm far from perfect, but thanks. To be honest, I was never comfortable with my looks. People always told me I was pretty, but I never felt that way. I'm still working on that with my shrink." My right hand automatically reached up and skimmed the side of my face where I felt like the biggest scar still stood out like a burning rim of fire along my jawbone. I knew that wasn't true, but whenever

I met someone from my past, I suddenly felt seriously self-conscious.

He didn't seem to notice I was on the verge of an anxiety attack, so I kept talking, babbling actually, hoping that would help. "It all started when I was an undercover cop in North Carolina. After six years, I quit the force after being ambushed, shot and nearly left for dead. I was supposed to have back-up, but it never materialized, leaving me completely exposed and in harm's way. Eventually, I sued the city, the police force, and the police chief personally. They were smarter than to face off in court, so I got a nice settlement. I had no idea it would take two years and multiple surgeries on my face before I could start living again." I leaned back and let out a deep breath, having told him the whole story without intending to.

He motioned for me to go on. "I started to blog about my experiences with plastic surgery, and it seemed to strike a chord with people, mostly women. I developed a significant following and became an expert on the topic. I successfully made the transition from reconstructive plastic surgery to cosmetic surgery of all kinds. Long story short, I put together an exclusive network of Cosmetic Surgeons who provide high-quality discount services, and I get a piece of every referral that results in a procedure."

"I'm impressed," he said, raising his eyebrows.

I looked uncomfortably at my hands and had to make an effort to make eye contact; I've never been comfortable being complimented. "The internet has been my salvation. I've been able to get a national reputation just by sitting at home in front of my computer. Sure, I've done a couple of interviews for national news organizations, but it's been easier than you might think. I guess I was in the right place at the right time." I stopped for a moment and my voice dropped when I said, "So to speak."

He grimaced, perhaps his expression of sympathy. "I sometimes regret becoming an attorney. There are days when I'd just like to be salaried. If I take time off, I pay for it in more ways than one. I lose revenue because I generate no billable hours, I get behind on my existing cases because I am off, and I'm so far behind when I return, I wish I never went in the first place."

Across the room, I saw a guy sitting alone at a table staring down his coffee mug as if he was mad at the world.

I whispered, "*Who is that guy? He looks kinda familiar.*"

Mark followed my stare. "He looks familiar to me too. Let me think. Um, Barry? Bob? No, Buck!"

"Shh. He's looking." I let out a groan. "We'd better go over there and say 'hi.'" We both stood up. I felt awkward, but at this point, we didn't have a choice.

"Hey, Buck, where ya at?" Thankfully, Mark spoke first. Funny how the local dialects come back when you run into a native. I had nearly forgotten the local expression which meant 'how are you'?

Buck stared at me. "Not so great. Not at all." With that as a starter, I couldn't imagine the conversation was going to go anywhere good. "Do I know you?"

"Yes, I'm Miranda Marquette." I stuck my hand out, and he glared at it. I put it back down, pretending not to notice his blatant snub. I babbled on. "I think you were in my math class in eleventh grade. Remember Mr.'Twitt'? We used to make fun of him something wicked." He almost smiled, but then thought better of it.

"Yeah, whatever. That's like decades ago now." He had perked up at the mention of my last name. "Are you any relation to Sabine Marquette?"

I looked at my feet and prayed for a good answer and then mumbled, "She's my cousin." I didn't feel like getting into the sister thing, and it was none of his business either way.

He spoke with a heavy New Orleans accent, somewhere between a traditional Southern drawl and a Brooklyn accent. "Hey, if you see her, tell her I want my job back, will ya?" I smiled sincerely. "I'll see what I can do." I didn't want to make any promises, but I couldn't help but feel sorry for the guy. He brightened slightly when I asked, "Didn't I hear you got an award or a medal or something for your heroic work during Katrina?"

Lines appeared across his forehead as his upbeat demeanor disappeared almost immediately. "Yeah, yeah, yeah, that and a buck'll get me a cup of coffee. Pretty soon I'm not even gonna have a dime since your cousin's ship captain fired me."

I saw where this was going. "I'm sorry to hear that. I hear Sabine is not that easy to work for so maybe it's a blessing." I smiled weakly.

Immediately, tears began running down his face. "I don't know what I'm gonna do." He stared at his hands. "I jus' don't have any skills an' since Katrina, work 'as been harder to come by. I don't know what I's gonna tell Sandy. She's gonna kill me. We've got three kids with another on the way."

I was surprised, to say the least, "That's right. You were dating Sandy Sully in high school."

"Yup, we tied the knot after we got out of high school for better or for worse." Talking about Sandy seemed to perk him up again. He smiled and shook his head. "I'm guessing she'd tell you it'd been for worse, but we get by okay. I guess we'll get past this too." Then the smile left his face in defeat. He hung his head.

He was suddenly quiet, and I seized the opportunity. "Hey, guys, I'll be right back, I have to powder my nose." I squeezed out of the chair between closely spaced tables. I was relieved to be heading to the bathroom and away from the conversation. I'd have to talk to Sabine to learn the whole story.

When I returned, Mark was finishing a conversation with Buck as I got back to the table. I was happy to see they had changed the subject. "I've got one in all three of my cars' glove compartments at all times. I've never needed to use one, but you never know, and, I feel better knowing I can defend myself if I need to."

Buck nodded in agreement. "I ain't never owned a handgun. I got a real temper so I always thought a handgun might get me in trouble that I couldn't get out of. I got a couple huntin' rifles, though." They both paused, either because I was glaring at Mark, or because they had run out of manly things to say about guns.

I didn't want to settle back in at Buck's table, so I said, "Hey Buck, I guess we'll get back to our brunch. I'll tell you what. Maybe there's something I can do." I gave him a card with my cell phone number on it. "Would it be okay if I talked to Sabine about this? Maybe she doesn't even know you were fired." Best case, I could talk to him after I started my investigation; maybe he knew something.

He brightened a little. "Sure. I'm pretty sure it's a done deal, but it can't hurt to try."

"Okay, take care." I smiled at him, and then headed back to our table.

Mark looked at me inquisitively. "That was interesting."

I frowned and whispered. "Probably more interesting for him. What were you doing telling him where you store your guns? Are you crazy?"

He brushed me off with his hand. "You've been away too long. Nearly half the population down here has a gun in their truck. That's not news."

Keeping my voice down, I changed the subject. "I'm not sure if you heard, but Sabine's got some business issues going on, so I'm here to see what I can find out for her." I had been spending so much time with family issues, I hadn't actually put a plan together. I'd been avoiding the reality that I'd be kicking back into investigator mode. My stomach churned as my mind started ticking off things I needed to get done. "That reminds me, I've gotta rent a car so that I can get down to Venice."

"Don't rent a car, Miranda." Mark's eyes lit up, "That's crazy expensive, and I've got two spare cars sitting at home. Granted, they aren't as sharp as my Porsche, but I have a Jeep Cherokee that I think would be perfect for you. It needs to be driven, so you'd be doing me a favor."

"That is a kind offer. Are you sure it wouldn't be too much trouble?" I asked.

He cocked his head to the side and said, "This is a 'no strings attached' offer, Miranda. I've got a spare car. You need a car. That's it. I have no other agenda."

Too bad this guy wasn't more my type in high school. I smiled at his perceptiveness. "Thanks, Mark. I really appreciate it."

As if on cue, my Blackberry chirped with a text message from Sabine. *Did you get all landed?*

I texted back. *Yes, I'm just arranging for a vehicle then I'll be heading down.* I didn't bother to go into detail since I'd be seeing her later. Mark seemed like a great guy. I hadn't gotten to know him as an adult, but it seemed to me that Sabine would eat him alive. I made a mental note to get the scoop from her.

"Okay," I said to Mark, trying to ignore the phone distraction. "Let's get outta here and go get that Jeep!"

Chapter 5

Mark lived in Chalmette, just upriver from Meraux. I was surprised when we rolled past a group of modern, post-Katrina ranch-style houses. The hurricane must have wiped out his neighborhood because they all looked brand new.

"Wow, not bad for a homeboy," I said, figuring his house was the one with the Jeep in the driveway.

The smile that he gave me was the widest one yet. "I like it. Would you like to come in?"

"Nope, gotta get to Sabine's. I'm late already." I tapped my pocket. "She's already texting me to see what my ETA is."

He looked disappointed as he tossed me the keys to the Jeep, but I didn't have the time or inclination to worry about the implications of his invitation.

I rolled my eyes, pointing at his vanity plate: "Law Guy."

He reddened a little and chuckled at my reaction. "Well, this is who I am around these parts. It's cheap advertising."

I smiled at the banter between us. It felt comfortable, like home. I crawled into the driver's seat of the Jeep and sat for a minute, familiarizing myself with the critical knobs and switches like those that operate the windows, the power seat, the mirrors, the satellite radio, and the air conditioning.

Mark surprised me when he came out of the house and ran down the driveway as I was backing out.

I hit the brakes and rolled down the window.

"There's a handgun locked in the glove compartment, just in case you need it. It opens with the ignition key."

"Thanks for telling me."

He waved and headed back up his drive.

Hoping I'd never have to use it, I unlocked the glove compartment and opened it up to see a ten mm Glock. I picked up the gun briefly. Considering I had been a cop for six years, it felt strange in my hand; I hadn't touched a handgun since I'd been shot. I carefully set it back in place and then headed to my mom's house to get my bags. Surprisingly no-one was home, but I made a mental note to give her a call later letting her know I was with Sabine. I used the few miles on the local streets before reaching LA23 to get used to the large SUV. It felt far different than my little Mazda convertible. Soon I was motoring down LA 23 for the nearly two-hour drive to Venice.

I put all the windows down so I could smell the Bayou air I had missed so much. The wind blowing through my incessantly messy hair reminded me of how much I missed my motorcycle. It was probably better that I wasn't riding though. Rather than paying attention to the road, I was making a checklist in my mind of what I needed to do first to carry out this investigation. I wanted to impress Sabine by already having a game plan in place. It seemed like interviewing Sabine's employees was the logical place to start. I was making progress. This was the first time I had thought about questioning potential suspects without breaking into a cold sweat.

Two hours was barely long enough to plan out my next couple of days. My mind was racing in anticipation of the investigation when I finally saw the shabby sign welcoming me to Venice, population 202, that loomed before me. I had driven down here once on a dare in high school, but that was another story for another time. I felt like I was driving to the end of the world, because I was. In about a mile, the road would end; there was nothing past Venice except water.

Sabine lived between Sooner Road and the L turn. After that, it was just the marina and some oil tanks. There never had been a building boom down here, so it was a mishmash of businesses, shacks, and closed-down gas stations. Her house number was

1224. When I found it, I pulled off the road and blinked in confusion. She used the term 'house' very liberally. Frankly, it looked like a fish shack. *Man, what a way to live. What was she thinking? What was I thinking, agreeing to stay with her?*

Just when I was starting to wonder if I was in the right place, or if I should head for the hills, I heard a familiar voice, "Hey, Cuz! About time you got here. I was just about to send out the authorities to see if you were wrapped around a tree somewhere."

I hopped out of the SUV and ran to throw my arms around Sabine.

"Are you okay, sweetie?" She held me at arm's length after I released my death grip on her. "We just saw each other a couple of weeks ago."

"Sorry, I had worse-than-typical family drama at my mom's house, and I needed a hug." I decided to spare her the details of my anxiety about getting started on her case. I just needed to take action and I'd be fine.

She peeked over my shoulder and then frowned. "Hey, how'd you get Mark's car? That plate is, what should I say? Unmistakable." She apparently didn't like it any better than I did. She gave me a look that was somewhere between quizzical and melancholy. "I didn't even know you knew Mark."

I felt a pang of guilt like I had been called into the principal's office. "We ran into each other, and I happened to bring up that I was gonna rent a car and he offered me this." I didn't want to touch the topic of Mark with a ten-foot pole. "Nothing planned. It just happened. I'm happy about it, though, since I don't know how long I'm gonna be here and I didn't want to spend a fortune on a rental car."

Thankfully, she seemed satisfied with the explanation, so I didn't have to go into detail about how I hadn't been completely sure about his intentions. I grabbed my bags out of the back, and she grabbed my carry-on, grinning, "Are you planning on staying a year?"

It felt good to laugh. "I told you. Whatever it takes."

She opened the front door, and I dragged my bags in. I stopped in my tracks, "Hey, this is really cute. Actually, it's better than cute; it's gorgeous."

I was shocked. Everything was brand new and tastefully done. Sabine took me on the ten-cent tour, and it just got more amazing in each room. There were hardwood floors throughout with tasteful Oriental rugs, a gourmet kitchen with granite countertops and a cooking island, and marble floors in the bathrooms. There were two decent-sized bedrooms, each with a full bath, and an office off the kitchen. Her living room boasted a big screen—it had to be at least 80 inches—TV mounted on the wall and a comfortable sectional couch. It was the last thing I expected to find inside a fish shack.

She explained. "In this part of the world, you don't flaunt your good fortune. When I bought this place, I decided to keep the outside just as it was, so I wasn't drawing attention to myself. I had the inside completely gutted. I was lucky to find a couple of artisans down here who were super affordable and did amazing work. I'm sure the neighbors and the fishermen passing by every day wondered why it was taking so long to get my remodeling done, but what they don't know won't hurt them, and it won't hurt me."

"You always were the smart one, Sabine," I said with love and affection.

She beamed with pride, but there was a hint of sadness in her eyes that I hadn't seen when she was out in Malibu.

I rubbed her shoulder. "Let's sit down and talk about how we're gonna tackle this problem, okay?"

She attempted a smile, but the corners of her mouth turned down. "You want some coffee?"

She hit my hot button, "I'd *kill* for coffee. There wasn't a decent place to stop in the last hour or not any place I dared to stop anyway." I plopped on the most comfortable couch in the world.

She called from the kitchen with a lighthearted lilt. "You're getting soft, *mon amour*. There was a time that nothing scared you."

"That Goth stuff was just a front. I was scared to death." I smiled sheepishly. "It's funny. I love to take physical risks. I love to sky and cliff-dive, street luge, motorcycling on or off-road, but I'm still scared of people. After all, all it takes is an encounter with one crazy person, and you're dead." I had scoffed at my therapist's suggestion that I had post-traumatic stress disorder, but maybe she wasn't so off base.

"I'm sorry you feel that way, but I need you to get over it if you're going to help me figure this out." She sat down next to me now that she had the coffee started. "You're likely to come into contact with people who aren't gonna be happy that you're here and would love nothing more than to intimidate you right back to California."

I smiled and gave her another hug. I hadn't realized how much I missed her. "I'm here for you, Sabine. We all have fears inside that we have to conquer, even you."

She hugged me tightly. "Nope, not me. I can't afford to be afraid."

I thought that she protested too much, but I let it go. "Okay, you need to tell me everything you know about your shrimping problem, so I can do whatever I can to help." Now that I had my marching orders from Sabine, I was ready to move forward. "Oh, by the way, Mark and I ran into an ex-employee at the Déjà vu earlier. Buck?"

"Oh yeah, Buck. I hated to see him go, but according to Emil, the captain, he was stealing from us. He was damned lucky we didn't prosecute." Her distracted look contradicted her reaction. I wasn't sure I bought her explanation. "Really? What did he steal?"

"Money and some equipment. He was caught red-handed." She wasn't looking me in the eye, and I felt like she was either lying or trying to reconstruct what happened while she spoke. My six years as a cop had me leaning toward lying, but I'd give her the benefit of the doubt for now.

"That's funny. Buck never mentioned that," I said. Not that we talked all that much, but the whole thing didn't smell right to me.

She looked over at the blank TV screen as we talked, "Um, well, makes sense, I guess. Who would want to admit they're a thief?"

I followed her eyes until they were focused on mine. "Are you okay? You seem kind of distracted." I said, concerned.

She snapped back to reality. "Oh, sorry, just thinking about business stuff."

"Okay, can you give me some details about what we discussed when you came to visit? You know, like who was aware you got the contract, personnel changes since you got it, stuff like that." I got my Blackberry out to type notes as she spoke.

We settled into client/investigator roles, and she did her best to provide me with the information I needed. "Just before I signed the contract, I hired a new captain . . . Emil Abel. My last guy couldn't handle the responsibility of a fleet. He was okay

69

when he wasn't drinking, but he usually was and that wouldn't do. I finally had to let him go before he killed someone. Emil was a captain upriver for more than thirty years, so I knew he'd be able to help me out."

"I wonder why he was available after all that time."

She nodded, understanding my concern, "I had the same question. Evidently, there was a fall-out between him and the owner of the company. Rumors are that it was about a woman. I didn't care about the details as long as it wasn't about addiction or work performance." She shrugged.

"Fair enough," I said. "How's he been so far? How has the crew reacted to him?"

"Emil is a tough character who doesn't take any guff from the crew, and they respect him for it." Then she grinned, "Or maybe they're scared of him. Either way, it works for me. Many of the issues I had been having with my employees not showing up to work, showing up late, or showing up drunk, have gone away. All in all, I'm happy with how things have turned out."

"That's good. Can't make money if no one does their work, right?" I said, paraphrasing one of Grandpapa's favorite sayings.

"Absolutely. And the work's getting done, but production has still dropped," Sabine sighed heavily. "I can't blame Emil. He's fishing in all the right areas. We've had successful catches there for years, but these days after we have a good haul one day, there's suddenly no shrimp the next day. We normally get days and days of good catches before we need to move on to a new place. Catching shrimp is as much an art as a science."

I had a nagging feeling, "I know you haven't known this Emil very long. Are you sure that you can trust him? The 'there are no shrimp to be found' story sounds too convenient."

"Well, *mon amour*, you know I don't completely trust anybody. However, he hasn't given me a reason not to trust him yet." She then shifted gears. "Let's have lunch and strategize after that. You want a glass of wine?

"I'd love some wine. Anything red? I'm a Cab Sauv nut, but anything red will do."

She headed for the kitchen and her well-stocked wine rack. "Hmmm, I have a 2005 or 2006."

"Definitely 2005. Perfect." Knowing Sabine as I do, I wasn't surprised to see her under counter wine cooler set at sixty degrees, perfect for a dry red.

She grabbed a bottle and poured a couple of glasses. She pulled out two prepared salads from the fridge.

I was relieved to be taking a break. I felt like I could use some downtime. "Looks delicious."

Soon afterward, we were both lounging on her couch. Lunch was fabulous, but the wine sealed the deal. Her house was surprisingly comfortable and quiet; I didn't want to ruin the moment, but I was bursting to get my new-found information off my chest.

I started slow. "Hey, how much do you know about the circumstances that brought you here from France?"

"Hmmm, well at the time, I was told that I was to come over here and live with my grandparents so that I could have a better life in America. My parents explained that they needed to stay back in France to run the fishing business and to raise my younger brother. He was only three when I left. I have learned since then that there was no love lost between your father and mine. I'm not sure what it was, but I have my hunches." She flipped her hair back with an air of indignance. "I honestly haven't thought about it much lately since I have my own life here and I have only seen my family a few times since I left France."

I shifted nervously on the couch. *I'm not sure I should be the one telling you this. Then again, if not me, who?* "Well, um, I got some interesting news from my mom when I was at the house. It was kind of, er, surprising, so I hope it's okay for me to tell you."

I had her attention now. She grabbed my arm and gritted her teeth, "Just spit it out, Miranda!"

"We are . . ." I started and hesitated.

"Sisters." She finished my sentence.

I stared at her, stunned. "How did you—?

She leaned back on the couch. "I figured it out years ago, but I knew you weren't ready for the news. I'm not quite as naïve as you are, Miranda. The story my parents dreamed up as an excuse never made sense to me. They had a good life in France. There had to be more. And the way you and I bonded, it just made sense. I never said anything because they all wanted to keep it a big secret, so I decided not to rock the boat. I would have asked your mom at some point, but she's been downright cold to me lately, so there was never a good chance for that. Quite honestly, blood or not, you have always been my sister, so this just makes it official."

Tears welled up in my eyes as I hugged her again. "I should have known you would take it better than I did. I was so angry about having been lied to all these years, that I walked out of the house and all the way to the Quarter."

"Oh my god, that's almost ten miles," she said, wide-eyed.

"Twelve, to be exact," I boasted. "In flip-flops."

"I guess you *were* mad." She put her hands on her hips. "I would think you'd be happy to have a sister."

I shrugged and said, "I'm thrilled about that. I just think my parents could have handled it better. It certainly explains the issues I have had with my dad." *Now I have a whole new father to have issues with.*

Sabine looked up at the ceiling, thinking back. "It sure does." Her voice trailed off, and she seemed like she didn't want to talk about it anymore

I cleared my throat following her lead. "Hey, would it work out if I spent the day interviewing the staff? I'm not sure what your routine is and how schedules work with three boats."

Sabine rubbed her eyes and scratched her head. "They normally all leave port by seven a.m., heading downriver to the Gulf and then splitting up. Why don't we do this? You can interview the crews of one boat each day so that we don't lose a whole day of production. I'll have Emil stagger their shifts tomorrow."

I jumped up and started to pace the room. "Have you told them that I'm coming or anything?"

Sabine stretched out on the part of the couch that I vacated. "I talked a little about it to Emil, but I didn't tell the crew, so they won't have time to make up any stories."

Finally, after all my apprehension, I was itching to get started. "Sabine, do you have your personnel files here or do you have another office?"

Sabine said in a confident tone, "The files are all in my office off the kitchen, but I probably have most of what you need right here." She pointed to her well-coiffed head.

I headed toward her office and pulled out her desk chair. "I'll tell you what—I'll pull the files, and you can give me some background information." She smiled, so I took that as a 'Yes' and I grabbed the alphabetical files starting with 'A.' "Okay, how about Tommy Albans?"

Sabine looked at the ceiling, searching her memory. "He's a mid-twenties kid from Buras. A local kid. He's typical for his age, needs more supervision than the older guys and looks to them for leadership. He comes off as a shy kid when you first meet him but has come out of his shell since he's been here. He's got an adorable girlfriend from upriver and plans on getting married as soon as he saves some money up."

"Wow!" She knew a lot more about this kid than I would ever know about an employee. "It says in here that he's got a criminal record. What's that about?"

Sabine brushed off the seriousness of the infraction with a simple hand gesture. "From what I can tell, it was one of those high school pranks where he and several of his buddies defaced a statue of their school's founder. Seemed harmless enough."

I frowned. "That judge must have been having a hard day not to let him off with a warning." I pulled the next file. "Okay, tell me about Juan Asteria."

Sabine dialed in her fantastic memory. "Grew up in West Texas, the son of a Mexican immigrant. His father had him pegged to take over the family's Taco Truck, but Juan wasn't having any part of it. He moved to the bayou a few years ago and did odd jobs, janitorial work, house painting, stuff like that. His friend, Charlie Orlando, worked here for a while and recommended Juan. He's been a great asset, comes to work early, leaves late, volunteers for overtime when we need it. I'd give him an A if he were being graded."

I looked at her with my mouth open.

Sabine punched my arm. "What? Did you think I was just a pretty face? I do own the company, you know."

I was impressed. "I just can't believe the detail you know about your employees. I figured you owned the place and let your captain run the show."

"Oh, I see." She pointed at her chest. "You thought I was like you and just sat back while the money rolled in." She winked.

My face reddened a bit. I started to respond with a defensive remark, but who was I kidding? She worked way harder than I did. "Touché, Sabine."

Sabine could tell that she'd hurt my feelings and came over to hugged me. "No offense intended, my dear."

I hugged her back and smiled. "I guess sometimes the truth hurts. I feel guilty sometimes about the amount of money I make compared to how much work I do."

Sabine exclaimed, "Believe me, if I could get a job like that, I'd catch the next boat out of town."

We spent the next three hours reviewing her employees one by one until I was on information overload. "I'm done!" I exhaled dramatically for effect, as I collapsed on the couch.

Sabine cooked while I laid on the couch trying to absorb everything she had told me. I took notes, but it was hard to capture all the detail that Sabine provided with a pen and paper, but I did my best to summarize the information I had inputted into my Blackberry. Not surprisingly, she served fresh shrimp for dinner, and we went off to bed early.

When the sun peeked through my bedroom window, I couldn't believe that it was only six and I wasn't grumpy. It had everything to do with sleeping in the most comfortable bed. I made a mental note to ask Sabine what kind of mattress it was. I spent a mint on the one I had at home, but it was nowhere near as comfortable. I jumped out of bed and made a beeline for the shower. I couldn't wait to get these interviews started.

I took a nice, long shower. I hoped Sabine didn't have a small water heater or she was going to be an unhappy camper if she hadn't showered yet. While I squirted some shampoo on my locks, I thought about our discussion yesterday. I was glad the cousin/sister thing was out in the open. I guess I either overreacted when my mom gave me the news or Sabine was just better adjusted than I am. Or maybe the fact that she suspected we might be sisters had something to do with her lack of reaction.

After my shower, I took my time toweling off and drying my hair. I never wore much makeup, so that took almost no time. I knew from growing up here that my hair was going to be an issue due to the humidity. Add the salty sea air to that, and it was going to be a bird's nest. I decided to opt for a baseball cap and a ponytail. After all, I wasn't trying to win a beauty contest.

I could smell coffee wafting under the door. It was enough to make me want to go out in the kitchen right now, but I still needed some clothes. Jeans and a pink Breast Cancer Awareness T-shirt worked fine. I nodded in approval when I looked in the mirror and headed out of the bedroom.

When I got out to the kitchen, Sabine was in her office reviewing spreadsheets with lots of graphs and charts on them. I had no idea how to do that stuff, and it amazed me that she did. I looked over her shoulder. "Can you teach me how to do that some time? I'm pretty good at Word, but I'm completely lost when it comes to Excel."

She said, "Sure. I'd love to." Then, smiling, she stood and led me to the kitchen where she had already served up crab omelets, fresh squeezed orange juice and an Ethiopian coffee that was to die for. While she flitted around the kitchen, she asked, "Do you want butter or cream cheese on your bagel?"

"Cream cheese," I said. "Wait." I giggled, "give me both."

She slid her knife into the cream cheese and then the butter and spread them on the recently toasted bagel. Sabine then raised her head, followed by a raise of her eyebrows. "I'm really proud of you. I probably don't tell you that enough. You are successful, confident and a survivor. After all you went through, you could have bought that house with the money and thumbed your nose at the world, but you turned a tragedy into one amazing success story."

I smiled. "Thanks, Cuz, er, I mean, Sis. Whatever, let's eat."

We had a pleasant and comfortable breakfast. We talked about our childhoods and how we got to where we were today. She hadn't even told me much about her life as a young teen in France. In many ways, her country life seemed idyllic compared to the rat race we were so accustomed to here in this country.

I reflected for a moment and then remembered my conversation yesterday. I blurted out, "Hey, whatever happened with you and Mark? He seems like a nice guy now that he's gotten past the geeky stage."

She paused and seemed to study the wall behind me for a moment. "I haven't really thought much about him lately. I guess we just weren't right for one another."

I drummed my fingers on the table. "There had to be a reason you broke up. Right?"

She continued, "We'd dated a few times and things were comfortable between us. We talked and laughed and told each other stories from our past. So, we decided to go away for the weekend. There was nothing untoward about it. We had booked separate rooms."

She had the faraway look of someone trying to remember details from the past. "A couple of days before the trip, Mark was dropping me off. He walked me to the door, as usual. But then he unexpectedly kissed me. I didn't think about it that much at the time, but the more I thought about it, the more I thought this was a precursor to him wanting more intimacy on our trip. Well, to make a long story short, I texted him my regrets the next day. I haven't seen him since."

I stared at her, waiting for more, but she was silent. I finally said, "Wow, that was cold." I looked her in the eye. "Have you ever had second thoughts? It must be lonely down here."

She avoided looking me in the eye and got up and puttered around the kitchen instead. "Never. I'm not one to look back. I guess it wasn't meant to be."

We didn't talk much after that. After I finished eating, I helped Sabine clean up the kitchen, and then we moved to the living room and back onto her comfy couch. "So, Miranda, I'm gonna run over and talk to Emil and finalize plans for today. I was going to call, but I want to be able to read his reaction. When do you want to get started with the interviews?"

"Well," I responded, thinking while talking, "Around eight would be good. I was originally thinking seven, but it's already 6:59. I'll interview the first crew and finish up with Emil. He can probably help answer any questions I have after talking to the rest of them."

Sabine continued. "I don't know if anyone will give you anything you can use. Even if they know something, they are a pretty tight group."

I thought back to my law enforcement days. "One thing I have found with interrogations is that they usually yield some outcome, although not always a direct one. Guilty people have a way of showing their hand."

Telltale lines crossed her forehead. "I hate to put you in harm's way, but I guess there's no completely safe way to handle something like this." She thought for a minute. "You should be able to use *Fergie* for the interviews."

I cocked my head. "Who's Fergie?"

Sabine laughed. "I had to come up with a quick naming scheme to the fleet, so I picked female pop singers."

If I were naming ships, Fergie *wouldn't have been my first choice, but whatever.* It seemed better not to voice my opinion, so instead, I said, "I feel like Emil will be the key to my success since he's the eyes and ears of your operation. If I can get his cooperation, I have a chance. I know you said you mentioned it to him, but how much does he know exactly?"

She looked up at the ceiling, "Well, I didn't tell him that I'd be bringing you in to investigate if that's what you mean. He does know that I'm very concerned and frustrated with the catch in the last month or so. We've talked about it several times, but not since I came back from the conference. I'm honestly not sure how open he'll be to you. He's very old-school, and I get the idea that he doesn't care much for women, especially women in the shrimping business."

"So, why'd you hire him?" I couldn't help but wonder.

"There's not a lot of options around here, especially with thirty years' experience. I figured I could handle him." She responded in typical Sabine fashion.

I was getting antsy. Too much talk and not enough action for me. Before I could voice my opinion, Sabine looked at her watch.

"Oh my gosh, where has the time gone?" She rushed to the door. "I need to catch Emil so we can finalize the schedule." She ran out and across the road to the marina.

I sat back on the couch and started reading through the notes I took earlier. I grimaced; I was out of practice, and it was making me feel very unprepared.

Within ten minutes, Sabine was back. "Well, Emil wasn't thrilled that I was disrupting his day, but we're all set. You can interview on the *Fergie*. Emil will take the *P!NK* and Sam will take the *Avril*. You'd better get over there. The first group is already lining up to talk to you."

We hugged, and I said, "Wish me luck."

Sabine kissed both of my cheeks. "Thanks so much."

I turned and headed for the Jeep. Honestly, it would only have taken me two minutes to walk over there, but it was always good to have transportation. You never knew when you might need to make a quick getaway. It was already eighty-five degrees and brutally humid. As I suspected, it took me less than a minute to get to the docks. Sabine's fleet appeared to be the only commercial boats left at the docks, and the ships that weren't staying in port were motoring out as I approached, diesel smoke billowing from the vertical exhaust pipes.

There were about ten young men on the dock, talking, smoking cigarettes, and doing whatever else it is that guys do when they are bored or nervous. As I approached, they all turned and stared at me in unison. Maybe I was getting paranoid, but it felt more like they were glaring, except for the couple who were smirking, nodding, and poking each other. The one in the front of the line whistled, which prompted several others to laugh and start catcalling.

I needed to get things under control, so I figured I'd start with a cordial approach. I walked quickly to the front of the line. "Good morning, gentlemen."

The apparent leader of the group interrupted. "We ain't no gentlemen, ma'am."

I didn't want this to deteriorate any further, so I raised my voice hoping I sounded like an authority figure and not like a nervous and, quite frankly, out of practice, amateur sleuth. "My name is Miranda. I'm working for Sabine. We can do this the easy way or the hard way. It's up to you to decide. We can play nice, and you can respectfully provide the information I request, or we can start by requesting background checks on each of you."

A couple of them shifted nervously from one foot to the other and looked anywhere but at me. I happened to know from Sabine that it was likely that there were some with arrest records out there that she had hired anyway even though they hadn't disclosed it on their application. And, I already knew of a couple based on my conversations with Sabine.

I continued, having gained their attention, "Since Sabine required all of you to swear on your job application that you had no prior record, that approach might not be the most positive thing for *some of you*." I glared directly at the ringleader who had already had an immediate attitude adjustment.

I motioned him to climb aboard with me. "I guess you're first."

He followed me with no further smart remarks. I led him to the navigation bridge, a mahogany-lined space which doubled as the captain's office and where the huge steering wheel was. I recognized it from when I used to sit on my Grandpapa's knee, and he'd let me steer his shrimping boat. I felt a stab of guilt and remorse for not being able to tell him goodbye and how much I loved him. I pushed the feeling down.

I turned to find the young man right behind me. "Johnny Vazquez."

He stuck out his hand. "No hard feelings about before. I was just kidding around." He winked, and I had to admit he softened my heart just a little.

I smiled. "Do you know why you're here?"

"I don't know much. Heard a rumor that the catch is down and there might be some foul play involved."

I looked at Johnny. "That's pretty much it. Do you know anything about that?"

He looked thoughtful. "Can't say that I do, ma'am."

I had this guy's number. I'd seen it a thousand times. "Okay, Johnny, as I said, we can do this the easy way or the hard way. I know that you think you can charm me and walk off this ship smelling like a rose. If that's how you want to play this, let me tell you one thing. If I find out later that you withheld information or lied to me, I will make sure I come down on you twice as hard as I would have if you told me the truth up front. And you can tell your buddies the same thing."

His smile faded. "I like my job, and I don't want to get fired. All I can say is that this is between Sabine and Emil. Don't know why you're involving any of us." We both sat staring at one another for what seemed like an eternity. I didn't know what I was waiting for other than a better answer, but that was all he had. With minor variations, the rest of the morning went the same way. Either no one knew anything, or they were all great liars. I didn't have a clue which at this point. At around noon, I walked back over to Sabine's to get a change of scenery and some lunch. Sabine was buried in paperwork in her office and waved to me but didn't get up.

I made myself a sandwich and the hour went by quickly as I was lost in my thoughts and trying to think of a better angle to garner more information from the remaining group. I yelled to Sabine, "See you tonight," as I walked out the door toward the Jeep. I assumed Sabine waved from her office but offered no comment.

There were just six more guys to talk to. In this day and age, I was surprised there weren't any females among them, but I supposed it was probably too physically demanding. The afternoon was just as pointless as the morning. I was about to give up on getting anything more useful than the standard story when Bob Lynch walked in. He was very different from the rest of the group. Number one, he had at least twenty years on all of them, and number two, he wasn't taking the party line.

He started before I could even ask a question. "Okay, Missy, let me tell you a couple of things. First, there is not one guy here who trusts you as far as they can throw you. You are a bad combination of Sabine's cousin and an amateur. If you put yourself in their position, you can imagine why you're not trusted. I get it. But, I'm not afraid of being accused of anything because I know I haven't done anything wrong. So, if there's anything I can do to help, I will. I've had to change jobs more than I like to admit, so I'd like this one to work out."

"Well, that's refreshing." I smiled. "So, what have you got?"

"I'll give you my opinion." He looked around the room like he was checking for hidden cameras. "You can't tell Emil I told you this or I'll be toast."

I smiled. "It's all confidential. You don't have to worry." I did have to share everything with Sabine, but I wanted answers.

He seemed to relax a little. "Okay. One day a couple of weeks ago, I was over at the CrawGator after my shift ended. I sometimes go over there for a beer before I head back upriver. I remembered that I left my hat on the boat. It had gotten wet, and it was drying below deck. So, I ran back out on the dock, and the boat was gone. When I left the boat, Emil was the only one aboard, so he had to have taken it."

I was missing the point. "So, couldn't Emil have been going to fuel it up for the next day?"

He scratched his head. "Honestly, no. Once we dock, our catch is weighed. It's a process control to prevent theft and to keep the catch fresh, so it gets cooled, cleaned and to market as soon as possible."

"So, where do you think he went?" I asked.

He continued with such an intense look on his face, he seemed to be in pain. "I was curious, so I hung around. About an hour later he returned to port, tied the boat up and left in his car. I went back on board, and there were no shrimp in the hold. It was like we never went out that day."

"Couldn't there be another explanation? Maybe there is another customer who bought some or all of that particular catch." I pressed.

He rubbed his chin. "I suppose, but I've asked around, and that's not how they do business here. Everything we catch is supposed to be earmarked for the Costco contract."

I honestly wasn't sure it meant anything. "I'll see what I can find out from Sabine without mentioning your name."

"Thank you," he said. "I'd hate for her to think I was a snitch."

"Is there anything else?" I asked.

He thought for a minute. "Nothing I can think of. I'll let you know, though, if I think of something else."

I handed him my card. "Call my cell number day or night if you think of anything else. And, thanks, Bob."

He tipped his hat and left the ship. My day was almost done. I only had Emil to speak to. Just as I had that thought, the door to the navigation room opened. A man, in his sixties, at least, with the ruddy wrinkled face of a lifetime drinker entered. He seemed disoriented for a moment like he wasn't expecting me to be there.

I walked toward him and stuck out my hand. "Emil?" He nodded. "I'm Miranda Marquette. I'm Sabine's cousin here to help her out with the shrinking catch." I smiled hoping he would smile back.

He didn't. I could swear that he was slurring his words slightly. His face reddened as he spoke. "You can go back to wherever it is you come from. Everything is fine, and I told your dang fool cousin the same thing." He walked toward the door, obviously hoping I would follow him.

I didn't move. "Then how do you explain the lack of shrimp?"

He raised his voice. "I've been shrimping my whole life. Some years are good. Some years are bad. You can't wish shrimp to arrive. They will arrive in their own time. If she'd," he motioned over toward Sabine's shack, "been in the business more than five minutes, she'd understand that. It ain't my fault that she signed that damned contract. She never asked my opinion so now she has to lie in it."

I wasn't sure the analogy worked, but I knew what he meant. "So, you don't believe that anything is wrong, just her business sense, is that what you are saying?"

The veins at his receding hairline bulged. "What I'm saying is that you can go back and tell her that she don't know nothin' about the shrimping business and she shouldn't be looking for people to blame for her bad decisions. Now, you need to get off my boat." He, not so gently, grabbed my arm and guided me toward the door.

"But . . ." I tried to protest and suddenly found myself on the dock with several onlookers from today's interviews who were curious about how my conversation with Emil would go. Johnny Vasquez was one of them.

Embarrassed at being summarily dismissed by Emil, I yelled back at the door. "We will discuss this later!" and I stormed off the dock. My face was red and hot when I got behind the wheel of the Jeep. How could I go back to Sabine and tell her that Emil threw me off the boat? Since Sabine lived across the street from the marina, I didn't have much time to figure it out.

When I got to her house, I walked in without knocking. She was intently working on her desktop and barely acknowledged my return, but that was fine with me. "How'd it go?" I responded weakly. "Fine," and went to my room. I plopped down on the bed. *What just happened back there? You blew every part of that interrogation! You let him take control. You weren't assertive. You weren't prepared. You . . . well face it, Miranda, you messed up.* I closed my eyes and tears ran into my ears.

I heard a knock on my door. "Miranda, are you okay?" Sabine had come out of her business-induced coma.

"I'm fine," I said.

"Can I come in?" she insisted. She walked in and stared at me like I was crazy, crying with tears running down my cheeks. "You don't look fine."

"Emil threw me out." I nearly ran out to the living room to escape her questions and plopped down on the couch feeling dejected and defeated.

"He did what?" she asked indignantly, following me out of the bedroom with her hands on her hips.

I sniffled. "Now don't you get mad at me too."

"I'm not mad! I just find it hard to believe that Emil *threw* you off the boat." She sat in a chair across the room.

"Well, he did. And there were witnesses." I closed my eyes, wishing this day would just go away.

"For heaven's sake, Miranda, you are so dramatic." I could only imagine what hand motions Sabine was using because I refused to look at her.

I pouted like the child I felt like at that moment. "He did throw me off the boat."

"Well, what did you say to him?" Sabine was indignant. "Why are you taking his side? He said some mean things about you too." I had finally stopped crying. "He said that you and I are crazy and that ups and downs are just the nature of the business."

She stood and sat next to me on the couch. "Oh, he gave me that line too. That was just Round One. You need to go back and talk to him tomorrow before he's had time for his afternoon snort."

"You *knew* about that?" I was amazed, especially since she mentioned firing her previous captain for the same reason

"I've suspected for a while. He seems like a functional alcoholic, though," she said, casually.

"Is there anything else you might want to tell me before I go back tomorrow?" I rolled my eyes.

She smiled. "I didn't want to prejudice your investigation."

We ate munchies for an hour or two, skipped dinner, and went to bed. The next morning came much faster than I would have liked. I could remember a strange dream about being trapped on a shrimping boat, not Sabine's exactly, much larger and darker. Whenever I tried to get off the ship, we were further and further from shore. When I finally made it to the navigation room, there was no one driving, but the steering wheel was moving like the captain was invisible.

I got up at 6:30 so I could catch Emil before the boats left port, so I didn't have time to evaluate the dream, but I was sure it meant something that I should be paying attention to. Where was my shrink when I needed her?

Sabine was already up and reviewing stacks of reports in her office. She had coffee made already by the time I stumbled into the kitchen. I groaned, "Don't you *ever* sleep?"

Sabine stood up, stretched and yawned. "Of course, I do, but I do have a business to run, plus I have to watch you every second."

I sauntered into her office and gave her a morning hug. "You won't have me to watch today. I'm just grabbing some coffee and getting out of your hair. I want to catch Emil first thing." I walked out the front door.

I decided to leave the car since I didn't want to get there any sooner than I had to. As I shot past the car down the dirt driveway, I noticed a can sitting on the rotted post of a wooden rail fence running along the north side of the property.

Suddenly I was ten years old hanging out with my Grandpapa. *"Go ahead youngin,' take a shot. See if you can knock that sucker off the fence."*

I smiled to myself at the memory and walked back to the Jeep. My heart did a little jolt when I realized I had not only left the vehicle unlocked, but the glove compartment as well. *You've got to be more careful* and prayed the gun was still there when I reached into the glove box. I breathed a sigh of relief when I felt that curved handle.

The Glock felt more natural in my hand than it had at Mark's. I thanked my Grandpapa for the good memory. There was no one in sight and nothing but an abandoned gas station in the lot behind the fence, so I raised the gun slowly and got the can lined up in my sights. I squeezed the trigger and braced myself for the kick which almost knocked me over. The sweet sound of the gunshot reverberating around the marina was nowhere near as rewarding as watching the can fly 50 feet toward the boarded-up building.

"You've still got it," I whispered as I shoved the Glock into my oversized purse. I looked back to see if the shot had disturbed

Sabine, but she apparently remained buried in her work in the back of the house.

It felt like Déjà vu as I walked out on the dock. Butterflies fluttered in my stomach after my last experience with Emil. I expected to see more people around, but for once I was happy to be wrong. At least if I got thrown off for a second time, there would be no witnesses. When I got to the top of the stairs to the navigation room, I could see through the window in the cabin door, and my heart dropped. Emil lay face down on the floor. I opened the door, ran over, rolled him over and instinctively put my ear to his chest checking for a heartbeat.

The early stages of decomposition were already settling in. Emil's skin was a purplish color and felt waxy and cool to the touch. I figured he'd been dead for an hour since not all the blood had dried up, but lividity had already begun to set in. At least it was clear that no one had tried to move him. I pulled out my phone and hesitated before I called 911. Based on my conversation with Sabine about local law enforcement, God only knew how long it would take to get someone down here. While it wasn't urgent since he'd been dead a while, I needed to be smart about it.

From my time as a cop, I knew that the person who reported the person dead was the first and most tempting suspect for them to hang their hat on. There were several reasons for that. Primarily, most of the time, the person reporting the death *was* the murderer. And second, it also took absolutely no effort to find the suspect since they were already in custody. I needed to think clearly and use my police experience to my advantage. I closed my eyes putting together the details about everything that happened before, during, and after I arrived here. At least I had

Sabine as an alibi; I was in bed and then eating breakfast before I came over here. I figured I had better just bite the bullet and call; the longer I waited, the worse it would look. I hit the send button.

"Plaquemines Parish, 911 operator." She sounded perkier than most 911 operators I had spoken to while on the force. *Here we go.* I took a deep breath. "Hello, I need to report a death."

"Before we go any further, are you sure the person or persons are deceased? Have you checked for a pulse or if the person is still breathing?" She seemed unusually cheerful, considering I just reported a murder.

"Yes. I am a former law enforcement officer and dealt with several deaths during my tenure. I would estimate that this individual has been deceased for at least an hour." I was trying to sound authoritative and in control, but even I could tell it was fake.

"Thank you. Before we continue and I take the rest of your information, let me connect with the sheriff's department. Can I get your location, please?" Her upbeat tone never faltered as if she were an announcer on a game show.

"I am at the marina in Venice. I found the body aboard a boat with the name of *Fergie.*" I rubbed my head just above my eye where it was starting to throb.

"Fergie?" If it hadn't been for N'Orléans accent, I would have pegged her as a valley girl.

"Yes, F-E-R-G-I-E. *Fergie,*" I said with some aggravation in my voice.

"Fergie. Got it. Can you give me the location of the vessel so that the officers can locate it more easily?" She took no note of my tone, which meant to me that she was either very good at what she did or was utterly oblivious.

"From the parking lot, you take the dock the furthest to the left. *Fergie* is at the end of the dock on the right side." I spoke as slowly as I could so that I wouldn't have to repeat myself.

"Okay. Please hold while I contact the sheriff's office, and then I will get your information." She continued to bubble over with enthusiasm.

"Okay. I'll hold." I was sure she was supposed to take my information first, but who was I to tell her how to do her job?

I wondered how long it would take the police to get down here. Port Sulphur, where they are based, was a half hour from here at least, but I decided that I shouldn't leave here just in case they could get here sooner. However, I thought it would be best if I let Sabine know what was going on before all the activity with sirens and ambulances started blowing into the marina.

As if on cue, the operator came back on the line, "Okay. Thanks for holding. I guess I should have done this first, getting your information. I'm new here, so I forgot. The sheriff was not happy that I hadn't gotten your name."

"My name is Miranda Marquette." Having had a few seconds to collect myself, I tried to sound more pleasant.

"No! Are you any relation to Sabine?" Bless her heart.

"Yes, we're cousins." Finally, a topic I could get behind.

"Okay. What is your address, dear?" I started questioning why I was so irritated earlier. She seemed nice enough and was just going her job.

"47 Malibu Colony Road, Malibu, California." Just saying my address made me feel homesick, and I was sure I sounded it too.

"Really? I've always wanted to visit California. Could you spell that, please." I almost asked if she needed me to spell California, but the joke would probably have been lost on her.

"Malibu—M-A-L-I-B-U—Colony—C-O-L-O-N-Y—Road and then Malibu again." I finally got over myself and smiled.

"I'm Daphne Masson by the way. Maybe we can meet while you are visiting." She sounded so sincere that I almost started making plans to get together. "Anyway, can you give me any details that you have about the dead person? Name, if you know it, how you found them, You know, that sort of thing."

"Nice to meet you, Daphne. I was in town to help Sabine. She's been having a business issue she wanted me to investigate. I met with the captain of her fleet yesterday, and I was going to follow-up with him this morning. His name is Emil with, of course, a French last name, but I can't think of it right now." I strained my brain and finally came up with it. "Oh, wait a minute. It's Abel, like Cain and Abel. I came down to the marina to talk with him before the fleet took off for the day. There was no one around, so I climbed on board and went to the navigation room, where we met yesterday. When I looked through the window in the door, I saw him lying on the floor. After I checked if he needed help, I called you."

"Thanks, honey. I was supposed to let you know that this call is being recorded, but I'm guessing you already knew that." She laughed. "Let me call the sheriff back to see what their ETA is. I'll be right back after another brief hold."

"Okay, I'm gonna put you on speaker, so don't say anything confidential when you come back on." I pulled the phone away from my ear and switched to speaker mode.

"Okay, dear. I'll be right back. The sheriff wasn't in a very good mood, so I don't think we'll be chatting long." She didn't sound concerned about the sheriff's mood. I guessed that the sheriff was never particularly pleasant to this woman.

God, I wish I knew if I would have time to go over and tell Sabine before the law arrived. I decided I shouldn't chance it.

"Miranda? I'm back. They will be there directly. Less than five minutes, so just sit tight. I let them know your name so you can get acquainted." I was pretty sure they wouldn't care about getting acquainted with me, but it was a nice thought.

"Okay. I'll go down on the dock so they can see where I am. Is that everything you need?" I felt like I was in the twilight zone—this was the strangest 911 call ever.

"Yes, it is, sweetie. I hope to meet you before you go back to California. Take care of yourself," she gushed.

"Bye, Daphne. You too." I chuckled to myself.

I didn't feel right just calling Sabine to let her know her captain was dead. On the other hand, once the cops got here, the cat would be out of the bag. This town was way too small, and she lived across the road. The call took me longer then I had planned so I broke into a run to let Sabine know what was going on before the cops arrived. As I was halfway across the parking lot, a sheriff's car pulled into the lot. No lights or sirens. Since I was expecting them and I knew they were expecting me, I gave them a brief wave as I ran by. So, nothing could have surprised me more than when I heard the car slide to a stop and car doors open and more than one voice yell, "Freeze."

I turned around and was stunned to find two officers of the law standing with their pistols aimed at me. "Face down on the ground! *Now!*"

"What the . . ." There had to be a misunderstanding of some sort. I stayed standing and fished around in my purse to find my phone. "You know I called 911 and have been waiting for you for 45 minutes, right?"

"Throw down your purse and face down on the pavement *now,* ma'am, or we will help you." He was dead serious; Despite

Daphne's hospitality, it was clear they weren't going to want to visit with me or get acquainted any time soon.

The second one tackled me, put his knee on my back and shoved my face onto the blacktop. "Hands behind your back now."

My purse dropped to the ground, and the Glock fell out. This was not my day. The younger of the two officers cuffed me while I was on the ground and not so gingerly helped me to my feet. It wasn't until I was standing again that I remembered that my blouse was stained with blood from listening to Emil's chest, and they had just recovered a weapon from my purse.

They shoved me in the back seat of the patrol car. The sheriff explained, "We would normally take your statement now, but due to the unusual circumstances of this case and the evidence that has been confiscated, we are obligated under the Louisiana State Police Community Support Program to take you to the nearest State Police facility so that they can assume responsibility for your case. In the meantime, you have the right to remain silent and refuse to answer questions. Anything you do say may be used against you in a court of law. You have the right to consult an attorney before speaking to the police and to have an attorney present during questioning now or in the future. If you cannot afford an attorney, one will be appointed for you before any questioning if you wish. Do you understand these rights?"

I tried to think of something smart to say, but the only thing that came out was, "Yes."

Chapter 6

Two hours later, the Sheriff's cruiser pulled in front of the State Police Headquarters in New Orleans, but the ride felt like a lifetime.

I had plenty of time to relive the last few hours, trying to figure out where I had gone wrong. I settled on tossing the gun into my purse after target practice as my biggest mistake followed closely by appearing to be running away from the crime scene. I admonished myself for not thinking like a cop.

State Police Headquarters were right across from the Superdome. I had visited here on a school field trip once years ago. That was the first experience that had made me want to become a cop.

My captors didn't waste any time pulling me out of the car. They seemed to enjoy manhandling me. I hoped I wasn't this abusive when I was a cop.

The building was intimidating, gray, and dated back to the thirties. It looked like they'd given it a bit of a facelift since I was in grade school, but it was as I remembered it. The entrance had ceilings that were at least five stories high. These days, they would never design anything this beautiful for the police or any government function. It made me wonder where they got the money to build this one back during The Great Depression. As they led me into the building, I decided that I should focus on the problem at hand as opposed to admiring the architecture.

They shoved me into the elevator. The taller one pushed the button for the eleventh floor. When the elevator stopped, I was tempted to say something like 'housewares and home furnishings,' but it didn't seem appropriate. We took a right out of the elevator and walked down the hall to the second door on the right. The floor was much more utilitarian than the lobby and far less impressive. There were two well-dressed detectives, I assumed, sitting at the far end of the table. I hoped I was in better hands than with these small-town cops.

The sheriff and deputy removed the handcuffs and left without comment. The two detectives stood. They both shook my hand and introduced themselves as Detectives Sansone and Bricker. Sansone was a sandy-haired athletic type in his late thirties or early forties. Bricker probably put away more burgers and fries, but he had kinder eyes than his partner. I pegged Bricker as the 'good cop.' Time would tell. They motioned for me to sit across from them. No bare light bulbs hung over my head. I took that as a good sign; it was all I had.

Bricker spoke first. "Miranda. Can I call you Miranda?" I nodded without saying a word, and he continued. "Miranda, would you like something to drink, some coffee or water perhaps?"

I tried to smile, but to be honest, I wasn't feeling it at that moment. "No, thanks."

He continued, "First of all, I want to explain why we're here and why they didn't question you locally. We recently started a new program with some of the more rural Parishes, where the Louisiana State Police assume responsibility for serious, non-routine cases. We find that it works better since the local law enforcement agencies have significantly less experience and much smaller budgets when it comes to dealing with these cases. We prefer to deal with the case from start to finish as opposed to being brought in in the middle where we then have to take time getting up to speed. Honestly, there have been some issues in the past concerning the integrity of crime scenes and the handling of evidence. We already have a team at the scene as we speak. Okay. That being said, we have some questions we want to ask."

"I want to have an attorney present." I forced a smile, hoping they wouldn't push back on my request.

"Well, Miranda, you certainly have the right to an attorney. Although that might be premature at this point since we haven't charged you with anything. We're just on a fact-finding mission. Since we aren't accusing you of any wrongdoing at this point, we thought you might have a conversation with us." The fact that he wouldn't look me directly in the eye when he addressed me in his monotone voice did not make me feel all warm and fuzzy.

I couldn't count the times I had used that line on a suspect. "Detectives, I appreciate your honesty. However, you may or may not know that I have experience in law enforcement. I am aware that the last thing you want me to do is to call an attorney. You want me to take you at face value and believe that you're just trying to get clarity about the situation all the while, hoping that I paint myself into a corner. Unfortunately, I've been on the other side of the table too many times to fall for that. So, we can either get my attorney, you can let me go home, or you can charge me with something. Of course, I'm pretty sure option three isn't happening once I explain what happened." So much for staying friends.

They both kept straight faces but were giving each other side glances, probably trying to decide what road to take next. Bricker finally replied. "Okay, Miranda. Feel free to call your attorney. You can use the phone here on the table."

I smiled sweetly with a touch of sarcasm. "I'm sorry detectives, but I don't have my attorney's number with me. I don't usually need an attorney. I'm also not from around here, so any attorney I would know wouldn't probably practice in Louisiana."

Then it hit me. Mark. Didn't he say he was a defense attorney? I was sure he did. Maybe this was my big break, "Wait a minute. I do know a local attorney. Do you have an attorney directory or some way I can look up his number?"

Bricker was disappointed. Sansone didn't wear his emotions on his sleeve, so I couldn't tell what he was thinking. He spoke for the first time. "Give us a name, and we will see about getting a number for you."

"Mark Peterson," I said weakly. I felt like a scared child calling their parents after getting arrested for DUI at sixteen.

"Mark Peterson. I'll be right back with the number." He said and left the room quickly with a sour look on his face.

Bricker stayed with me. He tried to make small talk or at least pretended to try to make small talk. I remembered this from my days on the force too. The goal was to pretend to have a casual conversation while your perps let their guard down. Ironically, a part of me would have liked to spill my guts. I had nothing to hide. I had done nothing wrong despite being caught with a recently fired weapon and blood-stained blouse. Unfortunately, the way our legal system worked, your guilt or innocence didn't necessarily matter; it was whether the evidence supported the case. The perceptions and recollections of the detectives could make the biggest impression with the jury in court.

"So, what brings you to town? You're from California?" He seemed pleasant enough, but I knew not to get sucked in.

I considered how to respond to this or whether I should respond or not. I decided it was a safe enough question to answer. "I'm from here originally, and I still have relatives here. Yes, I live in Malibu."

He seemed surprised, "Malibu? Nice. You must be doing okay for yourself."

I pondered that question for a while. "I'm doing okay, I guess." Thankfully his partner returned with Mark's number before I needed to dodge any more questions.

They both stood, and Bricker took over again. "We'll leave you alone while you make the call. We'll be right outside if you need anything."

I was sure they would be right outside. I was surprised Bricker and Sansone were letting me call alone. It was probably a trick; I would bet it was a recorded line because the detectives were hoping I would spill my guts on the call after they left the room. It was a good thing I knew how this stuff worked. I hadn't even noticed the two-way mirror behind me. They'd probably be on the other side watching and listening—good thing I didn't have anything to hide.

I dialed Mark's number hoping I wouldn't get voice mail. A receptionist answered, "Mark Peterson, Esquire, can I help you?"

"Yes, this is Miranda Marquette." I tried to keep my voice even and business-like, but what I heard coming from my mouth was fear.

"Oh, yes, Ms. Marquette. He told me if you called to put you right through. Hold on," the receptionist responded.

"Mark Peterson." He sounded clipped and distracted.

"Mark, this is Miranda Marquette," I said, on the verge of tears.

"Miranda. What a pleasant surprise. Is everything okay with the car? It's been known to do some weird things. I should have warned you." I secretly resented his cheerful tone but did my best to hide it. "The car is fine. I do have a problem, though. I'm at the State Police facility downtown, near the Superdome." I took a couple of deep breaths, trying not to come across scared to death.

"What happened? Are you okay?" He sounded worried, which at least made me forgive him for his earlier cheerfulness.

"I'm okay. I need you to meet me down here as soon as possible. I'll explain when you get here. Can you come?" I tried to sound like I wasn't begging but failed.

"I'll have to juggle a few things, but I'll be there in about ten minutes." His distracted voice was back, but I was glad he'd be here.

"Thank you so much. Hurry." I hung up the phone. For the first time, it hit me in the gut that I might be in trouble. I knew I hadn't done anything, but that didn't mean they knew that. It could take months to straighten out something like this. What if they arrest me? I could sit in jail for months just waiting for a trial. What if I'm convicted?

Miranda, breathe. Just breathe.

The police knew by that point that they wouldn't be getting anything from me until my attorney arrived, so they left me alone in the interrogation room. Of course, that gave me plenty of free time to panic. The sweat running from my armpits, soaking my blouse was a not so attractive indication that I was pretty worked up by the time Mark got there.

He came in without an escort. "Mark!" I ran to him and threw my arms around him. I had to give him credit for hugging me back even though I left sweat stains on his white shirt.

He then held my shoulders at arm's length. He scowled and then put his finger to his lips.

He whispered. "I know this room is bugged and recorded. We need to request a private room and, by law, they have to provide it to us. When we get a room where we can talk, you can let me know what's going on, okay?"

His confident demeanor was calming. He left the room but came back in a few seconds, with a uniformed officer who led us to a small glass-walled conference room. I guessed if they couldn't listen to us, they wanted to make sure they could watch us. He sat across from me, looking very lawyer-like. It was like he wasn't the same guy I had shared breakfast with just the day before yesterday. I reminded myself that there was a time for laughs and time for tears or however that verse went.

He finally spoke. "So, what's going on?" He smiled briefly, "I didn't expect you to get in trouble this quickly."

"Funny. Anyway, as I told you earlier, I came back home to help Sabine because she has been having an issue with her shrimping business. I interviewed her employees yesterday, and I finished the day with Emil Abel, the captain of her fleet. My interview with him was less than a success; in fact, he threw me out."

"Well, you do tend to have that effect on people." He half-smiled.

I groaned. "That's not even remotely funny."

He returned to his business-like demeanor. "Then what happened?"

"He'd only been with her a couple of months, but Sabine seemed to trust him. After a restless night, I went back down to the marina to talk to him again, hoping for a better outcome. I guess that's the definition of insanity." I groaned again. "When I got to the boat, there was no crew around. That seemed odd to me since they were supposed to head out to the Gulf any minute. I climbed onto the boat and then up to the navigation room. When I looked through the door, I saw Emil lying in a pool of blood, shot in the head. While I was reasonably sure he was dead, I went in to confirm that he had no pulse, and I ended up with blood on my hands and my blouse."

He noticeably cringed and glanced at my blood-stained blouse as if he hadn't seen it earlier.

101

I ignored him. "Oh, I almost forgot. On the way over to the Marina, I shot an old rusty can sitting on a fence bordering Sabine's yard. Then I threw the gun in my purse and—"

He jumped out of this chair his face immediately turning an unpleasant shade of red. "Why wasn't the gun locked in the glove compartment?"

Sweat was running down my back. I couldn't look him in the eye because I had no easy answer for that. "I-um-guess I wasn't thinking."

Mark sat for a minute with his head in his hands. "So, let me get this straight. You left the glove compartment unlocked after you left here. It was unlocked overnight— "

"But the car was locked," I interjected. "I think."

"You think? You think?" he shouted at me. "Anyone could have entered or broken into the car and found the gun. What's wrong with you? Of all people, you should know better about securing your weapon."

I hung my head, not exactly in shame, but pretty close. "I kind of forgot it was there. I haven't owned a gun since I quit."

"That's no excuse." He was talking with his hands and pacing the room like a wild cat in a cage. "You shot the gun, put it in your purse, and then found the captain, evidently shot in the head. Do you know how that looks with the blood on your blouse?" He clasped his head like he was trying to keep his brains from falling out.

"I'll just explain to them what happened. I didn't shoot Emil, for God's sake. They'll eventually come to that conclusion when the bullet didn't come from your gun."

He finally sat, taking deep breaths. "Yeah, I suppose."

I glared at him. "Hey, I'm the one in trouble here. You're supposed to be doing your damned best to convince me it's gonna be fine."

He looked at the ceiling as if he were looking for a sign from God. "Well, at least they haven't arrested you yet."

"Yet? Thanks for the vote of confidence." I rolled my eyes and wondered for the first time if he was the best choice for an attorney.

He stood again and walked straight over to me and grabbed my upper arms like he was trying to shake some sense into me. "Think about it for a minute. Allegedly, you found the body and called 911. You have a recently-fired weapon in your possession." He glowered. "Did anyone witness your argument yesterday?"

I felt like I was in the principal's office again. "Well, yes, there were a bunch of guys on the dock when I got off the boat."

He ran his hands through his hair. "Did the Sheriff's deputies swab your hands for gunshot residue?"

"Of course, they did." I rolled my eyes again. I was starting to feel like a Valley Girl myself.

"You know what that means to your case, right?" Veins bulged in his forehead. If he didn't calm down soon, I feared he'd have a stroke and then where would I be?

"Mark, I'm not stupid. I didn't shoot him." They could probably hear me through the two-way mirror without any microphones in this room.

His face was stone. "But you did shoot my gun."

I was getting a sinking feeling. Oh my God, I *am* stupid. And dead.

There was a loud knock on the door. The detectives were getting impatient. "Five minutes," Sansone said and closed the door.

I sat down. Mark sat across from me at the table. "Okay, real fast now, what happened after you found the body once you confirmed that he was dead?"

I sighed. "I called in to report the body and had a nice conversation with the 911 dispatcher who turned out to be a friend of Sabine's."

"Daphne."

"Yes, Daphne. Anyway, she stayed on the call for quite a while, while the Sheriff's department was heading my way." I was racking my brain to find a way to save myself.

He asked, "Plaquemines Parish?" I could have sworn I saw him grimace.

"Yes, but what I read between the lines is that these rural cops have messed up so many cases, that the State Police are taking over when it's any more serious than a traffic infraction."

"Well," he continued, "I had heard the state was implementing something to protect people from these bozos. As a defense attorney, I'm not thrilled about it, but I understand the logic. Their tendency to ignore simple protocol got a bunch of my cases dismissed. Although, I guess the good news is that we are dealing with professionals instead of hacks. That probably helps us all in the long run."

After this exchange with Mark, I looked forward to the real interrogation. "After I got off the 911 call, I decided to run over to Sabine's to let her know about Emil in person, but they arrived before I got out of the parking lot. They immediately started treating me like a criminal. My purse fell on the ground, and your gun fell out. It was all downhill from there. They had me face-down in the parking lot while they handcuffed me. They were rough with me. They hit my head on the squad car when they shoved me into the back seat."

"That sounds about right. Did the officers say anything to you? Did they read you your rights? Did they say that you were under arrest?" His panicked tone was making me feel worse every second.

"They cuffed me and shoved me in the vehicle. The officers read me my rights then nothing was said during our terrific car ride from Venice to here. They confiscated my cell phone and my purse while they cuffed me, so I haven't been able to let Sabine know what's been happening." I suddenly felt exhausted and put my head on my arms, folded in front of me, like kindergarten nap time.

"Is there anything else that you remember?" I shook my head, and he continued. "Judging from what I've heard so far, I'm worried, but maybe you made it sound worse than it was. So, let's go have a chat with the detectives so we can hopefully get you out of here."

I dreaded talking to these detectives, but it probably wouldn't be as bad as getting cuffed with my face down on the pavement. They were ready for us when we were escorted back into the interrogation room. I described what happened just as I had to Mark ten minutes earlier. They nodded and took notes until the phone rang.

Bricker answered. "Detective Bricker."

He listened for a while without saying anything. I started getting a bad feeling in my gut as he glanced at me repeatedly. Mark sat quietly, but I could tell by the bead of sweat dripping from his forehead he didn't like it either. Eventually, Detective Bricker nodded to whoever was speaking, even though they couldn't see him, and then abruptly hung up and motioned to Sansone to follow him outside.

The detectives returned in less than a minute, and Bricker started speaking before the door had even closed. "Miranda Marquette, you have the right to remain silent. Anything you say can be used against you in a court of law. You have the right to an attorney and to have him or her present while you are being questioned. If you cannot afford to hire an attorney, one will be appointed to represent you at no cost to you."

My mouth gaped open in horror. I looked over at Mark for help but said nothing. He had his hands folded like he was praying. I felt like I was going to be sick.

Detective Bricker continued, unfazed. "You can decide at any time to exercise these rights and not answer any questions or make any statements. Do you understand these rights?"

Mirandized twice in one day, and I still didn't have a better response than, "Yes."

"You are under arrest for the murder of Emil Abel," he concluded.

The room went dim. I felt like I was having an out of body experience. Suddenly I was in a police station, but it wasn't this one. I was standing in the dark hallway at my old precinct in North Carolina. Two officers rushed by with a young woman in cuffs. As she passed, our eyes met. I couldn't look away, and suddenly I realized that she was me. I closed my eyes and shook my head. There was nothing I could do now but put my hands out in front of me. I said nothing as they cuffed me; the ringing in my ears made it too loud to speak.

Mark finally woke up. "What exactly is going on here? She was nothing but a Good Samaritan contacting the police because she found a dead body."

"You might not want to say much at this point, Mr. Peterson," Sansone snapped. "She was driving a vehicle registered to you. She had a recently fired weapon of a similar caliber as the murder weapon, which was licensed to you. And her gunpowder residue test was positive."

Mark looked at me but said nothing in my defense. As they hauled me out of my chair, I grumbled, "Of course, it was positive, I shot at a can before I went to the marina."

The detective ignored me. "This is all just too coincidental to let Ms. Marquette go free. We have debated holding you as well as an accessory. Please do not leave town. We will be processing Ms. Marquette now, so your presence is no longer necessary."

The detectives escorted me from the interrogation room. As they led me to the elevator, it seemed like a bad dream, but everything was too real. I was led down a long hallway painted drab yellow. On the right, a sign read 'Processing,' and behind the corresponding desk sat a portly woman, probably in her mid-fifties looking incredibly bored.

"I'll take her from here, boys," she grunted in their general direction and pointed for me to sit in a folding chair in front of her desk. They retreated down the hallway after being summarily dismissed.

She looked over her glasses at me. "Name?"

I smiled nervously. "Miranda Marquette, ma'am."

"Date of birth?" She asked, typing it into her system.

"March 29, 1974." Now was not the time to be embarrassed by my age.

She shuffled some paperwork and pointed to the wall. "Stand over there facing me with your back to the wall."

I complied meekly, muttering a quiet, "Here?"

"Turn to your left. To your right." The woman barked, and I briefly felt like I was posing for a new driver's license as she snapped my picture.

After I was processed, the model-like guard led me to a small cell that smelled like a combination of urine, disinfectant, and something else unpleasant I couldn't place. When I saw that I would be alone in the cell, I thanked God for something finally going my way. Spending the night with a stranger or strangers in a cell would have been too much. My home away from home featured a cot and a small but private bathroom for which I was also thankful.

As night approached, I laid as still as I could on the cot so the guards wouldn't know I was awake. I had noticed them chatting with other prisoners, and that was the last thing that I needed. All night, I felt every heartbeat, every breath, and heard every sound, from voices in the distance, someone snoring in another cell, and even an owl hooting, sounding even lonelier than I felt. Finally, just after sunrise, a guard, probably in her fortics, reminiscent of Susan Powter in the nineties during her butch haircut days, came to escort me upstairs. She didn't bother to tell me why, and I didn't bother to ask. She led me to a room half the size of the walk-in closet adjacent to my bedroom at home. Mark sat in a corner at a miniscule table. He attempted a smile but failed miserably. "Hi, Miranda. How are you?"

After everything I have been through in the last twenty-four hours, this was just enough to put me over the edge. "Exactly how do you think I am? I've been falsely arrested, cuffed, poked, prodded and thrown in a cell, like a common criminal," I shrieked at him.

He jumped up, sending his chair crashing against the wall, and after realizing there was barely enough space to stand in, much less pace, he sat back down. "Try to stay calm, Miranda. I'm not the enemy here."

"Well, you didn't do so well keeping me out of here, did you? It was your gun that got me in here." I kicked the leg of the table.

He blanched and looked down at the floor. "True, I am sorry about that. But it was there for your protection, not for target practice."

"Yeah. What was I even thinking of going out to breakfast with you? Borrowing your car? Defending you to Sabine?" I didn't care if he had no idea what I was talking about.

He blushed, but then reached across the small space and put a hand on my shoulder, "This isn't getting us anywhere. I need to prepare you for what you'll face during the arraignment. Your part is easy. You just need to stand and plead innocent when asked by the judge how you plead. The prosecution will be pushing for no bail since you're accused of murder and are a potential flight risk."

"That's great, Mark." Sarcasm will get me everywhere.

"I'll do everything I can do to get you out on bail. You have no record. The evidence is circumstantial. You had no motive. You're not a flight risk and were planning on staying in town indefinitely. You don't even have a plane ticket back. Of course, it's all going to depend on the judge. Unfortunately, it could take a couple of days to get the ballistics results back on the bullet. At least you and I know for sure that you didn't shoot him. The recently fired gun and your positive gunpowder residue test will be less relevant to the case when we prove the bullet that killed Emil came from another gun." He hesitated. "It did, right?"

"Of course!" My head was throbbing. "Do you know how outrageous this is? How did this even happen? What is wrong with people around here? No wonder I moved out of here as soon as I turned eighteen. I'm going to be railroaded right through to a conviction, aren't I?

His face didn't give anything away. I guess that was one reason he was a defense attorney. He spoke slowly and softly as if he wanted to soothe me into submission. "Let's just take this one step at a time. I know you're scared, but I'll be here every step of the way."

Maybe I wasn't thinking clearly, but I had yet to hear anything that would make me believe this situation would be resolved quickly in my favor. I was even starting to feel like I was guilty. That would be written all over my face at the hearing.

There was a knock on the door. We both looked up. It was another guard I hadn't seen before. She was a sweet looking girl who looked like she ought to be in college studying early childhood education. Just as I wondered how she got into this line of work, she slapped handcuffs on me and grabbed my arm. "Let's go."

I caught Mark's glance as I was escorted out. He said, "Sorry. See you in a couple of minutes."

The "student" led me to a long hallway and downstairs to the basement and a well-lit concrete tunnel that, I learned later, went under the street to the courthouse. She didn't say a word to me, which I was thankful for because the lump in my throat would have made it hard to speak.

As she led me upstairs and into the courtroom, there were way more people than I had expected. Sabine was there. My mom and Tom were too. Tom looked stoic, but my mom's face was puffy, and tears ran down her cheeks. I wanted to run to her and tell her I was okay, that this was all a mistake.

Assorted ex-classmates and ex-neighbors filled the rows. How humiliating. There was a part of me that wanted to smile and wave at people in an attempt to show that I was innocent. I always thought defendants looked guilty when they were too serious. On the other hand, I didn't want the judge to believe that I was making light of the proceedings.

The female officer led me to a table where Mark was sitting. I briefly wondered how he got here before I did, but then the judge's chamber door opened.

The clerk announced the judge, "All rise for the Honorable Judge Samantha Cantrese."

As the petite brunette judge, probably in her early forties, climbed onto her bench, the clerk continued, "Please be seated.

The first case is number 25631-1 the State of Louisiana against Miranda Marquette."

I tried to get a read on the judge by looking at her facial expressions, but she gave nothing away, so I listened intently as she spoke. "I see many of you came out for today's spectacle. It'll do you well to keep your comments and any other emotional outbursts to yourself. Do I make myself clear?"

I turned to see the gallery nod in agreement.

"I don't like how this is starting," I whispered more to myself than Mark.

The judge turned her attention to me. "Ms. Marquette, you have been charged with the first-degree murder of Emil Abel. How do you plead?"

"Not guilty, Your Honor." Good thing I've seen Law and Order fifteen thousand times.

She continued, "Mr. Prosecutor, what say you in terms of bail in this case?"

The prosecutor was the District Attorney as opposed to an assistant. It wasn't a good sign that he hadn't delegated this case. "Your Honor, the prosecution feels strongly that there should be no bail offered in this case. The defendant is a significant flight risk and has the financial resources to flee the country if she is released."

"Mr. Peterson?" The judge addressed Mark with a slight smile on her face. Maybe having a young, attractive male attorney wasn't such a bad idea.

C'mon, Mark, get me outta here! I snarled in my head.

"Your Honor, my client has been an exemplary citizen. She runs a successful business. She gives substantial donations to charity. She is a native of the area and has significant family connections here. The evidence tying her to this case is extremely circumstantial. After she discovered the deceased, she remained with him for forty minutes while the police were responding, certainly not trying to flee the scene. Most importantly, there is no motive." Mark was on a roll.

"Mr. Peterson, this is an arraignment and bail hearing, not a trial!" She snapped him out of his tirade.

Ugh! Why did I think this guy would be a good attorney?

The judge then addressed me. "Ms. Marquette, you seem like a responsible young woman. You do realize if you leave the area, you will be arrested for contempt of court and that you will then have no possibility of bail, correct?"

I nodded and spoke meekly, "Yes, Your Honor."

"You also realize that the press will eat me alive if I allow you out on bail and you don't hold up your end of the bargain, correct?" She stared into my eyes, and I held in a shiver.

I nodded again. "Yes, Your Honor."

The judge continued, "Ms. Marquette. Miranda, is it?"

"Yes, Your Honor," I replied.

"I am going to choose to believe you, so don't give me a reason not to." She held my gaze a moment longer then shifted gears. "It's important that you realize you are accused of a heinous crime and the court takes this very seriously. However, because you have no criminal record and do not seem, to me," she looked directly at the Prosecutor, "to be a flight risk, I am going to set bail at one million dollars." She referred to some notes in front of her and almost as an afterthought said, "Just so I can sleep better, please surrender your passport to the court."

"Your Honor!" yelled the prosecutor as he jumped to his feet.

She responded immediately, "Watch out, Bill, or I will find you in contempt. This hearing is adjourned."

It took time to process me again to get me out of there. They had returned my clothes and personal effects if not my dignity.

Being arrested for murder was one of the worst experiences of my life, although it paled in comparison to being shot in the face and left to die. Two hours later, I burst through the double front doors of the combination police station and jail for prisoners in transit and onto the street.

One thing I knew without a doubt; I was not going back to jail. Unfortunately, that meant I had to shift gears from working on Sabine's case to solving my own. The police had their suspect. How much easier could their investigation have been? I found a body, called 911, and told them who and where it was. They arrested me. Case closed?

Not by a long shot.

I had never been arrested before, unless I counted that student demonstration in North Carolina, so I couldn't say I ever gave any thought to what I would have done when I got out of the slammer. However, we were in New Orleans. So, of course, we all went to a bar. We decided to go to Bourbon 'O' on Bourbon Street. Honestly, we locals usually avoided the Big B, but, what better place to party, especially when you considered that they served root beer floats made with rum and butter pecan ice cream?

It felt great to be surrounded by happy people as opposed to detectives, judges, and prison guards. I was only out on bail, but I was learning to be thankful for small favors. We even got Mom and Tom to join us. I wasn't sure if Sabine would come since she and my mom weren't on speaking terms, but she did. She seemed to be trying to make the best of it like I was. Mark and about ten others from our graduating class, some I remembered, some not so much, came along for the ride, probably figuring if I could afford bail, then I could afford to buy them a couple of drinks. And I did.

I had the non-alcoholic version of the root beer float because I wanted to keep my wits about me. Sabine and I had been having fun taking turns fighting off potential suitors for a couple of hours, and I was doing my best to stay in the moment and not get too far ahead of myself.

Mark's cell phone rang a while back, and he was outside on the phone. I could tell he was none too happy. I couldn't help but feel that this conversation had something to do with me since he kept looking at me through the window. When he finished his call, he didn't come inside. He just stared through the window at me.

After five minutes of feeling his stare, I decided that I should go outside and find out what was going on. I hated to leave Sabine since we were having fun and I felt the most relaxed I had since I got into town, but I could tell something was very wrong.

When I got outside, Mark was running his fingers through his hair, staring at nothing. He looked like his life was flashing before his eyes. Finally, he focused on me like he just came back from a million miles away. "We need to talk, Miranda. Jackson Square is a couple of blocks down. Let's get out of here."

I smiled even though he couldn't muster one. "Great! I haven't been there since I was a kid."

He said nothing, just walked slightly ahead of me.

We found a bench and sat down. I braced myself. "Okay, shoot," I finally said after he sat staring at the ground for a while.

"Miranda, we are in trouble. And I mean we. They got back the results from the ballistic test. My gun is the weapon used to kill Emil Abel." He said in a weak voice.

I grabbed his arm, "No way! How?"

"Tell me the truth, Miranda. Did you shoot Emil?" He begged.

"No! Why would I shoot him? I didn't even know the man." I was angry and indignant, up and pacing the sidewalk with my hands on my hips.

"It gets worse." He couldn't look at me.

I closed my eyes and started to pray. I didn't even know if God believed in me at this point, but I needed all the help I could get. I asked slowly, "How can it get worse?"

"Your fingerprints and mine are the only ones on the gun." He said as much to himself as to me.

I opened my eyes and looked Mark right in the eye. "Mark, did you shoot Emil?"

"No." Then he looked away.

"You were in love with Sabine, at least at one time. She was having business issues coincident with the hiring of Emil. From everything I have heard about Emil, he wasn't the easiest person to get along wi–"

"Stop, Miranda! I didn't shoot him!" He yelled.

After a long silence, he continued. "If neither of us shot him, we have another problem. Remember how you said that you left the key in the glove compartment lock?"

I stared straight ahead, knowing this wouldn't be good.

"Okay, so neither of us shot him. If someone stole the gun from the Jeep, you could be found guilty of breaking the Louisiana concealed weapon statute which is a $500 fine, six months in jail or both. Emil's estate could also sue you for any manner of things like loss of revenue or pain and suffering. I've seen awards in the millions for cases similar to this."

I stood up and started pacing back and forth. My mind was running wild. I am in serious trouble here. I am the one out of bail. I am the one charged with first-degree murder. I was the one who grabbed the murder weapon from the glove compartment of Mark's Jeep. I'm the only one with fingerprints on the gun other than him, and he owns the gun. Now I'm in cahoots with this Mark, and I don't know him from Adam except that we spent a morning having brunch and went to high school together. Can I trust him? He's my lawyer for God's sake! He could manipulate this case almost any way he wanted to. Oh, My God. What if he did it? It's the perfect storm. Is this why he lent me his car? Did he have this planned all along? I stopped pacing.

I tried to slow down my mind and spoke slowly. "Mark, I need some time to think. This new information would be a lot to process under normal circumstances." I started walking, but I had no idea where I was going. "Maybe you need to do some thinking too, Mark." I left him sitting on the bench with his head in his hands.

As I walked, I remembered I had no vehicle. Mark's Jeep had been impounded as evidence. I headed around the block and back toward the bar since Sabine was my ride. My mom could tell I was upset when I got back to the bar and suggested that I go home with her and Tom. I decided to take her up on it. It was fun sitting at a bar with Sabine flirting with guys, but I wasn't in the mood to talk with her all night about the murder when we got back to her place.

As we left, I could see Sabine watching us through the window. I waved to her and gave her the 'I'll call you' sign. She looked curious but stayed put and blew me a kiss. She went back to a conversation with the guy who was now sitting in what had been my seat. She would be fine.

When we got back to the house, my mom's protective hug told me she was ecstatic I was staying with them. But I immediately had second thoughts when she released me and started pummeling me with questions about the murder, about jail, about Mark and anything else that crossed her mind.

I held my hand up. "There will be plenty of time to go into all that. Right now, I just need a bath and a nap." I yelled down the stairs as I ran up, "I'll be down later."

I just wanted to get out of my clothes. They hadn't been washed since I left home and now, I'd worn them for two days. I needed a bath so badly I couldn't stand it. I checked my room and found some gym shorts and a Nirvana tee-shirt that I hadn't taken with me when I moved out. I was thankful my mom never threw anything out.

I grabbed the clothes, went into the bathroom and sat, exhausted, on the edge of the tub while I ran the water as hot as I could stand it. I didn't know if I would ever feel truly clean again after being in jail. But, as I stepped into the tub, I felt some of the tension flow out of me. Gosh, it felt good. It was dangerous to fall asleep in the bathtub under normal circumstances, but after not sleeping a wink, I closed my eyes and let myself slip away.

"Miranda!" I awakened with a start as my mother started rapping on the bathroom door. "Are you okay in there?"

I looked around in confusion before I realized what had happened. "Yeah, I'm fine. I'm taking a bath. I may have dozed off."

"Well, be careful." She sounded disapproving. "We don't want you drowning. You've been through enough."

"I'm going to dry off and go to bed, Mom," I said sleepily.

"Okay, dear. See you in the morning."

The water was barely lukewarm now, so I had been asleep for a while. I donned my clothes, dragged myself down the hallway to my room, and lay down on the bed. Reflecting on everything that had happened today, I still had a nagging concern. I still wasn't convinced that Mark didn't have something to do with Emil's death. I was pretty sure he hadn't pulled the trigger but was he somehow working with Sabine? Before I got up that morning, it would have been possible for Sabine to unlock the Jeep. She may very well have had a key to Mark's car. She could easily have taken the gun from the Jeep, walked over to the marina, shot Emil, and returned it to the glove compartment without me knowing.

That thought raised a thousand more questions. Why did Sabine ask me down here if she planned on murdering Emil? Was she trying to frame me? Was she trying to frame Mark, and I got in the middle? Was Sabine even involved in the murder? All I knew was that I didn't have much time to get these questions answered because we were moving full steam ahead toward a trial where I was afraid I would be convicted.

While I felt terrible doubting my friend and my sister, I was feeling very alone and vulnerable. The best thing I could do for all of us was to find out the truth.

Chapter 7

The sun shining through my bedroom window woke me up at eight a.m. I'd been home less than a week, but it felt like a year. I let out a groan and slid the covers over my head. My whole body was screaming at me to stay put and curl up into a ball, and that things were only going to get worse because I still had a trial to go through. But I realized, even half-asleep, that I needed a plan other than keeping my head under the covers and hoping that all my problems would just go away.

No question, there could be plenty of people who wanted Emil dead. He didn't seem like the easiest person to work for. It could have been any of his present or past employees or even his ex-boss. Suddenly, Mark's gun flew back into my memory. I had to figure out how negligent I was concerning the concealed weapon law. I knew I had left the glove compartment unlocked, but had I really left the car doors unlocked as well? Coming from California, I always locked my car at home. But had I locked Mark's in Sabine's driveway? I wasn't sure. Who could have had access to the gun the morning of the murder? Who else besides Mark and Sabine knew he kept a gun in his car? He hadn't been shy about sharing that when he and I went to the Deja Vu.

I wanted to get out of the house without having to be on the receiving end of twenty questions from Mom and Tom. I knew what I would be facing. What was jail like? How am I? What happened anyway? Why do they suspect me? And on and on. I would talk to them when it wasn't so raw.

I was grateful to my mom, though, and I needed to thank her. Somewhere between my bath, falling asleep and going to bed, my mom had laundered my clothes and left them folded on my

119

dresser. Thank goodness, because if I had to wear them again without washing them, I was sure they would have been able to tell I was coming before I entered the room.

Before I ventured downstairs, I called Mark. Thankfully, it didn't go to voicemail. "Mark Peterson," he responded.

"Wow, I can't believe you don't even know my number yet," I sassed him trying to keep it light after our last encounter.

"Sorry, Miranda, I was in the middle of something and didn't even look. It's a hazard of the profession." I pictured him shrugging. "So, how are you doing?"

"As well as can be expected, I guess. I got a good night's sleep, so I'm feeling much better than yesterday." I didn't feel like rehashing our last meeting, and it sounded like he didn't either. "Just calling to see if you might consider giving me a ride down to Sabine's."

"What about my Jeep?" he began and then it hit him. "Oh yeah, the police have it."

I groaned. "Once their people tear it apart looking for evidence, you may not want it back."

He didn't acknowledge the fact, but I was pretty sure he knew he wouldn't have his Jeep for a while. "I'll pick you up. You're at your mom's house, right?" I heard him shuffling around, probably for his keys.

"Yup. Can you come soon? I'm trying to avoid having to discuss this whole mess." I looked over my shoulder as if my mom were waiting in the shadows to pounce as soon as I emerged.

"I'll be right over." He was cheerful, which made me feel for the moment like things were normal. I wanted to hold onto that feeling.

If I took my time getting ready, I'd be able to use Mark as an excuse to avoid Mom. Ten minutes later, she called from downstairs letting me know that Mark was here.

As I ran downstairs, she gave me the look. "Leaving so soon? I was hoping we could talk."

"Sorry. Gotta run." I called and ran out the door. I didn't look back, but I knew that she was standing in the doorway with her hands on her hips and her mouth open.

"Hi," Mark said, looking a little sheepish.

I felt that I needed to clear the air. "I guess I got a little freaked about the gun yesterday. I need to believe in someone right now, so I'm choosing you. I understand what it's like to be accused based on circumstantial evidence. So, can you accept my apology and we can move on?"

I thought I caught a look of relief cross his face, and I felt a little better. "Apology accepted. Now we need a plan to get you out of this thing."

"I was just going to say the same thing." I leaned toward him and patted his hand on the steering wheel. "Okay, Sweetness, how are you planning on getting me out of this?"

He evidently wasn't in a flirty mood because he ignored my gesture, flicking my hand away as if it were an annoying fly. "Since you came down here to investigate the issue with Sabine's business, I think it would best if you to continue the investigation but focusing a little more on the captain's murder than on the missing shrimp for the time being."

"Believe it or not, I was thinking the same thing. I'm not one to sit on the sidelines while my life hangs in the balance. The good news is that I have the distinct advantage of knowing beyond a shadow of a doubt that I'm innocent. I'm wondering, though . . ." I figured that I might as well address this sooner than later. "Since the murder weapon was yours and was in your vehicle, doesn't that make you a prime suspect also? It certainly does in my book. So how would you feel about me investigating you as part of the process?"

He frowned. "I thought you said you had chosen to believe in me."

I responded coolly. "I'm closer to believing you than I was yesterday, but the wound is still raw. I don't know who to trust. Logic tells me you have nothing to do with it, but logic doesn't always lead to the right answer. I'd be doing you a favor by investigating you because if there is anything to uncover, I'll get to it before the cops do. If I were you, I'd be a little concerned that your gun disappeared out of your car, was used to kill Emil and was returned to the glove compartment in a very short period of time. Granted, I still have to face the fact the I violated the concealed weapon statute, but I'm hoping the judge will let me off with a slap on the wrist."

I put down my car window for some fresh muggy air. "This is my life we're talking about here. After you, Sabine is the next suspect I need to clear in my own mind. I mean, she's my cousin," well actually my sister, but he didn't need to know about that, "but I also know that she's not someone you should mess with. If she found out that Emil was stealing from her, he wouldn't have wanted to be on the receiving end of that gun. On the other hand, if I find out that she killed him, and she let me take the fall, she's gonna learn what it means to mess with me."

He cringed. "I wouldn't want to get on the wrong side of either of you."

I decided to let him off the hook for the time being, but if I found anything contradictory along the way, I would have no mercy.

I glanced out the car window savoring my freedom and asked, "So what are you going to be up to while I'm doing all your legwork?"

"I'll be working behind the scenes to find out what kind of case they're building against you. The prosecution will probably ask for all sorts of discovery documents that I'll need your help with retrieving."

"Yeah, of course," I muttered, lost in my thoughts.

As we rode along, I was overwhelmed by the infinite possibilities of suspects and scenarios leading to Emil's death. While it could be weeks or months before the preliminary hearing, I could hear the seconds ticking by.

When he pulled into Sabine's yard, I smiled and gave him a quick hug before I got out of the Porsche. "Do you want to come in?"

As I struggled to climb out of the sports car which sat inches from the ground, he said, "I think I'll take a rain check. I gotta get going."

Before I could respond, he shifted into reverse, backed out onto the road and was gone. I turned and headed up the driveway, but as I neared the front door, my heart began to sink, and I suddenly felt sick to my stomach. Sabine's car still sat in the driveway, but the house lights were off, which didn't make sense unless something was wrong. I wielded the key Sabine gave me as if it were a weapon, wishing I had something better to protect myself and praying that I wouldn't find Sabine lying on the floor like I had found Emil.

The front door was locked, so I took a moment to unlock it before flinging the door wide if I needed to surprise an attacker. But no one was there. I cleared the rooms; nothing was out of place. I took a few deep breaths and sat on the couch. This experience of the last several days was more traumatic than I had been aware of.

Now that I knew that she wasn't dead, I was relieved Sabine wasn't home. I loved her, but she had the opportunity, the means, and the motive to kill Emil. How had she been so sure that the fleet would still be at the marina when I went over to meet Emil that morning? Why was no one else around? Shouldn't the crews from all three boats have been hanging around waiting for the fleet to leave?

Before I left the house, I changed into a pair of white shorts and an L.L. Bean Madras blouse that I'd been waiting for the right occasion to wear. Since I'd been wearing the same clothes for three days now, it seemed like the right time. I decided to walk up to the marina to see what I could find out. Without a captain, all three of Sabine's boats were docked. One piece of evidence in Sabine's favor was that the murder had to be costing her a bundle. Even if she had discovered that Emil was doing her wrong, killing him would have been cutting off her nose to spite her face. As I reached the parking lot, Sabine and a man dressed in an Armani suit disembarked the *P!NK* and headed for the CrawGator, the bar/ restaurant adjacent to the marina. No ship captain I knew could afford clothes like that, so whoever he was, was not a candidate to captain the fleet.

I hung back and waited a few minutes before following them. Sabine and the mystery man sat engrossed in conversation by the window overlooking the marina. The place was mostly empty, except for two weathered older men sitting at the bar, so it wasn't too hard to overhear what was said between them. But as the lone waitress ran in and out with drinks and food, I could only get bits and pieces from my table near the end of the bar, but I needed the cover of the wall between the bar and the restaurant.

The waitress surprised me when she stopped at my table. "What can I get you?"

"What?" I strained my neck to try and hear a little better. The waitress didn't move, so I blurted out, "Can I have a Diet Coke, please? Hold the ice."

"Sure, coming right up." She frowned at me and headed to the kitchen. I wasn't her dream customer.

The man in the suit was doing most of the talking; I took notes on my Blackberry with the hope of piecing it all together later. "It's all right . . . give it some time . . . the police . . . lay low . . . you are amazing. . . just need to hold on . . . we can get the best price . . . could be set for life."

Get the best price for what? The business? If so, it might have been considerate of her to mention that to me before I traveled a thousand miles to help save it. They asked the waitress for the check, and the guy in the suit paid. I darted to the bathroom and hid in one of the stalls. After counting to sixty, I pushed the door open to peek out. Good. No sign of them. I peeled a few bills from my wallet to pay for my Diet Coke and headed back to Sabine's.

When I hung out with Sabine after the bail hearing, I didn't get the feeling that she was grieving much about Emil's death. Granted, he was a short-term employee, and she had had nothing but problems since she hired him. It made me wonder even more who the mystery man in the suit was. I had no choice but to ask her.

But she wasn't home when I walked back from the Gator. I wanted to talk to Emil's old boss, Ronnie, and there was no time like the present. I scribbled a note and snatched her car keys off the hook in the entryway. I crossed my fingers that Sabine wouldn't need her car over the next hour or so. I headed to Boothville. Sabine never mentioned Ronnie's last name or the name of his company, but I did know that Boothville was as small as Venice and it was only five or six miles up the road, so I didn't think this Ronnie would be hard to find.

A few minutes later, I was pulling into the tiny port. Their marina only had two docks; one had a sign that read, 'Shrimp Unlimited, Ronald Hamill proprietor,' next to which was a small office with windows on all sides. Every window and door was propped open. I could see an older man sitting at a desk working with what appeared to be ledgers. The deep lines on his face told me that he was at least seventy, and those years were not easy ones.

I knocked on the screen door. "Mr. Hamill?"

He looked up from his work. "Who wants to know?" After looking me up and down, his tone softened a bit. "Hello, little lady. Call me Ronnie. What can I do for you?"

I smiled as sweetly as I could. "I want to talk to you about Emil Abel."

His face went sour. "Now why would you want to ruin my day by bringing him up?"

I stumbled over my words. "You know that he was, um . . ."

He stood and walked toward the counter. "Killed? Yeah, I know. Served him right if you asked me. Whoever managed to kill him deserves a prize as far as I'm concerned. The world will be a better place without him."

He paused and scratched his balding head. "Okay, I don't know who I'm kidding. That's my anger talking. I shouldn't say anything bad about Emil. For most of the time I knew him, he was a decent man."

"He worked for you for you . . ."

"Thirty years. Hard to believe. Then he just left me in the lurch. Went to work for that woman downriver, I heard. Now he's dead. Looks like he got what he wished for and then some."

He laughed and coughed like someone who had been smoking his whole life. His yellow fingers and the full ashtray on his desk confirmed my suspicions. He followed my gaze. "Sorry, darn cigarettes."

I shrugged. "To each his own."

He flipped up an opening in the counter and let me into his cramped office. "Hey, who are you anyway? A reporter or somethin'?" He motioned for me to sit in the lone ancient lawn chair opposite his desk.

"Sorry, I'm Miranda Marquette." I put out my hand, and he shook it briefly.

He pondered for a while. "Am I supposed to know you? Judging from your wardrobe, you're obviously from upriver, but the name rings a bell."

I smiled. "Well, among other things, I'm the one they arrested for killing Emil."

He laughed and coughed harder than before. "Well, ya didn't do it, did ya?"

"No, I didn't." I said firmly.

"Ya know what, Miranda Marquette? I believe you. You got a real sincere way about you. Now, what can I do for you?" I was surprised at how quickly he trusted me.

"I'm Sabine's cousin." I winked, "You know, 'that woman' that Emil went to work for."

He cringed and reddened a little. "That's why your name sounded familiar."

I resisted rolling my eyes. "Anyway, I am just talking to anyone I can find who might know something, anything, about Emil and the circumstances of his death. Sometimes the truth gets out on the street long before the police or the prosecutors hear it and sometimes, they never do. I have the advantage of knowing that I didn't kill him, so I'm already one step ahead of them."

He laughed again. "You've got gumption. Ya can't say that for a lot of women these days. Granted, I love women; I just can't stand them most of the time." He coughed another laugh. "I'd like to help. I'm just not sure I can."

"Well, can you tell me about what led to Emil leaving your employ after thirty years? I know he left to work for Sabine. But how were things before that?" I wondered if Emil had been as rude to Ronnie as he was to me.

"Emil started out as a deckhand back in the eighties. I'd only been in the business for a few years and had gone through a bunch of ship captains at the time. He got the job by default. He just kept doing what he needed to do." Ronnie seemed almost proud of him. "After a couple of years, he was First Mate. He did such a good job that he was pretty much acting as Captain already. So, when I fired his predecessor, Emil took to it like a fish takes to water. The men respected him. He didn't take any guff, even from the old-timers. Of course, we had our disagreements over the years. He always thought I should modernize, but I'm pretty set in my ways." It seemed to me like he had told this story a thousand times.

I nodded. "Sabine said something very similar about how Emil was with all her men."

He continued as if he hadn't heard me. "We're a small operation, and that's how I like it, not like that woman who keeps buying out everyone in sight. She's not gonna get this one even after I'm dead. I guarantee you that." He waved a gnarled finger at me as if I somehow intended to steal his business.

I felt like I needed to defend her. "Sabine's just trying to make a living like everyone else. She's also helped a couple of old shrimpers retire I understand."

He almost stood up again but thought better of it and scoffed instead. "Made them retire is more like it." He narrowed his eyes at me. "Wait a minute; you don't work for her, do ya?"

"No." At least, not in the way that he was thinking.

He nodded and appeared satisfied that I could be trusted and continued. "So, everything was good until about six months ago. We had survived Katrina and were nearly clearing a profit again, but then things started going bad. I keep track of every single shrimp that we catch and everyone that we sell. Things stopped adding up. The catch was down a lot. Sure, we had seen difficulties over the years, but this was different. I started asking around, and no one else seemed to be having the same problem. They were catching more than they had in the recent past."

He coughed and continued. "When I asked Emil about it, he always had one excuse or another. The weather wasn't good, or the oil rigs were seeping into the deep water, or the normal places were getting fished out. He also seemed different, somehow. He had always been a hard man with the crew, but he seemed to have cranked it up a notch or two. I was starting to get complaints from the men. I had always gotten some complaints, but it was getting worse. I even asked him about it, but he just shrugged it off like everything else. Then three months ago, he just up and quit. There was no fight and no notice. I asked him if more money would help. He said that he had made up his mind and he was gone. I haven't seen or heard from him since."

His body posture was very open, he was maintaining eye contact with me, and he wasn't sweating. I've been wrong before, but all the non-verbal cues told me that he was telling me the truth. Things changed abruptly with my next question. "Did he have any family, a wife, or close friends nearby?"

He immediately looked as far away from me as he could. "I make it a policy not to mix business with pleasure. It's less messy that way. I do know that he was married for a while. Divorced at least ten years ago. No kids. Since then, I've seen him with a few women, but I don't know of anyone permanent. I'm pretty sure he lived alone. All I can tell you is that he was not a happy man. Some guys are free and easy, but he wasn't one to take things casually. Especially during the last year."

I knew he was lying about the last part, but I didn't need him to clam up on me, so I didn't call him out. "I guess you haven't heard anything about who might have killed him?"

He shook his head. "Not a word. I'd be happy to keep my ear to the ground though. Why don't you give me your phone number, just in case?"

I smiled. "I was going to ask, but I appreciate you offering first."

He laughed. "I'm a sucker for a pretty woman, especially one as kind and honest as you seem to be." I handed him my card, and he examined it. "California? I'll bet you'd like to get back there about now."

"You can say that again. But, let's say I have a knack for being in the right place at the wrong time." This time is a bit over the top, though, even for me. "Thanks so much for your help, Ronnie. I hope to see you again under better circumstances." I shook his hand and stood up to leave.

"Good luck to ya." He waved me off and went back to work.

I hoped Sabine was free now. I wanted to talk about what I saw, but I still didn't know how to handle the situation without her thinking that I'd been spying on her. I pulled out my phone to give her a call and found an unopened text from Heather, "I heard you were in jail. Are you okay?" It would take far too long to explain by messaging her, so I dialed her number. She sounded like she was near tears. "Miranda, talk to me."

"Hey, sorry I didn't call to let you know what was going on." It was good to hear her voice, even though she sounded upset.

"You don't have to apologize to me. Gosh. Jail? I was so worried about you." She paused. "You didn't actually kill this guy, right?"

"I hope you're not serious," I grumbled.

Heather relaxed again and laughed. "Well, I have seen you mad enough to kill someone, so I just wanted to make sure."

"Funny." It was good to be connected to back home. "It's just a bunch of circumstantial evidence that I'm sure will get straightened out eventually." I sounded more confident than I was.

"Okay. Are we still going to have our weekly call on Sunday?" She sounded hopeful.

"Yes, unless there are things we need to discuss now." I was torn; I wanted to talk to her longer but was hoping nothing was wrong with the business.

Heather seemed to be back to her old self. "I'm good. I was just too worried not to make sure you were okay. I'll talk to you on Sunday."

"Okay, bye." I hung up and shoved my phone in my pocket.

When I pulled into Sabine's driveway, the lights were still out. I put the keys back, threw out my note, made some coffee, and flopped on the couch. When my coffee started pouring out of the machine, I heard her fiddling with the lock, so I got up to let her in.

She looked worried. "I'm so glad you're back. I kind of expected you last night. I wanted to make sure you were okay."

We hugged, and I said, "I was really overwhelmed and had just gotten some unfortunate news from Mark, so I decided to

131

crash at my mom's and take a long bath. I couldn't imagine coming all the way down here. Besides I didn't have a car. Sorry I didn't fill you in."

"Of course, it's fine." She took my hand and pulled me to the couch. "So how are you really doing, Miranda? And what are you going to do now?"

I pondered her question for a minute. "I get the feeling the prosecutor's office believes they have an open and shut case. Since I didn't do it, I'm quite sure I can poke some pretty big holes in it. Mark is working the paperwork side while I work the street. Paperwork was never my strong suit, so it seems like a good division of labor."

"Oh, thank goodness you didn't do it." She exhaled a relieved sigh.

My mouth gaped open, "Seriously? You thought I might have actually done it? Thanks for the vote of confidence."

"I just wanted to hear it from you. You know how things go sometimes. Arguments happen, they spiral out of control, one thing leads to another, and before you know it, somebody's dead." She said matter-of-factly.

"Um, actually no, I don't." Sometimes she worried me.

"Before I forget, guess who I just met with." She was suddenly excited and wide-eyed.

Hmm, some rich guy who you couldn't keep your eyes off at lunch? I thought, but said, "I don't know." I tried to sound casual even though I was excited she was telling me before I had to ask. "Who?"

"Warren Banks. He's a commercial realtor who also sells businesses. He was telling me that there is some interest on the street in buying my business now that I was able to secure the Costco contract." She sat next to me on the couch.

I glared at her in amazement.

She had a faraway look in her eyes. "I don't know if I would ever sell, but it's a great offer . . ."

"Okay, hold on just a minute, mademoiselle!" I couldn't control my voice getting louder with a severe edge. "You dragged me back to this god-forsaken place to help you save your business. I get arrested for murder, and now you are thinking about bailing on the business? Have you lost your mind?" Or have I?

She put her hand on my arm. "I thought you'd be excited for me."

I was livid. Sabine came all the way to California and never mentioned, oh, by the way, even though I need your help to save my business, I might be selling it. I stared at her, unblinking. "Sabine. If I were still working on trying to figure out what was happening to your shrimp volume, I'd be happier than a clam if you sold. I could get back to what I do, and we could get on with our lives. Unfortunately, this murder charge is putting a little cramp in my style right now."

Deflated, she just sat for a minute with hunched shoulders. "Okay. I get it."

"I have to ask you this." I couldn't wait any longer to address the elephant in the room. "Did you have anything to do with Emil's death?"

She jumped up from the couch, "NO! How could you even think that? I don't even know you right now, Miranda. I am sorry that this happened to you, but you will not hang this on me! How dare you after everything I've done for you?"

Odd that she didn't have any problem thinking that I might have done it five minutes ago, but that was Sabine. I guess I needed to mend fences for now. "I'm sorry Sabine, it had to be asked. Like you said, sometimes one thing leads to another. Are we okay?"

"Yes, I'm sorry too. I guess I'm a little sensitive." We hugged, and she sniffled. "I don't like the looks I'm getting out there. I'm pretty sure everyone down here, and most everyone up in town believes I did it. No one is saying anything, but you know how that goes. I swear on Grandpapa's grave; I had nothing to do with Emil's death. I'm as anxious as you are to get you cleared and find out who did this. Let me help you."

"Of course, Sabine. Thanks." I hoped that I wouldn't live to regret that decision.

We spent the rest of the day reminiscing and watching old movies; one thing we were good at was avoidance.

Over crabmeat and feta omelets with French Roast coffee the next morning, we strategized our next steps. I wasn't completely sold that Sabine was not involved in Emil's death, and I felt guilty about that. On the other hand, I couldn't afford to be stupid. If, in fact, she wasn't involved, I needed her help. And if she was, I would find out soon enough. The truth had a strange way of revealing itself in time.

After a couple of hours of brainstorming, I was starting to feel better about how to handle the investigation. I decided to re-interview all of Sabine's employees and circle back with all the ex-employees I could find. The staff at the CrawGator could also be helpful since they were the eyes and the ears of the marina.

I said, "Thanks, Sabine. Mark said I needed to head back to the city today because we need to go over some things relating to the upcoming hearing. Can I take your car?"

"Okay, ma chérie. I'll arrange the meetings with the staff. Are you coming back tonight or in the morning?"

I wasn't sure how I'd feel after my meeting with Mark. "Do you mind if I play it by ear?"

She looked a little pained. "No, that's okay. Just let me know when you figure it out, so I know what to plan on. And remember your meetings with the employees will start first thing."

The suspicious part of me wondered why she cared whether I came tonight or tomorrow morning. Maybe her social life was more active than I knew, or perhaps she just wanted to figure out if she needed to buy more food. Although, I was happy Sabine was arranging the meetings with her employees. I had hoped that she wouldn't be resistant to that. I didn't know how I'd manage to do all that and take care of everything Mark needed from me, but I'd figure it out as usual.

We said our 'goodbyes' and I was on the road again. I had just enough time to get to Mark's for the meeting. The drive was getting old; another nearly two hours one-way. The monotony of the commute and how my back was starting to hurt told me that I wouldn't be going back down until tomorrow morning. Even though I would need to leave by 6:15 in the morning to make my first appointment with Sabine's staff, it was just too much driving in one day. Thank goodness for the Garmin in this thing, or I would have been completely lost trying to find Mark's office. I made it with about thirty seconds to spare.

His office was nice, but not gaudy. It was tastefully decorated. If he had a decorator, my gut and the soft colors and attention to detail told me it was probably a woman. He walked out to the lobby just as I walked in.

I grinned at him. "Nice digs."

Mark smiled, surveying his kingdom. "Thanks. That means a lot coming from you."

He headed toward the back, and I sped up to join him. He led me to an oversized conference room with a bunch of legal boxes stacked in the corner.

"What's all this?" I asked.

"Discovery, my friend," Mark said with a sigh. "More accurately, it's the prosecution's discovery request."

"You've got to be kidding. What could they possibly be asking for?" I stared in amazement at the sheer volume of items.

He sat at the table and motioned for me to do the same. "This is a textbook case of 'keep the defense as busy as possible with meaningless work.' What it means to me is that they have a weak case, and they don't want us to have enough time to find the real culprit. What they don't know is that we have a two-pronged approach and that you've got a lot of investigative experience. It'll still be a challenge getting this stuff together, but it may buy us some extra time. They are asking for things like school records and information from prior employers that can take weeks or even months to get. The longer they delay, the better, as far as I'm concerned."

I studied the boxes. "How long are they giving you to get all this stuff?"

"As of right now, two weeks, but they can't have it both ways. That's one of the things I wanted to discuss with you. I want to request a continuance of at least two weeks. I'm asking for four weeks, but I don't want to get on the wrong side of the court either, so we need to be reasonable." He had a piece of paper in his hand that he slid in front of me. "I also wanted to discuss this." His serious face grew into a half-grin. "We had to run a background check to see if you had any priors. It was clean except for this resisting arrest conviction."

I knew this would come back to bite me at some point. I must have turned twenty shades of red. "Really, what does this have to do with my murder charge?"

"It points to character." He sounded like the prosecution to me.

I was exasperated but said nothing.

136

"I'm sorry, Miranda, I need to know anything and everything that they may throw at us during the trial, assuming it gets that far. Of course, I'm still hoping they drop the charges before we get to trial, but we need to be prepared." He scribbled some notes on a yellow legal pad.

I glared at him, and then relented, "Okay. you knew that I worked undercover for several years in North Carolina, right?"

"Right." He sat on the edge of the conference table, preparing for the extended version.

"As I told you before, after I got shot, I quit the force. Although, I didn't officially quit until I got my settlement which was nearly a year, and many surgeries, after my accident. My partner, Melissa and I had gotten really close during that time, and she came to visit me every day I was in the hospital. By the time I quit, she was so fed up with the life of a female undercover cop; she quit too. The day after we quit, being young and stupid, we decided to join a protest at the University of North Carolina. It was in favor of women's rights."

I shifted in my seat. "To make a long story short, the protestors got a little out of control. We clashed with some frat guys who were giving us a hard time, but it got serious enough that the police were called. We ended up blocking off the student union, and we were all arrested. We were sure our arrest was directly related to the fact that we had recently quit the force. She and I were leaving the next day for Vegas, and we blew off the trial, so we were convicted by default."

I crossed my arms. "Do you need anything else on that? Admittedly it was stupid, but I don't believe it's a mark on my character. Besides, we need to talk about the other thousand-pound gorilla in the room—your gun."

He noticeably grimaced. "I've never made it a secret that I keep handguns in my cars. But I always keep my cars and glove compartments locked especially since the local police started cracking down on concealed weapon violations."

I glared at him. "You might have wanted to mention that." I felt a little guilty blaming him since I knew, bottom line, it was my fault that the glove compartment hadn't been locked.

He ignored my dig. "Since Sabine and I were seeing each other for a while, anyone in Venice could recognize my car, especially with the vanity plate. It's plausible that almost anyone on her crew could have known about the gun in the Jeep."

"You're right. Letting the whole world know you kept guns in your vehicles wasn't the smartest thing you ever did." I decided to eat crow. "Just as not locking the glove compartment wasn't the smartest thing I ever did.

He nodded. "I guess we both were at fault, but hopefully when this is all sorted out, the judge will cut us some slack."

I sighed, ready to get back to the case. "I'm interviewing her crew again, one by one, tomorrow. I'll work in some questions about their use and knowledge of handguns. That might reveal something important."

Mark spoke quietly, grasping at straws. "Maybe this helps us . . . we certainly can make the case in court that there were potentially many people with knowledge of and access to that gun besides you and me. Anyone could have worn gloves, jimmied the car door lock, stolen the gun from the glove compartment, and killed Emil without completely wiping off our prints." He smirked. "Who am I kidding? Saying it out loud, it doesn't even sound plausible to me. How am I going to convince the judge or jury of that?"

The lines on his forehead told me even more about his state of mind. I touched his arm. "If we didn't kill Emil, someone had to have stolen the gun. The truth will set us free."

He smiled at me like I was the most naive person he had ever met, but took the opportunity to change the subject. "Andrea has some specific questions regarding the discovery documents. She'll be in to meet with you in a couple of minutes." His confident demeanor had returned. "I'm going to petition the court to have the charges dropped. They have the weapon with your fingerprints on it and a bullet matching the gun from Ballistics but are lacking a motive. You had barely even met the man."

"Thanks. I'm sorry I bit your head off earlier. I think all of this is catching up with me. I haven't had time to stop and process it. It's a lot a deal with."

"Don't worry, Miranda. It'll be all right. We just need to take it one step at a time." He left the conference room while I sat lost in thought.

After a minute or two, perky twenty-something Andrea cruised efficiently into the conference room. She had a legal pad with several pages of questions that took three hours to get through, leaving me feeling exhausted. I couldn't imagine what any of this information had to do with prosecuting a murder case. Mark was right; most of this busy-work was designed to distract us from mounting a decent defense. It was working. I was going to be exhausted for my day-long interviews with Sabine's staff.

Since I felt more than a bit cranky after my ordeal with Andrea, I stopped only briefly in Mark's office on the way out. He looked fried too, so I decided that I wouldn't engage him any further today. "I just wanted to let you know I'm going to head out. I have the worst headache right now." I hoped he wasn't as discouraged as I felt. He certainly looked it.

"Thanks for spending the time." He glanced up wearily from his desk. "We can do this, Miranda. We just need to work a little bit harder than they do. I'll give you a call when we get the new date for the preliminary hearing." He clearly didn't want an extended conversation either, so I turned and walked out.

Chapter 8

Despite my earlier inclination to spend the night in Meraux, I headed back down to Sabine's. I gave her a call to let her know. She sounded energized; that made one of us.

When I got to her house, she looked perfect as usual, dressed in another sundress I hadn't seen yet. "Gosh, you look like something the cat dragged in. Did your workday not go so great?"

"I've had better. Three hours of discovery with Mark's assistant, Andrea, pronounced *ondraya*, not *andreya*, made me feel even older than I am." I rolled my eyes, and Sabine laughed.

"Right, you're so old, Miranda! How do you think I feel?" She winked.

"If you feel as good as you look, I think you feel really good. My day was grueling, how about yours?" I asked, wondering about her company sale.

"I had another meeting with Warren today . . ." Sabine had another one of those far away looks on her face.

"Oh, it's just Warren now. I see how it is." I tried to sound light and amused but didn't feel that way.

"He's a very nice guy, and very good looking, but I just don't think of him that way." She flipped her hair. "Yes, I admit I might be flirting with him a bit, but that's so he gets me the best deal if I decide to sell. There's no harm in him looking as long as he keeps his mind on the end game—my business and his commission."

"Sounds like you're a lot closer to selling than I thought." I said it with a smile, but underneath I fumed with anger.

She was thoughtful for a minute. "I guess maybe I am. I only met with the guy on a whim, to see what it was worth. Now that I have some idea, my imagination is running wild."

"I have to be honest with you about something." Her happiness was making my insides burn with guilt. "Yesterday, I came down here before I went up to Boothville to talk to Ronnie. I saw you and Warren walking off the dock and into the restaurant." I looked away and bit my lip. "And I may have followed you."

She stopped in her tracks. "You spied on us? So, you *do* suspect me of killing Emil? Is that it?"

"No. Well, not really . . ." I didn't sound very convincing.

"Not really?" Her face turned red as her lips disappeared in a scowl.

This wasn't coming out right. I tried setting it straight. "I saw you with a guy that I didn't recognize who you hadn't mentioned to me, and I panicked. To be honest, from what I heard of your conversation, I didn't walk away with a warm and fuzzy feeling."

"Great. Just what did you think you heard?" She was pacing like a wild animal. She was livid. Telling her might have been a mistake.

"Sabine, listen," I begged.

"You need to get out of this house! Now!" She pointed to the door to make sure there would be no confusion.

"Sabine, hold on." I reached out for her arm.

She pulled away. "Out! Now!"

Stunned, I rushed out the front door. She slammed it behind me. Tears were rolling down my cheeks. By the time I got to the end of the driveway, I was sobbing uncontrollably. My legs were weak, and I had to sit down on a boulder marking the end of her driveway. I stared up at the sky, wondering how things had gone so wrong. This had been the worst week of my life. The only good news was finding out that Sabine was my sister, and now she would probably disown me. My butt was falling asleep as I balanced on the rough stone, hoping Sabine would come after me; she didn't.

After twenty minutes, I figured I had better go. But where? I didn't want to go to my mom's under any circumstances. I still needed to be back early in the morning. That was assuming Sabine didn't cancel the interviews. As I sat and pondered, I couldn't kick the feeling that Sabine was lying about something. I could only think of two reasons why someone would get that mad—either because I was calling her a liar or because she had something to hide. I hoped it was number one, but why did I keep questioning her involvement in this?

I guess I needed to face the facts. If I were still a cop, Sabine would be my number one suspect. She was awake before I was that morning and could have easily slipped over there and come back undetected. She knew that Mark had a gun in his vehicle and may have had motive since she suspected Emil of ripping her off. I needed to get past this whole family connection, or I wasn't going to be effective in my investigation. And frankly, now that I had a few minutes to collect myself, her reaction made me question her innocence even more. I took some deep breaths in an attempt to curb my increasing anxiety.

Seconds later, her door opened, and she walked outside. She no longer gave the impression of a wildcat stalking her prey but of a lioness circling her victim after the kill.

She finally settled on the boulder next to mine. "Miranda, let's talk."

I nodded like the child I often defaulted to in her presence.

Sabine started in a calm voice. "I am so sorry I reacted that way. You may not realize it, but I look to you for approval."

I gaped at her blankly. That didn't even compute with me.

143

She continued, "You have grown into such a beautiful, intelligent and competent woman. I am so proud of you. I am more than proud of you. I don't feel like I'm superior anymore. Sure, when we were kids, I had the upper hand. You were so sweet and open to everything I had to say."

She paused, and I kept quiet and let her continue. "You may not realize it, but when you spied on me, you might as well have accused me of murder. You hurt me so deeply that I lost control. Honestly, Miranda, I'm scared to death. I know that you didn't kill him. The evidence will never support the murder charge against you. You will be exonerated. I am sure of that.

"I also know that as soon as that happens, who the next suspect will be. Moi! It only makes sense. I knew Emil. He worked for me. Everyone knows that work relationships can create their own set of issues, especially since I was his boss. It's all circumstantial, but honestly, I believe if they had taken more time to investigate, they would've come after me, not you."

Tears welled in her eyes. "I need you, Miranda. I need you in my corner. If you suspect me, what is the rest of the world going to think? But along with that, I feel tremendously guilty. I asked you to come out here. You dropped everything to help me and now look where we are. If there is anyone who should be angry, it's you, not me."

I had been staring across the street at the marina while she talked. She grabbed my shoulders and turned me to face her. "Please look at me, Miranda. If you look in my eyes, you will know that I would never lie to you. I truly believe that this is our moment of truth. How we resolve this will affect our relationship for the rest of our lives."

She looked deep into my eyes. "I had nothing to do with this. I am devastated by Emil's death. He was a good man, Miranda. God knows what the crew will say about him. Sure, he was tough, but he was also fair. Some people could never live up to his expectations, and I imagine those people will take this opportunity to talk him down. I really hope that doesn't happen. He was like Grandpapa in many ways."

She sobbed and hugged me like she was holding on for dear life. I hugged her so tight I thought I might break her. We stayed that way for what felt like an hour but was only minutes. It took me some time to process everything she said, but I finally believed her. This was not the desperate plea of a guilty woman. I was a cop long enough to recognize that. I felt ashamed for doubting her.

I pulled back a little so that I could see her face. "I believe you, Sabine. I am so sorry for doubting you."

She breathed a sigh of relief even as the tears streamed down her cheeks. That confirmed one final time for me that she was innocent. We stood up and headed back inside, hand in hand. The rest of the evening, we spent laughing about the crazy things I did in high school. I had almost forgotten about my brief acting career when I was a freshman before I went Goth. When I saw the video of my performance, I wanted to hide under a rock and never come out. I was horrible—more wooden than a statue and less genuine than a friendly drug dealer. It's a wonder I made it into the undercover division at all.

After years of separation, it was great to be back together; just Sabine and I, the way it used to be. Only now, it was better than when we were younger. We were both women now—equals. Our recent struggles had brought us closer than we had ever been. We stayed up past midnight because neither of us wanted the evening to end.

I slept dreamlessly and woke up refreshed. Sabine was already up when I entered the kitchen. She handed me my coffee, and I smiled. "You really know how to get my day started. Thanks."

We had a companionable breakfast, and she filled me in a little more about the crew members I would be interviewing today. She gave me some insight into each of their relationships with Emil and their work history. I wished I had this much background when I met with them the first time, but she said that she didn't want to prejudice me. I decided to meet with them at the CrawGator as opposed to the boat where Emil was murdered. It just seemed like a more respectful thing to do.

The CrawGator was nearly empty, so I took a table by the window, next to where Sabine had been with Warren. One by one, the men came in around ten minutes later. If I thought they were closed-mouthed and suspicious the first time I interviewed them, I wasn't prepared for the stonewalling I received this time. No one had seen anything, heard anything, or knew anything.

Even the couple of guys who had been somewhat helpful the first time were downright uncooperative. I held onto hope of the possibility that an ex-employee might spill their guts, but that was for another day. I was packing up my laptop when one of the waitresses asked if she could talk to me. She was probably in her mid-forties and was, perhaps, feeling her age, considering the amount of makeup plastered across her face.

"Miranda?" she asked.

"Yes, that's me." I smiled. "I'll be out of your hair in a bit. Sorry for taking up one of your tables all day."

She nervously chewed on the dirty blonde hair that hung in front of her face and ignored my apology. "My name is Becky Fisher. I need to talk to you. Is there anywhere else we can go?"

I extended my hand to her. She shook it with the grip of a woman who knew what she wanted or at least wanted to give that impression. "Sure, Becky, we can walk over to Sabine's."

She glanced around nervously. "Let's go walk on the dock."

I was curious and somewhat apprehensive at the same time. This girl felt like bad news. "Sounds good." We left the CrawGator and walked to the end of the dock. I gestured at the benches I imagined were used mostly for fishing. "Want to sit here?"

"Sure," She once again scanned the area. No one was within earshot. "You're investigating Emil's death, right?"

"Yes," I said more impatiently than I should have.

She leaned close to me as if someone might be listening even though she'd already checked the area. There was no place for anyone to hide nearby. The smell of smoke on her uniform and mints on her breath were overpowering. "That's what I need to talk to you about."

"Have you contacted the police or the prosecutor's office?" I was curious as to why she was opening up to me, especially after I heard nothing of value all day from the crew.

"No. I would have, but no one ever came looking for witnesses or anything. I thought it was strange since we were open all that morning. I thought they would eventually come, but I haven't seen anyone yet." She piqued my interest, but I pulled away slightly so I could breathe.

I wasn't surprised they hadn't come looking for witnesses. "They think this is an open and shut case. They have botched this from beginning to end, so nothing would surprise me at this point." In an attempt to sound wide awake and perky, I asked in my best Valley Girl voice, "So, what do you have for me?"

"That was a strange day. I get to work at 5:30 every weekday because we open at six for breakfast. About 6:15, I saw all the guys leaving. Normally the fleet is out by 6:30 am. Sometimes, if the weather is bad or predicted to be bad, they won't go out, but it was beautiful that day with clear blue skies and low humidity, which is almost unheard of this time of year. At about 6:30, I saw Sabine walk over from her house and out to the dock. She seemed in a real hurry. It was rare to see her there. She was usually hands-off when there was shrimping going on. I guessed that she must be meeting with Emil and that was why he sent the crew home. She came back down the dock less than five minutes later, still in a real hurry. I watched her walk across the road, so I'm assuming she went back home."

"Did you hear anything? Any yelling or a gunshot?" I turned to face her straight on and listened intently, hoping for a negative answer. I believed Sabine earlier. I prayed she hadn't lied to me.

"No. Nothing, but honestly, when we are opening, there is a lot of noise, vacuum and floor cleaners, fans and stuff like that. I guess I would have heard a gunshot, but with the marina here, we hear lots of engines backfiring, so we get kind of immune to noises," Becky said. The lines on her face told of a rough life, and it was very hard to read. I had found this to be the case with hardened criminals and psychopaths.

Accusations about Sabine were not what I wanted to hear right now. "Anything else, Becky?"

She smiled but wouldn't look me in the eye. "No. I don't want to get anyone in trouble; I just thought that someone should know. I didn't tell anyone else that I saw her. There are plenty of people who would love to see Sabine go down, but I'm not one of them. She's always been super nice to me, and I'd hate to think she had anything to do with this. I just haven't been able to sleep since this happened. I feel terrible." Her avoidance of eye contact and the glint of sweat on her forehead told me she was lying, but I wasn't sure about which part or all of it.

"You did the right thing, Becky. I need to figure out how to handle this, so I'd appreciate it if you kept this quiet for now." I offered a reassuring smile and reached for her hand.

"Sure. I'd rather forget about it, to be honest." She took my outstretched hand glanced back toward the CrawGator.

We both stood up and walked back to shore. When we got there, Becky jumped in her car and took off. She wasn't lying about not wanting to be seen by her coworkers. I took a deep breath and sat alone for fifteen or twenty minutes on another bench overlooking the river. My head was pounding, and the slight ringing in my ears warned of a possible panic attack. I controlled my breathing and closed my eyes until it passed. This was way too much to process right now. There had to be a logical explanation. Even if there was, this would be very damaging evidence should Sabine come under suspicion for the murder. I was going to do what I needed to do to get myself acquitted, but I didn't want to do it at her expense. I was sure that Becky was lying, so I decided to pack the information away for future reference. I would mention it to Mark the next time we got together.

With that thought, I stood and ambled back to Sabine's house. She was in the kitchen, putting the finishing touches on dinner. I was sure I looked like hell after spending the day in a greasy bar while she looked great as usual. After this was over, I needed to take 'how to cook dinner without breaking a sweat' lessons from Sabine.

"Hey, Little Sister!" She sounded like our argument from yesterday was a distant memory.

"Hi, Big Sister," I responded, hoping I sounded cheerful.

"You look like something the cat dragged in." She didn't even laugh to make me feel better.

"I know. Do I have time to take a shower?" I whined, dropping the cheerful act.

"Sure, you do. I guess it must have been pretty slimy spending the day at the Gator."

"Ya think? I feel like a french fry right now. I'll be back." I was glad to have an excuse to look miserable. Honestly, it wasn't the grease as much as the information I was dealing with, but the shower gave me some time to digest it.

While I was showering, I tried to focus on what I was missing. Sabine couldn't be that good a liar, and I couldn't (or wouldn't) believe she would let me take the rap for this if. I needed to pursue every angle, and there had to be one that I missed. After stepping from the shower, I put on a happy face and pulled on a floor-length casual summer dress. The hot water and clean clothes made me feel immeasurably better. We ate the salmon croquettes, Potatoes Almandine, and a Caesar salad in silence until she interrupted.

"Miranda! I almost forgot."

My heart sank. What now? "What?"

"We're supposed to watch Casablanca on TV tonight."

I dropped my fork onto my plate and laughed with relief that she didn't have anything of substance to share—no monkey wrenches to make things worse. "When is it on? We'd better move to the living room and get comfy."

We went to bed at nine-thirty because I nodded off half-way through the movie. Then I fell asleep in bed almost the instant that my head hit the pillow.

I woke up with a start and looked at the clock. It was only 11:30 p.m. I had hardly even had a respectable nap. But I laid awake for a while trying to put the pieces together. I knew Becky was lying, but I didn't know about what. I didn't know anything about her. I settled again on giving it all to Mark tomorrow and getting his opinion; maybe he could run a background check for me.

The rest of the night was uneventful, or if I had any dreams, I didn't remember them. I called Mark first thing in the morning, and he was available at ten, so I had just enough time to dress and get up there. The ninety-mile commute was almost becoming routine. I said a brief good-bye to Sabine on the way out, but I was feeling unsettled and distracted.

She gave me a concerned look, but didn't say anything further except, "Have a good day, Miranda."

It was a hot and humid day, typical of the Bayou, so I cranked up the AC in Sabine's car and pointed the vents directly at me. While I tossed around everything that was running through my head, I felt more and more anxious. I was relieved to see Mark's Porsche parked outside because I didn't feel like sitting around the lobby or spending more time with Andrea.

When I walked into the office, Mark was waiting for me. "I saw you pull up. So, how are you doing, Miranda? You didn't sound so good on the phone."

"I've been better. Yesterday's interviews were pretty much a waste of time, but there is something I need to talk about."

He led me to his office. "There's something I need to talk to you about too."

That sounded ominous. What now?

"You first," I responded. I always like to get the bad news first.

"Okay. Remember how I was going to ask for a continuance?"

"Yes?" Dare I get my hopes up?

"I did." He took a deep breath and let it out slowly, "It was denied. Evidently, the judge's calendar is filling up, and she wants to keep this case on track. It's not really a big deal since we've almost completed the discovery request. Maybe we're better off moving forward. Do you have any more interviews planned at this point?"

I nodded. "I was hoping to talk to some recently terminated employees. The current employees are responding as one. Their answers were very well-rehearsed. I don't know if that means they have something to hide or if they just want to make sure that no one stands out as a potential suspect. It wasn't very satisfying, though. The general gist of their answers was that Emil seemed to be under a lot of pressure and that he was hard-nosed, but that was normal. They clearly did not trust Sabine or me and weren't going to provide their opinions."

"Did you learn anything at all you didn't know going in?" The way he leaned forward to wait for my answer made me feel like he was paying attention, more than most men I knew.

"Actually, I did. I learned that you should never do interviews in a greasy spoon with no air conditioning. Oh . . ." I paused to chuckle, "and I learned that I should probably change deodorants."

Even Mark, normally patient to a fault, was getting antsy. "Miranda."

"Okay. As I was leaving, a waitress from the restaurant at the marina approached me. She told me that she had seen Sabine going down the dock after the crews had been sent home, which is right around the time of death." I felt like a traitor ratting out Sabine.

"Wow. Really? Did she hear anything, like, say, a gunshot?"

He seemed excited. I wondered if Mark suspected Sabine, but I didn't mention it.

"No. She said it's pretty loud when they're getting the restaurant ready to open. But, before you get too excited, I don't know what to make of it. I know I have a bit of a bias where Sabine is concerned, but I'm not sure that I believe this waitress, Becky. It seemed way too convenient to me. She just happened to be looking out the window and just happened to see Sabine go down the dock? I don't know, Mark."

"You can't be worried about Sabine when you've got this trial hanging over your head." I could tell that Mark was frustrated with me. "She's a big girl and can take care of herself."

"Of course, I want to get off from this murder charge, but she's family," I said firmly. "Sabine and I had an earnest conversation about the murder the night before last, and she was far more convincing than Becky was. I know that gut feelings aren't worth anything in court, but that's all I have right now. Besides, Becky's body language told me she was lying about something."

"You're killing me, Miranda." He put his elbows down on the table and rubbed his temples. "I need evidence, real hard evidence, that I can slap down in front of the judge and blast their circumstantial evidence out of the water."

I remembered something else. "Here's another weird thing though . . . according to Becky, neither the police nor the district attorney approached anyone working at the restaurant for a statement. It's almost like they aren't even investigating this for fear that they'll find out that I didn't do it."

He looked thoughtful. "I'll do everything I can to use that to our advantage."

153

I sure hoped he could do that because it was my life on this line.

He nodded as if he read my mind, and I headed back to Sabine's wrapped up in silent thoughts.

Chapter 9

The next ten days went by like lightning as the preliminary hearing date approached. I spent the week interviewing anyone and everyone that I could who might be able to shed some light on who killed Emil, as well as anyone who might have had any insight on Emil's state of mind at the time of his death. In the final analysis, I hadn't come up with anything that made me feel like I was any closer to finding the killer.

No one else I spoke to at the CrawGator saw anything that day, nor did any of Sabine's recently terminated employees have anything of value to add. I did find it curious that Buck, the ex-classmate Mark and I saw at the Déjà vu, didn't show up for our scheduled interview, but I figured he'd found another job and couldn't get away. I even spoke to several other shrimping operations up-river to see if I could uncover the mystery of Emil's trips there after hours. While I figured it was unlikely that I was going to find someone who would admit that Emil was selling them shrimp out the back door, it was worth a try.

So, there I sat, back in Judge Samantha Cantrese's courtroom, at the table next to Mark. It was much better to be dressed in street clothes this time as opposed to a jumpsuit. I still had the same pit in my stomach today as the last time. It all seemed so surreal. I had myself convinced that between the arraignment and now, I would find the proverbial 'smoking gun.' But despite my best efforts, I hadn't found anything that I could use to save myself.

Mark whispered either to himself or me, "Let's get this done." The worry lines around his eyes and across his forehead did little to comfort me.

As we waited for the judge, I glanced around the courtroom. The gallery was not as full as it had been during my arraignment, and about half the courtroom was filled. I decided I wasn't as fascinating in my conservative grey skirt and jacket as I had been in the orange jumpsuit. I wondered who these people were and why they had this much free time on a workday. I studied the faces of the people in the first couple of rows, and there was not a hint of recognition. Of course, my mother and Tom were here, and Sabine was sitting in the back of the courtroom biting her lip like she does when she's worried.

I wished my mom and Sabine could figure out how to get along, but they were still miles apart.

With that thought, the judge breezed into the courtroom, and we all rose. It was hard to tell with the robe and the pomp and circumstance, but I guessed she and I would get along outside of the courtroom. She had a certain twinkle in her eye that made me relax a little bit. I briefly pictured the two of us sharing a couple of glasses of Cabernet at the Roosevelt Hotel Bar on Canal Street discussing torts and pleas or whatever it is judges talk about.

I was jolted back to reality when the bailiff announced, "The first case is number 25631-1, the State of Louisiana against Miranda Marquette. Please be seated." The judge motioned for us to sit with a wave of her hand.

Her Honor opened the session. "Welcome back to phase two of this trial. I'm pleased to see that we don't have as many spectators as we were blessed with for the arraignment. That will mean, I trust, that I won't need to provide any warnings regarding inappropriate outbursts or the like." She glared at the gallery but with a touch of a smirk.

"For the benefit of those of you who don't spend all your spare time at murder trials, let me explain the purpose for this preliminary hearing. Before we can proceed to the jury trial, we are required to determine if there is sufficient evidence to move forward. I value this opportunity to get a last crack at making the important decisions that could, potentially, be life or death."

I shivered as I realized the death she was referring to could be mine.

She scanned the courtroom, daring two people in the back row to continue talking. She resumed her introductory speech once they got the hint to be quiet. "Once it gets past this point, I pretty much lose control of the outcome because the jury is then responsible for the final determination of innocence or guilt." My stomach felt like it had lead balls in it. I hoped my face didn't show my fear as she laid it all out.

She took a deep breath and then continued, "There are some judges who, frankly, consider the preliminary hearing as a mere formality. As far as I'm concerned, that couldn't be further from the truth. Considerable taxpayer money is wasted annually on jury trials that never should take place. These trials clog up the court system, expose the defendant to unnecessary hardship, and end up with the same result, assuming the wrongly accused defendant is acquited. Even more distasteful are those who are wrongfully convicted and spend needless years in prison."

She seemed to look directly at me when she made the last statement. I couldn't decide if that was good or bad.

She completed her introduction. "With that in mind, Mr. Prosecutor, I turn the proceedings over to you."

"I'd like to call my first witness: Sheriff's Deputy James Patrick," the prosecutor announced, with a touch of arrogance.

I realized now that I never even knew the names of the arresting officers. I couldn't wait to hear what he had to say, though. I was tempted to stick my tongue out at him, but that wouldn't be lady-like. Besides, I didn't want to risk the judge seeing me.

The prosecutor ambled from his table to within a couple of feet of the officer. "Deputy Patrick, can you please provide us with the sequence of events that led to the arrest and apprehension of the defendant?"

He puffed up his chest and glanced at the judge. I couldn't tell if she actually rolled her eyes or if I had just hoped she had. He was the older one of the two and the deputy in charge. "At approximately eight a.m. on the thirty-first of May of this year, 2007, there was a 911 call placed from the area identified through cell phone records as the Venice Marina."

He leaned back and crossed one leg to rest his ankle on his knee, an arrogant posture if ever I saw one. "My partner and I were on patrol in Port Sulphur and were notified by the local dispatcher that there was a death, apparently by gunshot, on a boat docked at the Venice Marina. We were notified that a woman by the name of Miranda Marquette had made the call and would be waiting for us on the dock near the boat in question until we arrived. When we arrived at the parking lot for the marina, Ms. Marquette was fleeing the area by foot at a fast rate of speed. We stopped our vehicle, got out, and yelled for her to halt. While she did stop, she dropped her purse in the process, and a weapon fell onto the ground. When I saw the weapon, I immediately ordered her to get down on the ground, face down. When she refused, we were forced to restrain her physically. Because she did not respond to our instructions, we had no choice but to physically assist her to a prone position whereby we placed handcuffs on her and led her to our vehicle."

I nudged Mark and whispered, "Do something. This already makes me look guilty."

He looked too calm for my taste and whispered back, "We'll have time to cross-examine him. Until that happens, we need to be quiet and respectful. That will work to our advantage in the long run."

The judge looked at us briefly and went back to listening to the testimony without comment.

"As part of the new cooperative program with the State, rather than taking her back to our station for interrogation, we were instructed to take her to the State Police station across the street from this courthouse. We then turned her over to the detectives on duty and returned to Port Sulphur."

The prosecutor continued. "While you had Ms. Marquette in custody, did you perform a routine gunpowder residue test?"

"We did. I turned the swabs over to the detectives when we arrived. We found out later that the test was positive." He said this and finished with a smarmy grin and a gleam in his eye.

The prosecutor gave Mark a smug look. "Your witness, counsel."

Mark stood and walked quickly toward the deputy. "Thank you, Mr. Prosecutor," he said and then turned directly to the deputy. "Deputy Patrick, it is your testimony that you forcibly took Ms. Marquette into custody because you viewed her as a threat?"

"Yes. She did not respond to our instructions." He winked at me. I wanted to lunge at him but remained in my seat with a blank expression on my face.

"I see. Was there any reason to believe that Ms. Marquette was a threat, based on the information provided to you by the 911 dispatcher?" He sounded innocent enough, but I knew he had something up his sleeve.

"When there is a murder, more often than not, the perpetrator is the person who makes the 911 call." He said it as if he had testified the same information at a thousand other trials.

"I see. Have you listened to the 911 call?" he asked with interest.

The deputy blushed a bit and wouldn't look directly at Mark. "Yes, but not until it was provided to us by the prosecution."

Mark turned to the judge. "Your Honor, I know that this is unusual, but since the prosecution has provided the recording of the 911 call as evidence, could we listen to the call before I proceed with additional questions?"

The judge addressed the District Attorney. "Mr. Hanford, would you object to the court listening to the 911 call at this time?"

He didn't look thrilled, but he agreed to it. What could he say? It was his evidence. During the playback, the judge had to quiet the gallery a few times. I had forgotten just how 'down-home' the call was. My mom was beaming. Looking at her, I had an overall feeling of well-being. I didn't sound like someone who just killed a man. I had to admit that playing it was a brilliant strategy on Mark's part. This seemed to be causing quite a stir at the prosecution table. I had to wonder if they had even listened to this call.

The judge watched the District Attorney whisper to his assistant for a minute and then said, "Mr. Prosecutor, can we proceed here?"

He didn't look up. "Yes, your honor."

She motioned to Mark, "Please continue with your questioning, Mr. Peterson."

"That's all I have for this witness, your honor." Mark looked pleased with himself.

"You may step down, Deputy." The judge ordered.

The District Attorney was happy to move on, "I call State Police Detective Roland Bricker." He was sworn in, and the questioning began. "Detective Bricker, it's my understanding that a weapon was recovered near the scene of the murder."

"Yes, sir. That is correct. It fell out of Ms. Marquette's purse as was established earlier," he said with a half-smirk.

The DA hesitated for effect. "Do you have the ballistics report?"

"Yes, sir. The report states that the weapon produced the bullet responsible for the victim's death. We also determined that there were fingerprints consistent with the defendant on the weapon." He gloated.

The prosecutor was regaining his smug expression as if he had us on the ropes. "Was this a registered weapon?"

"Yes, sir. This weapon was registered to a Mark Peterson." He flashed us a brief smile.

The DA was having fun now. "Was this the Mark Peterson who is serving as the defense attorney?"

"Yes, sir." He smiled openly.

"Were his prints on the weapon as well?" The prosecutor asked, but we all knew the answer.

"Yes, sir," he responded.

The DA changed the subject. "Detective Bricker, have you had the opportunity to speak to any witnesses who can provide any pertinent information regarding this case?"

"Yes, sir." He nodded.

He asked as if he already knew the answer, and of course, he did. "Can you point out this witness in the court?"

He pointed to the middle of the gallery.

I turned around and was stunned to see Johnny Vasquez, Sabine's employee.

He smiled. "I'd like to call Johnny Vasquez."

The judge interrupted. "Bill, I know it's been a while since you've been in a court of law."

Bill glared at her, but then smiled when he realized who he was glaring at.

"Mr. Peterson gets a chance to cross-examine the witness before you call your next one," she scolded.

He retreated to his table. "Sorry, Your Honor, I got a little ahead of myself."

The judge nodded to the prosecutor and shifted her attention to Mark. "Your witness."

Mark stood. He still looked confident. "Detective Bricker, do you keep a weapon in your personal vehicle?"

The DA stood up. "Objection! Detective Bricker is not on trial here!"

The judge responded, "Mr. Hanford, in case you have forgotten, this is a preliminary hearing. Technically, no one is on trial here. We are here to determine if there is sufficient evidence to move forward with the trial. I will allow the question."

The detective responded. "Yes, I have personal weapons in my vehicles, locked in the glove compartment per the State of Louisiana concealed weapon statute."

I maintained my blank expression but was panicking inside.

Mark continued. "Are you aware how this weapon came to be in the defendant's possession?"

He spoke softly. "It's my understanding that you lent your vehicle to the defendant and that the weapon was in that vehicle."

Mark continued. "Are you aware that the defendant discharged the weapon the morning of the murder just before leaving Sabine Marquette's yard for the marina?"

Detective Bricker was stone-faced. "I believe Ms. Marquette mentioned that just before being escorted to the holding cells for processing, but we have been unable to authenticate her statement."

Mark sounded less than sure now. "Did you check out Sabine Marquette's premises for any evidence of this bullet?"

"We did and found nothing. Quite honestly, it sounded like the kind of story you make up when you've run out of the truth."

I was stunned. It was going so well. Mark seemed to have run out of steam just at the wrong moment. He stood there in what appeared to be stunned silence.

The judge finally interrupted. "Do you have anything else for this witness, Mr. Peterson."

He walked back to our table. "No, your honor."

I glared at him when he came back and hissed, "Are you trying to send me to jail permanently?" He didn't respond.

The judge directed her attention to Mr. Hanford. "Okay, Bill, I know you are chomping at the bit."

Johnny was too. He practically ran down to the front of the court to be sworn in. The prosecutor spoke confidently. "Mr. Vasquez. Can I call you Johnny?"

Johnny smiled. "Sure, why not?"

Hanford approached the witness like they were old friends. "Now, Johnny, can you tell me what you told the detective just a couple of days ago?"

He sat up and surveyed the crowd but avoided looking directly at me. "She . . ." He pointed at me, "came around asking all sorts of questions about our shrimp catch and why it seemed to be down. We didn't know nothing about that, and we told her so. Emil was the last one she talked to. A couple of us was sittin' on the dock, just shooting the breeze, and we could hear some yelling from the shrimper. When we looked up at the boat, she was coming out of the navigation room lookin' all flustered. She yelled something back at him and ran by us."

Bill spoke like a kindly grandfather. "Now, son, do you know what the yelling was all about?"

Johnny snickered. "We had a pretty good idea. He said something about her cousin being a bad businesswoman and blaming everyone else for her problems. He was mad. I'm not sure what he might have done if she didn't run out like a bi—like a female dog with her tail between her legs."

The prosecutor continued, "Would you say she was angry when she passed you by?"

He sat up straighter, enjoying being the center of attention. "Oh yeah! She was spitting nails. We all stayed out of the way." Several people in the gallery chuckled.

The judge picked up her gavel and slammed it down. "Order!" She glared.

The prosecutor purposely walked past our table on the way to his. "No further questions. Your witness, Mr. Peterson," He winked at me. My stomach churned. I didn't know if this winking was a strategy of the prosecution, but it was working to unnerve me.

Mark stood. I could see by the look on his face he was still trying to formulate a plan. "Mr. Vasquez, how long did you and your friends stay on the dock after Ms. Marquette departed?"

Johnny looked up in the air like he was trying to relive the moment. "We stayed probably a half-hour, I guess."

"Did you see anyone else come or go from the boat while you were there?"

"No." Then he looked up and to the left as if he were trying to remember something. "Wait a minute. Just as we were leaving, we passed what's her name?" He snapped his fingers a few times. "Um . . . that waitress from the Gator." He thought for a minute, and then he said suddenly, "Becky! Yeah, that's it. Becky."

Mark seemed like he was back on track. "Did Becky say anything as she passed you?"

"No. I don't think so. . . Oh yeah, she did. She said all happy-like. 'Just delivering a take-out order' And then she laughed. I remember 'cause I was thinkin', 'Why would I care what you're doing?' It was kind of weird, I guess." He scratched his head.

Mark pressed. "Did you see where she was headed?"

"Nope. We all jumped in our cars and headed up to Port Sulphur to have a couple a beers. I pretty much forgot about seeing her until you asked."

Mark came back to the table. "Nothing further, Your Honor."

The judge instructed Johnny to step down. "Mr. Prosecutor, do you have any more witnesses?"

He remained seated but sounded confident. "No, your honor."

She looked at Mark. "Mr. Peterson, are there any witnesses you would like to call?"

He hesitated. I kicked him and whispered. "Call me as a witness."

"No, Your Honor." He said, ignoring me. I kicked him again. "Ouch!" he whispered.

The judge glared but said nothing. She appeared to be taken aback by what had happened. My gut told me that she hadn't expected this case to go to trial.

After a minute where you could have heard a pin drop, she finally spoke. I felt like she was talking directly to me. "This morning, when I woke up, I would have bet two hundred bucks that this case was not going to trial. And, Bill, I can't say that you did that great a job making your case. Perhaps if we saw you a little more often, you'd be in better practice."

He blushed and nodded in acknowledgment.

She continued. "On the other hand, there is enough evidence against the defendant that I cannot in good conscience dismiss this case."

My mom gasped. Sabine slumped in her chair. I felt another out of body experience coming on. How could Mark let this happen?

Chapter 10

After hugging Mom, Tom, and a couple of other disappointed well-wishers, I headed out the back of the courtroom to find Sabine. While I was sad that my case was going to trial, after I thought about it, I wasn't surprised. Being acquitted during a preliminary hearing was rare. While Mark was a competent attorney, I couldn't count entirely on him to prove me innocent; I had to find the killer myself.

Leaving the courtroom, I was hoping I'd find Sabine in the hallway, but she wasn't there. Disappointed, I stepped outside for some fresh air. There were benches on opposite sides of the walkway from the sidewalk to the courthouse. She sat planted on one on the left, engaged in a hushed, but intense, phone call. I couldn't hear what she was saying, but I was glad I wasn't on the receiving end of that call. She was practically throwing the phone as she flung her arms and hands around while talking a mile a minute. A short while later, she hung up and remained on the edge of the bench staring at nothing. I walked down and sat next to her.

When she saw me, she snapped out of her staring contest with the landscape. "Hey, what's up? Is there a recess?" I shook my head, and she seemed surprised. "Sorry, I had to take a call. So, do we have reason to celebrate?" She smiled, obviously anticipating a more positive answer.

I settled in next to her. "It's going to trial." I sounded like a deflating balloon.

Her smile crumbled. "Oh, Miranda, I'm so sorry. You must feel horrible."

I reached out and hugged her, tears streaming down my cheeks. "What if they convict me of this murder? That judge seems pretty fair and rational, and if she thinks I did it, how is a jury going to acquit me?"

Her voice choked with tears. "I don't know, but we'll figure it out. We have the truth on our side. I'll do everything I can, and Mark is a great attorney. He seemed a little distracted today, but I know if anyone can get an acquittal, he can."

Sabine then laughed through her tears. "I hope I didn't have anything to do with his lack of concentration."

I pulled out a tissue to wipe my face. "Why? What happened?"

She smiled wryly. "We arrived at about the same time today and had a brief chat just before he went in. I wished him luck and kissed him. I afraid it wasn't just a peck on the cheek."

I mock pushed her away. "No! Way! Does this mean . . .?

She frowned. "I honestly don't know what it means. I didn't plan it, but it didn't feel wrong either. I guess we'll see."

I took her hand. "Was that why you were looking so freaked out when I sat down?"

Sabine paused for a minute and closed her eyes. "No, that wasn't it. I'm selling the business," she said as if she didn't quite believe it herself.

I couldn't believe it either. "What? Really? What're you talking about? That's your life!"

"True, but maybe there's more to life than shrimp. The last few weeks have made me think about what is important—friends, family, love." She held my hand tightly.

I was surprised and suddenly flooded with guilt. "This is because of me, isn't it? My goodness, you just went out to that conference to learn more and to network. Now Emil's murder . . ."

"In all fairness, Miranda, it has nothing to do with you, at least not in a bad way. You made me realize that there's a lot more to life than just working. I've been hiding away in Venice for too long, and for what?" She slumped back against the bench. "I feel like an outcast upriver. No one in the family even appreciates that I've sacrificed my personal life to make Grandpapa's business succeed. I just want them to realize that I'm a good person, but that'll never happen."

I often felt the same way, but now was the time to focus on her. "What will you do?"

"I'm weighing my options." She had a faraway look that made me feel like she knew more than she was letting on.

As we sat on the bench, I was distracted by the people streaming from the courthouse. I looked up to see Mark engaged in a deep conversation with some guy who looked like another attorney. Sabine watched him closely. She waited to greet Mark once their conversation ended. They immediately huddled together, chatting in low voices, and I felt like a third wheel, so I walked down the sidewalk.

I pulled out my phone and dialed Heather's number.

"Heather Macintosh, how may I help you?"

"You can stop being so formal." It felt good to laugh.

"Miranda! It's so good to hear your voice. How are you? How is your . . .uh . . . situation going?" She sounded worried.

I groaned. "Not as well as I had hoped. I just had my preliminary hearing, and let's just say it didn't go as planned." I paused, not wanting to sound too negative. In an upbeat tone, I said, "Well, it'll give me something else to keep me busy while I'm out here, right?"

Heather sighed. "You don't have to put on your everything's fine act for me."

I could feel tears welling in my eyes again. My voice broke. "What am I going to do?"

Now it was time for Heather to do her smiley-face act. "You'll figure it out. You always do. Besides, you didn't do it, so how can they convict you, right?"

Her attempt to cheer me up worked a little. "Yeah, right," I said. "Let's talk about something else. How's the business going?"

"I'm kind of bored. Thank goodness for your hot tub and the amazing view from your deck. I've done a lot of reading. Otherwise, it's business as usual. I'm loving Malibu. You've got such a great spot here. Thanks for inviting me to stay."

Her upbeat tone made me feel better. "I'm glad you like it. Hopefully, I'll be back before long."

Heather giggled. "I can't wait."

"Heather, have I told you lately how much I appreciate you?" I said it with a grin and a shake of my head. "Don't ever change."

She laughed again, "Just don't fire me when you see all the food I've eaten while you've been gone."

It felt good speaking with her and remembering what my real life was like. I reminded myself to call Heather more often. "Thanks so much, and I'll be in touch when I can."

In a slightly more positive mood, I started to work on a mental course of action. I had no idea what to do next—lots of options, but nothing definite. Should I go back to Venice and resume my investigation, or should I stay here and provide support for Mark while he worked on my case? Should I take some time for myself, or should I spend time with Mom and Tom?

After my internal debate, I decided two things. First and foremost, I was going to rent a motorcycle. I had been borrowing cars for too long and needed to clear my head, and there was nothing like a good motorcycle ride to ground me. I had seen a rental place within walking distance. Second, I was going back to Mom and Tom's again, at least for a night. I would get my bearings and start fresh. Maybe we'd make it through a whole day without fighting about something stupid, although my hopes weren't very high in that respect.

I called Eagle Rider Motorcycle rentals to see if was worth walking over there.

"Eagle Rider," Bob speaking.

I asked, "What do you have available?"

"We've got Harleys, Indians, BMWs, and Goldwings."

Ugh. Well, at least they had more than just Harleys, but the rest of the list wasn't much better. "No Ducati's? How about maybe a Yamaha YZF?"

"Nope, sorry, ma'am. We don't get much call for those around here." He sounded surprised at my motorcycle of choice.

"Okay, what are your rental rates?" I was ready to get down to business.

He sounded like he was fumbling with paperwork. "The BMW R1200RT or GS is $179 a day or $1,085 a week."

"Bob. Can I call you Bob?" I southerned up my accent, trying to sound like a good ol' girl.

He seemed pleased that I remembered his name. "Sure can."

I worked on hiding my irritation. "I grew up around here and have come back for an extended visit. I need a bike for longer than you usually might find with a typical tourist. Is there anything you can do about the pricing?"

"Tell you what, little lady. You come down here, and we'll see what we can do." I could almost see his sneer over the phone.

I gritted my teeth at the "little lady," but said, "You're on, Bob, but don't let me down. I'll see ya in a few." I was going to have to use my natural people skills to appeal to Bob's generous side. Or I needed another plan before I arrived there.

I headed down the street at a brisk pace, enjoying the smell of creole in the air. The walk was the first time this trip that I'd taken the time to absorb the sights and smells of the Crescent City, but I arrived sooner than I expected and felt slightly disappointed that it ended so quickly. Eagle Rider was a small place with a bunch of bikes lined up in front on the sidewalk. They didn't seem to be doing much business today, but it was still a bit early for the biker crowd. I walked in to find a guy behind the counter. His name tag confirmed it was Bob. I could see why he called me 'little lady' without even seeing me so I forgave him. Bob was easily three hundred pounds and was tattooed from head to toe.

"Bob," I exclaimed like we'd known each other for years.

"Hey, little lady."

"Miranda." I stuck out my hand and looked him straight in the eye. "We spoke on the phone."

"Well now," he smiled a toothy grin. "I like to make bets with myself when I'm on the phone. I have to say, you are even prettier than I imagined."

"Why, thank you, Bob." I smiled sweetly. "Now, let's get down to brass tacks."

He grinned like he was holding all the cards, "Well, little lady . . ."

"Miranda," I emphasized.

"Well, Miranda, I quoted our pricing on the phone." He was giving me the company line. I suspected this might be easier in person.

I stood my ground, "Bob, is that how we are going to play this?"

Sweat glistened on his forehead. His smile disappeared, "Ma'am, I just work here. I can't negotiate pricing."

"Well then, Bob, who can?" I maintained my smile. I didn't want to lose him, so I changed my tone. "As I said on the phone, I'm originally a local. I grew up in Meraux. I'm here for an extended . . ." I paused, "well, I wouldn't call it a vacation, but you know what I mean. I don't know just how long I'll be here, but I'll pay you, in advance, for a month if we can come up with a price we can both agree on."

I paused for effect, and then I threw out my offer. "I'll give you two thousand dollars for the BMW R1200GS for thirty days."

"I can't do that, ma'am." He avoided my stare.

"Miranda." My smile began to feel more like a grimace, but I kept it up, hoping I could get more with honey than vinegar.

"Miranda, I don't want to lose my job. That's over a fifty percent discount." He looked up at the ceiling, which signaled that he was at least thinking about a counteroffer. "Three thousand, and you got a deal. Nonnegotiable."

"Twenty-two fifty." I countered.

"Twenty-eight hundred." I knew I had him where I wanted him.

I headed toward the door. "Bob, it's been great doing business with you."

He yelled before I could get out the door. "Twenty-five hundred."

I kept walking. "Twenty-two fifty."

I could hear him coming after me from behind the counter as I opened the door. "The owner is going to kill me, but okay. Twenty-two fifty paid up front."

I turned around and reached out my hand with a smile. "Deal!"

It took another forty-five minutes of filling out paperwork, him calling and arguing with his boss, me insisting on free insurance, but then I was finally united with my 'new' bike. The Beemer was a little bigger than I liked to ride, but at least it wasn't a Hog. It was agile, fast, and had saddlebags in case I needed to carry any extra baggage.

I headed down to Mom and Tom's first. It seemed so long since I'd ridden, it was tempting to take a ride across the Lake Pontchartrain Causeway, but I'd have to save that for another day. When I got to Mom and Tom's, I was glad they were home. I parked the bike in the driveway and took a deep breath as I walked to the front door. I never knew if I should knock or just walk it. I decided to do the best of both.

"Yoo-hoo!" I knocked and walked in like a doctor after you've been waiting in the room for a half-hour.

They were in the kitchen as usual. My mom jumped up, ran over and hugged me. "Are you okay, honey? I was so sure this wouldn't go to trial." Her eyes were puffy from crying.

I didn't want to cry again, so I pretended that it wasn't a big deal. "It's okay, Mom. Mark said it would probably go to trial, so I was mentally prepared. We'll keep plugging along and find out who really did this before the trial starts."

She looked worried and confused but didn't comment then changed the subject, "I didn't see you pull in. Did you get dropped off?"

I knew where this is going, but I decided to play along. She hated the fact that I preferred two wheels to four. "No, Mom, I rented a motorcycle."

"A motorcycle? Whatever for? Did Sabine refuse to give you a ride?" she said in disbelief.

"No, Mom. She's been great, but it's time to take responsibility for my own transportation while I'm here." I used my most soothing voice so that I wouldn't sound as defensive as I felt.

"You know I hate those things. Are you doing this just to hurt me?" she said in her best guilt-evoking tone.

Okay, Miranda. Just count to ten. The relaxation technique didn't help; I couldn't help myself. "Believe it or not, sometimes I do things that have nothing to do with you." The anguished look on her face that followed made me want to shove the words back in.

She recovered quicker than I expected, probably because she had expected me to be more upset about the trial. "Before you run out to God knows where, can you stay for dinner?"

I suddenly felt exhausted. "I'd love to have dinner with you. I may have to meet with Mark later, but I think I'm going to lie down for a few minutes." I ran upstairs, laid on the bed, and fell asleep almost immediately. As I drifted off, I wondered if I would ever feel normal again, or I'd be exhausted for life.

When I woke up again, it was nearly four. I had to get out of this habit of taking naps. I was still groggy but felt the need to touch base with Mark. I picked up my phone and scrolled through my recent calls until I found his number.

It rang for a bit, and then he picked up, sounding as exhausted as I was. "Mark Peterson."

"Hey, it's me." I croaked. "So, how are you holding up? You sound terrible."

"I'm okay. Thanks for asking. I guess I should be asking you the same thing. I'm sorry this is going to trial. I really thought we had a chance at an acquittal." He sounded sincere.

I groaned. "I'm on an emotional roller coaster right now. I cry at the drop of a hat. Sometimes it's hard to imagine getting convicted of something I didn't do, and I feel like everything is going to be okay, but then moments later, I'm sure that I don't have a prayer. It's hard, Mark."

Changing the subject, he said, "Hey, where are you anyway. Sabine said you ran off."

"I rented a motorcycle. I was feeling the need for two wheels. It's in my blood, and I was tired of mooching off everyone," I said. I hoped I wouldn't hurt his feelings.

He sounded a bit distracted, but not hurt. "No problem. I just wanted to make sure you were okay."

"Thanks, Mark." He was a nice guy. "I guess I'll just continue the investigation where I left off. Does that work for you?"

"That's fine, Miranda, if that's what you want to do."

I insisted. "I'm pretty motivated to find out what really happened. Besides, I need something to do to fill my time. Did Sabine tell you she was selling the company?"

He hesitated. "Uh, yes, she did." I heard a garbled voice in the background like he was covering the phone. "In fact, she's right here. Would you like to speak with her?"

I was confused but then remembered they'd been hanging out together before I left for the motorcycle place. I was shocked when she told me she kissed Mark before court. They had been dating in the past and were both adults, so I didn't know why it had bothered me. Well, that wasn't entirely true. A little green-eyed monster raised its ugly head.

I took a moment to recompose myself and stuffed the jealousy down as far as I could push it. "No, I don't need to speak to her. It's good to know you are both in good hands. I'll give you a call tomorrow." I hung up feeling like an awkward schoolgirl. Sabine had struck again.

When I went downstairs, Mom and Tom were nowhere to be found. If she'd said something about them having to go somewhere, it had gone in one ear and out the other. At least I didn't have any obligations until dinner. I took the opportunity to take the ride across the Lake Pontchartrain Causeway I had been craving earlier. I couldn't even remember how many years it had been since I'd been across it, but I had never done it on a bike. It is so much better than a car—the wind in my face, the smell of the bog, the sound of the birds chucking, and diving for food. I loved it. On the way home, I stopped at the Bayou Sauvage National Wildlife Refuge, a favorite beer-drinking hangout when I was in high school. Back then, we called it the "B.S. Refuge" for obvious reasons. The empty beer bottles strewn around the edges of the parking lot confirmed that things hadn't changed much.

When I returned to the house several hours later, dinner was already underway, and the house smelled amazing.

While my mom bustled around straightening up, Tom sat down next to me. I was a little taken aback because he always seemed to take a back seat to my mom. He looked me in the eye. "Miranda, can we talk?"

I was intrigued. "Sure, what can I do for you?"

He hesitated and smiled nervously. "I know that we haven't had much of a relationship, but I'd like to start over."

I asked. "Start over with what?"

He continued, "Well, I know I'll never be a dad to you, and that's not really what I want, but I'd like to get to know you, and I'd like you to get to know me."

Alarms bells triggered. Mom's husband wanting us to get to know each other better? I felt myself leaning slightly away from him. "Go ahead."

He continued, "Well, we both know that your mom can be, well, a bit . . ." He struggled for the word. ". . . Well, let's call a spade a spade—controlling."

I said, "No way!" then laughed nearly spitting the water I'd been drinking on the table.

He was going to make his point no matter how hard a time I gave him. "Anyhow, I'd like to have a relationship with you."

All right. That's creepy. I folded my arms.

"You may not realize it, but we are more alike than you know. I have a dry sense of humor, not unlike yours. I love your mom, and I know you do too. I never had any kids of my own, and I would like to get to know you on your own terms."

I thought for a minute as I eyed him with suspicion. I had never really thought about Tom on his own. It was always Mom and Tom. He was right. The timing hadn't worked in our favor, but I supposed, grudgingly, it was nice that he showed some interested in me as a person. "I'm willing to try if you are," I finally said.

He had a twinkle in his eye that I hadn't seen before. Maybe I'd been wrong. He stood up and held out his arms as if expecting a hug.

I got up slowly and allowed it, still feeling cautious, but hoping for the best. The brief hug relieved me. Nothing weird about it.

178

When Mom finished cooking and served up dinner, she gave both of us a curious look. "Okay, what's going on with the two of you?"

We said in unison, "Nothing."

She then dominated the conversation from that point forward through dinner, and at least for the moment, we felt like a family.

Just as I was scraping the last of my Jambalaya off my plate, the door opened, and my brother sauntered through the door. "Mikey!" I jumped up and hugged him. He hugged me back in a 'why are we hugging now when we've never hugged before' sort of way.

"Hey, Miranda," he said awkwardly and then nodded at the rest of the table. "Mom. Tom."

He headed for the stairs, but Mom jumped up. "Can I get you some dinner, honey?" Her eyebrows were pointing at the table as if she were trying to get a jet to land on it.

"Um . . . no, I'm good. I already ate." He took another couple of steps toward the stairs.

"Well, the least you could do is have ice cream with us." She sauntered over and whispered something to him as she grabbed him by the arm and steered him into the kitchen. "And you can help."

After some more hushed whispering, barely covered by the clang of plates, my mom and brother came back toting a tub of vanilla ice cream, an ice cream scoop sitting in a dish of warm water, and four empty bowls. My mom did the scooping, and Mikey passed the desert around. I took the opportunity to stare at him while he concentrated on something else. God, I couldn't believe his hair was thinning. I hadn't seen him in years, and they showed on every inch of his face. It felt strange to be sitting at the dinner table and having an ordinary conversation with him.

He was essentially a stranger. Growing up, we never had any common interests, and the four years that separated us felt like a chasm. When I left for North Carolina, he was fourteen. It was as if I were getting to know him all over again.

After a while, he let his spoon hit the bowl with a clank, slid back his chair, and cleared his throat. "I'm going to go out for some air."

I was confused at his announcement until I saw my mom motioning for me to join him. So that's what the whispering was about. He slid open the back door, and I followed, closing it behind me. "So, Miranda, you're looking . . . different."

I wasn't sure how he'd react to my new face, and my fears were well-founded. We had talked on the phone several times over the years after he joined the Army, and he had always seemed angry. I never knew why, but I figured his life after deployment had something to do with it. This was the time to find out. I looked him in the eye, hoping that would evoke some honest answers from him. "You know I was shot in the face, right?"

He stared off into the distance for a few minutes silently as he puffed on a cigarette he had pulled from his shirt sleeve. "Yeah, and I'm real sorry about that," he finally replied but not with the sincerity I needed from him.

More silence prevailed as I followed him over to a bench by the back fence, and I thought that might be the end of our conversation. But I was not going to let this moment pass without at least trying. I touched his arm to get his attention. "Okay, Michael, just what is it? You act like my accident and surgery are somehow offensive to you, like I got shot on purpose of something." I could feel tears welling up in my eyes, but I held them back. I refused to cry in front of him.

He opened his mouth, but nothing came out. I could see he was struggling. I didn't know what to do, so I just waited. Finally, he spoke in a soft, almost child-like voice. "Why did you have to leave us? You didn't even say 'Good-bye' when you left for North Carolina. We never talked about you after you left. It was like you were dead." A tear streamed down his cheek, and he wiped it away quickly as if hoping I hadn't seen it.

"Criminy, now I have my twenty-nine-year-old brother crying." I put my arm around him, and we sat silently for a few minutes. Finally, I found my voice. "I'm so sorry. I was confused and young, and I knew I had to make it on my own. And I figured if I came back to the house, I would never go. Despite everything that happened, I don't regret it."

He put his arm around me too. "I wasn't angry, Miranda. I was hurt. It's only taken me five years of therapy to understand that."

I laughed. "You're in therapy too? That's great! I don't feel like such a freak now."

He tapped the excess ash off the end of his cigarette. "Twice a week."

I hugged him and whispered. "Who wouldn't need it, growing up in this house. Being able to differentiate anger from hurt is pretty advanced. It sounds like you are making progress."

"Speaking of progress . . ." he hesitated. "I hate to open this can of worms, but my therapist told me I needed to have it out with you."

I rolled my eyes but smiled. "All right, go ahead."

He took a deep breath and then blurted out, "I was so jealous of you growing up. That's why I always treated you badly. I felt like Mom and Dad favored you."

I jumped up with my mouth wide open. "The Mom and Dad we grew up with?" That didn't resonate with me at all.

"Who else?" He looked at me like I was crazy.

I scoffed. "I don't know what house you grew up in, but they didn't pay much attention to me at all—especially once the marriage started falling apart."

He slid down, stretched his legs out and took a long look at the sky. "One thing it's taken me a lifetime to learn is that perception is reality. I guess we're not so different after all."

I returned to my seat next to him. "Do you remember that camping trip?" he said.

I thought for a minute. "North Texas?"

"Yeah. We laid on our backs staring at the stars, just before you left town."

I smiled. "I was eighteen. You were fourteen? A world apart, for sure." We laid in silence, and then I asked, "Do you think we can start over?"

"Start what over?" he asked, still staring at the sky.

"Start our relationship over again," I offered. "As adults, not as damaged children."

He jumped up and then gave me a hand. "It's worth a try."

I hugged him, and we walked back to the house. The kitchen was dark. "Looks like they went to bed. I guess we were out there longer than we thought." I grabbed his shoulder. "Let's not be strangers anymore. Promise?"

"Promise." He walked out the door with a smile.

Chapter 11

The next morning, I opened my eyes just as my phone vibrated with a text. It was Sabine. "Hey, Miranda, are you still in town?"

I rubbed my eyes. What is Sabine still doing in town? I was suspicious, but I kept it to myself. "Yes. Just waking up."

It vibrated again. "Can you pick me up?"

I hesitated a moment before responding. "Did Mark tell you I rented a motorcycle?"

"Yes, that's why I'm asking, Silly." She sounded excited. "Do you have an extra helmet?"

I opened my closet door. "Yes, it's still here."

There was a pause, but I guessed what was coming next. "Can you *please* pick me up?"

I rolled my eyes. "You don't have to beg. What happened to your car?"

"Nothing. It's back home, so I need a ride back. It's not what you think. Mark had an out of town meeting in Houston, so he let me use his house. Can you pick me up there?"

I smiled. That was the Sabine I knew and loved. I reached down to pick up my helmet and then tossed it onto my bed. Then I typed, "Sure. How's 10 am?"

"Perfect. See you then."

I headed downstairs to find Mom sitting at the kitchen counter alone. I had been waiting for this moment since I'd arrived in town.

I sat next to her and said, "Mom, I have a favor to ask of you."

She looked concerned but replied, "Anything."

I didn't know how to say it, so I just began. "I want you to give Sabine another chance."

Mom looked at me but didn't speak.

I continued. "I don't know whatever happened, and I don't really need to. I just want you to know that it's important to me that we all act like family."

Mom wiped a tear from her eye and took my hand. "That was all I ever wanted with all of you, and nothing turned out like I planned."

I held her hand tightly. "That seems to be what happens with lots of families, but life is short, and you can never get the time back once you lose it."

Mom gave me a pleading look. "I don't know if Sabine will have anything to do with me the way that I've treated her over the years, but if she'll have me, I'll welcome her back."

I hugged her and said. "That's all I can ask."

She confessed, "I've always been jealous of the relationship you two had, especially when you were a teen. It seemed like I lost you as soon as she arrived."

I hugged her. "You never lost me. I was just so angry about the divorce, and I blamed you and Dad for ruining my life. I might have been a little dramatic."

Mom held on for dear life. "Let's all start over."

I nodded as tears ran down my face. "Let's."

Working as a cop had been a lot less emotional than trying to deal with family. After a domestic disturbance call, I could go back to my apartment and not worry about whose feelings were hurt, only relieved that someone hadn't been seriously injured or killed.

When I pulled up in front of Mark's, Sabine was sitting on his front porch in jeans, a leather jacket, and black boots.

I laughed and yelled to her as I powered down the BMW, "Wow, you must have done some quick shopping."

"Yes, I did," she said proudly. "I wasn't sure I could pull it off, but it all worked out. Thank goodness Mark had one more vehicle left. I wasn't sure if his MG would even run, but it started right up."

Sabine and I had a ball on the way back to Venice. We stopped a couple of times along the river to remove our boots and dangle our feet in the muddy Mississippi. It was nice to relax and de-stress from all the court stuff. I loved the wildlife, the seabirds, the abundance of fish in the river, and the smell of the freshwater and the sea mingling together.

When we were done mucking around in the outdoors, we were starving, so we went on the hunt for food. We found delicious Cajun homestyle food at Boutte's Bayou, a restaurant just a little out of the way in Lafitte. Neither of us had been there before, but it looked like it had been there forever, and the food was everything I loved about New Orleans.

We were so stuffed that we just flopped onto her couch when we got back to her house, laying with our heads on the opposite armrests. Finally, Sabine said, "Hey, Miranda?"

"Uh, huh?" I responded but didn't open my eyes.

"Why do you think this is all happening?" she asked, making me feel like we were having a sleepover at Grandpapa's again. "Do you think this is a wake-up call? I hate that Emil had to die, but I'm glad it brought us all back together."

I wasn't sure what to say. "Maybe someday we'll know. I hope so."

We went off to bed a little while later, and I fell asleep quickly, only to be woken up moments later to the sound of Sabine quietly weeping. I wanted to go and comfort her, but I knew she'd waited for me to fall asleep before letting everything out. She was never one to let someone see her cry. So instead, I just lay still and listened. Hearing her crying in the privacy of her room strengthened my resolve to pull this family back together. The next morning, Sabine was rushing around the kitchen, cooking, and making coffee as usual. There was no evidence of her tears from the night before.

As she served up breakfast, my cell phone rang; I didn't recognize the number, but based on the area code, it was local. "Miranda Marquette speaking. . ."

"Hey there, little lady!" a man said.

It was either Bob, the motorcycle guy or Ronnie, and I couldn't imagine Bob calling me after I nearly cost him his job. "Ronnie. I'm so happy to hear from you. What's up?"

He sounded serious. "There are some things I remembered that might be important to your case. Can we get together, say this afternoon?"

"That would be great." I grinned, feeling a spark of hope. "I'll come up to your office. Is one okay?

"Yes, that would be great," he replied. "See you then."

Sabine had already sat down to a breakfast of smoked salmon, fresh bagels, onions, capers, and cream cheese. I joined her. "Good news, Sabine. That was Ronnie, Emil's old boss. He says he has some information that might be helpful."

She frowned. "Hmm, from what I understand, I'm not the old man's favorite person. If he says he suddenly realized that I killed Emil, I want you to walk out, okay?"

I doubted that was his agenda, but I agreed. "You've got a deal."

"Thanks, Miranda." She smiled, but it held a hint of sadness. Then, she put on a happy face and playfully scolded me. "Now, eat something so you can keep your strength up." The food was tremendous; she even had a way of making bagels and lox taste special. She started picking up the dishes when I finished. I tried to stop her. "Hey, let me do that! You cooked."

She smiled. "It's fine. I just cut up some stuff I bought at the store. That hardly counts as cooking. You get out there and find that killer." She shooed me away from my plate.

"That's my plan. I'm also going over to the CrawGator to see if anyone besides Becky saw anything." That was partially true; what I really wanted was someone to refute her story.

I was about to go when I remembered my conversation with my mom. "Sabine, can I talk to you for a minute?"

She sat next to me. "Sure, what's up?"

I hesitated because I wasn't sure how she would accept my information. "I talked to my mom yesterday about you."

"Oh?" She bit her lip, looking distant and hurt.

"Listen, I don't know what happened between you two, and I really don't want to get into the details. But I asked her to welcome you back into the family and that it was crucial to me."

Sabine sat for a while, looking straight ahead. Her lips twitched and she frowned. She appeared to be remembering something painful as she bit her lower lip and shook her head slightly, as if arguing with herself.

I put my arm around her. She finally spoke, "Miranda, you know I love you more than anyone on God's green earth. And I would do just about anything you should ask me. But I just don't know about this one. She's been so cruel to me, and I've distanced myself from her to protect myself from the hurt she caused." She became more animated and louder. "I used to lie awake at night trying to figure out what I had done to that woman to make her hate me so much. I just don't know, Miranda. I just don't know."

I hugged her and spoke quietly. "I understand. Maybe this isn't the right time, or maybe there will never be one. She confessed that she was jealous of our relationship and that had driven a wedge between you two over the years."

She started to say something but then just shook her head.

"Just think about it, okay?"

She whispered, "Okay." Her tone wasn't very convincing.

I decided to walk over to the CrawGator rather than riding so I wouldn't draw attention to myself. I could hear people talking and cleaning. I tried the door, and it was open. When I walked in, I saw a teenage girl and a heavily tattooed skinny guy in his mid-twenties both working on opening the restaurant.

The girl approached me. Hi. May I help you?"

She seemed pleasant enough, so I figured I'd take a chance. "Is Becky around?" I hoped she wasn't, but she didn't need to know that.

"I'm sorry, she doesn't come in until nine today." It was music to my ears. "I'm Teri. Is there something I can do for you?"

I smiled, hoping for the best. "Maybe. Do you have a few minutes?"

She smiled back and said in a whisper, "Sure do. Anything is better than cleaning. I'll let Matt do it."

We sat down at Sabine's table. "I have some questions about the day of Emil's murder."

She looked back to make sure that we were alone, "I thought you might. You're Sabine's cousin, right?"

"Right, I'm Miranda."

She looked around again. "I'm glad you're here. A couple of detectives have been around several times, asking questions. They've pretty much been talking to Becky."

Becky said that no one talked to her. I *knew* she was a liar. "Oh, really?"

"Yes. She's been acting really weird since that day. I don't know what's going on with her. But after they left the last time, she went outside and made a call. I wasn't sure who she was talking to, but I heard bits and pieces of the conversation." Teri looked around cautiously.

"What did you hear?" I asked, getting excited.

"I'm pretty sure she said something about cops asking questions again and letting whoever was on the phone know that they didn't need to worry, that she covered for them. It's been bothering me since that day, but I didn't really know what to do. I know that she's been saying Sabine went out to the boat that morning, and I know I didn't see her." She shrugged, "then again, I didn't see anyone else go out there either."

Her information was way more than I hoped for. I tried to keep my excitement under control. "Is there anything else you remember about that day?"

She put a finger on her chin while she pondered. "There is. Becky and I were cleaning and prepping the morning of the murder about an hour before we opened, she said she had to go, and she'd be right back. I remember I was really angry because she was gone for about twenty minutes, and I had to finish cleaning the floors by myself."

"Did you ask her what she was doing?" I asked; puzzled.

She nodded and looked at the ceiling as if she was thinking back. "She mumbled something about having to help a friend. She seemed really upset, so I didn't ask her anything else." Teri looked me in the eyes. "I think she's lying to the police and that she had something to do with Emil's death. She told me last week that she thought Sabine did it. Yesterday she told me it was you. Something doesn't add up."

I could see she was uncomfortable. "I don't think you have to worry about Sabine at this point." I didn't want to go into detail about my situation and the fact that I was going to trial. "But, would you testify in court if we needed you?"

"Definitely!" She blushed and put her hand over her mouth, suddenly embarrassed by her enthusiasm. "I mean, I would if you needed me. I don't want to get anyone in trouble, but . . ." Her voice trailed off.

I smiled, shook her hand, and handed her my card. "Thanks, Teri. Give me a call if you think of anything else, okay? Either my attorney or I will be in touch."

Teri was almost whispering now. "Thanks, Miranda. And be careful. I wouldn't put anything past Becky."

I was so lost in thought as I walked back to Sabine's that I nearly missed Mark's Porsche parked in the driveway. I was surprised he was back from Houston. When I walked in, Mark and Sabine immediate retreated to opposite sides of the kitchen, looking like teenagers caught making out by their parents.

I laughed. "Wow, is there something you guys want to tell me?"

"We were just discussing your case." Sabine ignored the question. "I have a bone to pick with you, my dear." She wagged her finger at me. "Mark was telling me that waitress Becky was lying about me and saying that she saw me over there the morning of the murder. Why didn't you tell me?"

I tried to play it off. "Um, that day I was exhausted from interviewing all your employees, and she grabbed me just as I was passing. I was still processing what she said when I came back here, and there never seemed to be a good time to bring it up. If it makes you feel any better, she's now changed her tune. Now, she's telling the world that I did it."

She was still annoyed but softened with that update. "Miranda, you need to communicate with me. I know you're on trial here, but if and when you're acquitted, I'm pretty sure they're coming after me. Thank goodness at least Mark is straight with me." He smiled weakly and turned pink, probably due to some combination of getting caught kissing Sabine and ratting me out.

I continued, hoping to take the focus off her conversation with Mark. "Becky wasn't over there this morning, but there was a girl Teri who wanted to talk. She said that Becky has been acting strange since Emil's death. Better than that, though, she and Becky were opening the restaurant on the day of the murder. She said that around six, Becky left for about twenty minutes because she had to, quote, 'help out a friend.' When she came back, she seemed upset, but didn't tell Teri anything else about what she was doing."

Mark seemed to have regained his composure. "Do you think she would testify?"

"She definitely would." I explained, "She's no fan of Becky's, that's for sure."

He smiled, "Nice work, Miranda."

I thought for a minute, "My gut feeling is that Becky didn't kill Emil, but that she knows who did. Teri said she keeps having long phone conversations with someone, mostly out of earshot. But if she's already lied to me and the police, maybe she's backing herself into a corner."

Mark sighed. "While it would help to have Teri to cast doubt on her story, we need more."

I nodded. "I'm hoping that Ronnie, Emil's ex-boss, can give us something useful when I go up to see him."

Mark asked, "Do you want me to go with you?"

J. T. Kunkel

"No," I said, a little too quickly. "You're too lawyerish."

"Thanks." Mark crossed his arms.

"I just meant that he and I sort of clicked, and so I think I can get more out of him than you could." I smile sheepishly.

Sabine got very quiet and serious. "Let's remember one thing here. This detective work may be all fun and games for the two of you, but this is your life or possibly mine we are talking about here." Her voice cracked. "We need to find the killer and do it fast. Circumstantial or not, the evidence points at either of us. Until we find the killer, we are both vulnerable."

I went to Sabine and hugged her; it was so rare to see her emotional, and it made me want to succeed even more.

It never ceased to amaze me; the fresh seafood Sabine had access to. She served up a brunch of crawfish omelets for Mark and me, even though she had made me breakfast less than an hour ago. After brunch, they headed back to the Big Easy together. After my short bout with jealousy, I wished them well in my head and moved on. I spent the next hour working on questions for Ronnie. Since I didn't know what information he was going to be giving me, it was hard to formulate anything meaningful. I just hoped he had something I could use.

It was a great day, unusual for the Gulf Coast. Seventy-five and low humidity. I longed for the day I could go back home, but I wasn't leaving any time soon. But my ride upriver made me glad that I'd rented the motorcycle. Although I loved my little convertible in Malibu, if I never used four wheels again, I'd be okay with that. I arrived a little early for my meeting with Ronnie, so I walked around on the docks, looking at the boats and taking in the familiar sights and sounds of the river. When I got to the end of the pier, I noticed a set of buildings upriver from Ronnie's with a sign that read 'E and S Fish Wholesaling.' Interesting; I wondered if Emil had considered working there after leaving Ronnie's. The more I knew about his life before Sabine, the better, so I made a note to check them out later.

I headed for Ronnie's office. It was if he hadn't moved since I was last here. "I guess condolences are in order. I figured they wouldn't waste their time prosecuting you." He kicked the floor. "Seems like my sixth sense is on the blink."

"It just makes me even more motivated to find out who killed him. There's nothing like the threat of a life sentence or worse to get you motivated." I forced a laugh.

He winced. "Are you sure you didn't do it?"

I slugged him lightly on the arm. "Very funny." I laughed, but my smile quickly faded. "So, you said you had some information for me?"

He motioned for me to sit down. "I'm not sure how important it is, but it's been eating at me that I didn't open up more about Emil when you were here. There's a lot about the man I didn't know because he didn't share much, but over thirty years, you learn things."

"Just tell me what you can. You never know what might help." I said, trying to reassure him.

He looked at me directly in the eyes and spoke again, this time sounding as if he were pleading the case of the dead man, "First of all, he was a good man, Miranda. He wouldn't ever do anything wrong unless he had a very good reason."

I nodded, wondering what that comment was about. "I trust you," I said and held eye contact.

He settled into his seat. "Well, not long after Emil started working for me, he was in a bad car accident. He was driving under the influence; they weren't quite as strict back then as they are about DUIs today or he would probably have gone to jail and lost his license for life. He had some minor injuries, but his sister didn't fare as well. As a result of the accident, she was paralyzed from the neck down. Up until two years ago, she was living with their mother."

No wonder he was miserable. I couldn't think of anything appropriate to say so muttered a conventional, "That's so sad. What happened two years ago?"

He stood and paced around the tiny office. "Their mother died. Emil took his sister in for a brief period, but he didn't have a clue about how to take care of her and was working sixty-hour weeks. So, he decided that she needed to be taken care of full time. He found a home that was okay but couldn't afford it. It took me a little time to figure it out, but he was stealing from me, selling shrimp directly to a wholesaler, and pocketing the money so he could afford to take care of her. Once I found out, I had to fire him. I was very careful not to let that information get out, so we let Sabine think she was robbing him from me. It was the least I could do."

"Makes sense. People get close after thirty years."

He continued with a pained look on his face. "Even though Sabine agreed to pay him more than I was paying him, I doubt it was enough to cover her care. Emil probably kept up his racket of selling shrimp out the back door after he went to work for her. I figure she found out about it, confronted him, and one thing led to another. Sorry, kid, but that's the way I think it went down."

I thought for a while. "I have to admit there was a time when I thought that was possible. But if she already knew or strongly suspected Emil, then why bring me into the picture to investigate?"

He shrugged. "Maybe to deflect the facts and to give her an alibi."

I hesitated so that I could speak my piece without getting him angry. "Maybe, but something doesn't add up. While Sabine is passionate about what she does, she is not impulsive. There would have been so many more ways for her to deal with that information if she found out that he was stealing from her. She could have had him arrested. She could have sued him in a civil case. Why kill him? That's the reaction of someone out of control. That's not Sabine."

"Well, little lady, I'm afraid you know her better than I do, so I'll have to defer to you on that one." He shrugged. "I just hope this information helps you out in some way. You are a sweet girl, and I know I haven't known you long, but I feel like you are my daughter."

My face grew warm. "Thank you for saying that. I'm sure that this information will be very helpful. I'm just not sure quite how yet." We both stood and hugged. "You are a nice man, Ronnie, despite what you try to make other people think." He snickered and winked. I waved and headed back to Sabine's on my bike.

When I got back to Sabine's, I left the motorcycle in the driveway and walked over to the CrawGator again. I needed to figure out how Becky was involved in this. Did she kill Emil, or was she covering for someone, or neither? When she spoke to me, it was on her terms; who knows how long she'd been practicing her testimony. I could see Becky serving customers through the windows overlooking the marina. I walked in and sat down. She appeared to be the only waitress working. She walked up to my table and handed me a menu.

She refused to look at me, "Can I get you something to drink while you're looking at the menu?"

"Hi, Becky." I smiled. "Remember me?"

"Miranda! How nice to see you again!" Her feigned enthusiasm wouldn't fool anyone.

I paused. She shifted nervously from one foot to the other. She obviously didn't want to hang out. "I'll have a sweet tea. Do you have a minute to talk?"

She went white, "No, sorry. I'm swamped, and I don't have anything more to tell you." She hesitated, "And they told me not to talk to you."

I smiled. "Who would tell you that?"

Busted, she stammered, "T-the police."

"Huh, I thought the police hadn't spoken to you. Well, I guess my attorney can just ask you any questions he has when you are on the stand and under oath."

"No." Her eyes grew large as she glanced around the room as if seeking a hiding place. After a couple of seconds, she offered a grimace of a smile and said, "I mean . . . after that table by the window leaves, you'll be my only table. I'll come back in a couple of minutes."

I smiled and patted her arm. "Perfect."

I had some time, so I looked out the windows. It was beautiful here, with the view of the river, the boats, and the seagulls searching the docks for a stray french fry or potato chip. Staring out the window brought to mind something Buck said when Mark and I met him in the Déjà vu. He had seen Emil coming back from upriver several times after they returned from the Gulf. It would have been easy to see him with this view. It made me wonder if Buck was a regular here; maybe Becky knew when he'd be around again. I'd been meaning to talk to him since he hadn't shown up when I interviewed Sabine's ex-employees. I was surprised because he seemed desperate to get his job back.

After about five minutes, Becky returned with my sweet tea and sat down at my table. "I'm pretty sure I told you everything

I saw that day." She appeared to be a combination of nervous and angry. She wouldn't keep eye contact and was twirling and chewing on her hair. "I wish I never said anything, I've had so many people asking questions, I wish I'd just kept my mouth shut."

I tried to appear friendly and unthreatening. "Hey, the morning Emil was killed, were you here the whole time, or did you go somewhere?"

She shifted in her seat, granted these chairs weren't particularly comfortable. "I don't remember. It's been quite a while since—"

"Well, you clearly remembered seeing Sabine go out the dock, right?" I presented my case.

She avoided my stare. "Yes. But sometimes I take a cigarette break or sit in my car and listen to music, so I don't know if I was here the whole time."

I didn't want to bring up what Teri had told me, at least not yet. I might need that later. I changed the subject. "Hey, some of the crew from Sabine's boats come in here occasionally, right?"

A bead of sweat formed on her forehead. "I guess. I don't really know them."

"There aren't any regulars?" I asked, curious. "With you being right here on the dock, that seems strange."

"There are familiar faces sometimes, but I don't know any of them." She looked away, and beads of sweat dotted her forehead.

My line of questioning was clearly affecting her. "Do you remember a guy named Buck? He used to work here until recently."

She tried to act casual but seemed increasingly aggravated, talking faster as she clicked her gum, "Not that I remember, but they come and go."

"He used to come in here quite a bit after work," I pressed

"Um, maybe. Not sure." Her eyes kept flicking around the room like a cornered animal looking for a way out. "Do you need anything else? I gotta get back to work."

I offered a sweet, non-threatening smile. "No, but thanks." I was sure she wondered what I was thanking her for. I decided I wasn't hungry and left her three bucks for the tea.

As I walked back to Sabine's, I grabbed my Blackberry and called Mark. He sounded chipper. Spending time with Sabine seemed to agree with him. "Hey, Miranda!"

"That's better. You're learning caller ID." I laughed.

"What can I do for you?" He sounded like he was smiling.

"Remember when we ran into Buck at the Déjà vu? Did you get his phone number?"

He thought for a minute. "No, I wasn't all that interested in seeing Buck again any time soon. Maybe Sabine has it in her personnel files."

He handed her the phone. "Yes, Miranda?" She had a lilt in her voice too.

"Hey, can I get access to your ex-employee personnel files? I need some contact information."

"I don't keep those at the house, only the present employees. The ex-employees are in the files in the boat navigation room. The key is in the navigation room in the middle desk drawer, but the boat is locked right now. That key is in the coffee cup on my kitchen windowsill."

"Thanks, give Mark a kiss for me. Love you."

"Whatever, Miranda." She giggled and then said, "Love you too. Bye."

The key was right where she said it was. I took the bike over to the marina since I had already gotten my exercise for the day. Because I had been busy with other stuff, I hadn't taken the time to review the ex-employee files before this, and I knew should have. I figured I should take a cursory glance at them while I was here to see if I could find anything that would help in my defense.

Having found Emil's body, I wasn't wholly comfortable spending long bouts of time in the navigation room. I sucked it up and pushed open the door, scanning the area for a filing cabinet. The two-drawer lateral sat tucked into the corner next to a large black safe. The files appeared to be very well organized with all the personnel records together in the bottom drawer. The terminated employees were in a separate compartment, so I found Buck's quickly and scribbled down his phone number. Curious, I looked through the file. Oddly, there was nothing—no written warnings or investigations of theft.

I decided to search the rest of the room. It wouldn't do any harm, as the CSI crews had already been through and checked everything. Most of what I found was ordinary—navigation charts, schedules, and sales reports. One of the desk drawers had a lock on it, but thankfully it was unlocked, probably by the investigators. In the drawer was an unmarked file. I picked it up, wondering why it had been removed from the cabinet.

When I opened it, I was confused to see a bunch of test results. MRIs, CT scans, lab tests, EMGs, spinal tap results, and various neurological exam results, all with Emil's name on them. The dates on the scans went as far back as two years ago. I couldn't make heads or tails of the scans, but the file also had an information packet on ALS. I'd heard of that. Amyotrophic lateral sclerosis, also known as Lou Gehrig's disease. Oh, no.

Less than fifty percent of those diagnosed with ALS lived for more than three years, I read. Someone killed a man who was already dying. The ALS diagnosis explained his panicked desire to set his sister up in a place she'd be cared for—now that he was dead, there was no one left.

I need to go and talk to Ronnie again. He was my only link to find Emil's sister. I didn't even know her name. I hadn't thought she was critical to the case, but now I wasn't so sure. I didn't get the feeling that Ronnie got out much during the day, so I was pretty confident he'd be right where I left him. I kept my fingers crossed as I rode back to his office. As I pulled into the marina parking lot, I saw that I was right.

"Miranda, to what do I owe this pleasure?" He seemed surprised to see me, but he didn't look unhappy about it.

I smiled, hoping to get his cooperation. "Do you have Emil's sister's name and where I can find her?"

He looked concerned. "Now Miranda, I'm not sure I'm comfortable dragging her into this mess. She's been through enough, don't you think?"

"I don't want to upset her, but when I was going through Sabine's personnel files, I found out that Emil had ALS."

"What's that?"

I explained.

"You're kidding!" He looked shocked. "Why didn't he tell me?"

"I don't know. I don't think that Sabine knew either. It was stuffed in the middle drawer of his desk in a plain file, a drawer he probably kept locked at all times. I think his sister may have the missing link to this information. I really need to talk to her." I offered a compromise. "You can come with me if you'd be more comfortable with that."

He smiled and looked surprised that I was more perceptive than he thought. "I have to say I feel kind of protective of Amy now that Emil is dead. She has no one."

I pleaded. "Will you come see her with me?"

He patted my hand. "Yes, Miranda, but let me take the lead."

I nodded, "Okay, when can we go?"

He pushed himself up from his chair. "How about right now?"

"Perfect." Even as I answered, my mind was busy trying to drum up questions to ask Amy, but for all I knew, the crash had also left her mentally incompetent; I didn't know what to expect.

Since he wasn't thrilled at the thought of riding on the back of my motorcycle, he drove us in his rickety Ford pickup. The Riverbend Nursing and Rehabilitation Center was an hour away, so he probably made the right choice.

From the highway, it looked like a thousand other nursing homes with a dull brick exterior. I expected to go through the main entrance, but Ronnie walked past it, heading for a second set of doors with a sign that read The Sarah Reiss Memorial Wing. When we reached it, he pressed the intercom button; it was clear that he had been here before.

I gave him a sidelong glance. "What?" He tried to sound innocent, but then he relented. "Okay, since Emil died, I've been doing what I can to fill in."

I scowled at him to make my point. "I'm really trying to give you the benefit of the doubt here, but there was a whole lot of stuff that you left out last time we spoke."

"We were just beginning to reach an understanding then. I didn't say that I trusted you completely, but the fact that I brought you here should help with that."

I nudged him on the arm. "Okay, Ronnie, just don't play me or patronize me."

He smiled. "Okay, Little Lady." He winked.

"Don't 'Little Lady' me either." This time I gave him a less playful punch.

"Ouch. Deal." He nodded with a crocodile smile.

We were finally buzzed in after he explained to the voice on the intercom who we were and who we were there to see. The door opened to an elegant lobby with marble floors, a ceiling that went least three stories up, and an ornate circular stairway leading to the other floors.

Seated behind a granite desk was a woman who appeared to be in her early forties. She wore a designer dress. "Mr. Hamill, how nice to see you."

"Hello, Greta. You are looking fine as usual."

She came around the desk, designer heels tapping on the marble floor, and hugged him. "I'll bet you say that to all the greeters!"

He barked with laughter. "Since you are the only female greeter, I guarantee that you are the only one that I do this with."

She chuckled and then turned her attention to me, "And who is your guest today?"

"This is Miranda Marquette. Amy's brother worked for her cousin, so we are practically all related." He shrugged playfully.

"I've seen you on the news." She stopped dead in her tracks. "You're the Shrimp Killer."

Before I could react or defend myself, Ronnie beat me to it, "Don't believe everything you see on the news. Miranda is one of the finest people I have had the pleasure of meeting."

She looked unsure. "Okay. I'll take your word if you vouch for her."

His face got serious. "I do."

She seemed satisfied. "It must be terrible to be accused of something you didn't do."

I forced a smile. "It's been rough, but I truly believe in the justice system. We just need to let this work itself through."

With that, she led us down the hall to the first room on the right. I wondered who was paying for everything. This was not an average nursing home. The room was huge, at least twenty by twenty. Across from us was an antique four-poster canopy bed surrounded by twin dressers with matching mirrors, bedside tables, a dressing table, and a matching trunk at the end of the bed. The furniture had to be at least two hundred years old and was in immaculate condition.

Lying in bed with her back propped up with pillows was a beautiful woman in her early fifties. Her long auburn hair just barely sprinkled with gray, her porcelain skin had no wrinkles, and a wide grin formed on her face as we approached her.

"Ronnie, now who have you brought to meet me today? I hate to admit it, but my life has gotten much more interesting since Emil passed, God rest his soul."

Ronnie took my hand and led me to her bedside as Greta departed silently. "Amy, this is Miranda Marquette. You remember I told you about her and how impressed I was with her."

She spoke again, "Miranda, dear, come closer so we can talk. I trust Ronnie like, well, like a brother. He told me from day one, even before he met you, that you had nothing to do with Emil's death. I'm afraid, though, initially he felt that way because he was convinced that your cousin was responsible. However, neither he nor I feel that way any longer. So, if there is anything I can do to assist, let me know."

"Thank you." I was blown away by her hospitality. There I was, prepared to feel pity for her and she acted like a gracious hostess. "I'm so sorry for your loss."

She continued. "I'm afraid that Emil was a tortured soul. Granted, many years ago, when we had the unfortunate accident, I didn't believe I would ever forgive him. But, these many years later, I have come to appreciate what life is about, and it has very little to do with what we can do physically. The mind is an amazing thing, and I'm able to go anywhere in the world without ever leaving this room."

I shifted from foot to foot, not sure how to reply; I felt a little like an intruder to a simpler world, but I forced myself to ask for the information that I needed. "Can you tell me more about Emil? I imagine you knew him better than anyone."

When she answered me, tears glistened in her eyes. "First off, young woman, if we are going to visit, you must take a seat."

Without being asked, Ronnie immediately pulled up a comfortable arm chair.

"That's better," she said. "I have been very fortunate to have lived fully and loved deeply. Emil was never really able to do either as much as I tried to help him. He was so consumed with the guilt that he let it eat him alive." Then she sighed. "I'm sure you're wondering what I'm doing in a place like this."

I nodded. "It does seem a bit pricey."

She gave a small, sad smile. "It's almost unbelievable to me too. Up until his death, I was in the nursing facility that you went by on the way in. It wasn't the best care, but it was the best he could do. What I didn't know was that he had a five-million-dollar life insurance policy and a will that specified that I should be transferred to this facility immediately upon his death with the life insurance money put into a trust fund for my use." She looked up at the ceiling, but I knew she saw far beyond the bricks and mortar. "I hope that his final actions allowed him to enter the gates of heaven with a clear conscience and an unburdened soul."

The more I learned, the more confused I felt. "Did you know that Emil was ill?"

She sighed. "Yes, I did. He didn't want me to worry in case he suddenly stopped visiting. He seemed relieved to be quite honest. I think he saw the disease as a way to end his suffering without having to take his own life. I know he wanted to for many years, but he didn't dare; the life insurance policy would not have paid."

I felt like I had fallen into the rabbit hole. "It's, um, amazing, how little my cousin and I knew about Emil. I am very pleased to have met you. I know this would be a lot to ask, but, if needed, would you testify on my behalf in court?"

"There is nothing I would rather do. You did not kill Emil and should not go to jail for his death."

I smiled and caught Ronnie's eye. "We should probably go."

He nodded. "Can you give us a minute? I'll meet you out in the lobby."

I got up and leaned over to give Amy a brief hug, "I am so glad to have met you. I hope one day you can meet Sabine as well."

She smiled, "I'm sure I will."

I headed for the door, "Okay, Ronnie, I'll be in the lobby."

Greta was back behind the reception desk as I walked out. "Done so soon?"

"Yes, I need to be getting back," I said, with my hands in my pockets. "It's quite a facility you've got here."

She smiled, "Thank you. We have been very blessed."

Needing to process this visit, I walked over to a couch across the room and sat until Ronnie came out. He gave me a quizzical look. "Are you okay? You look, um, bewildered."

"You could say that." I let out a long exhale. "Are there any other surprises you plan on springing on me today?"

He smiled and led me out. "How about some ice cream?"

Delighted with the complete change of subject, I leaped to my feet. "I'd love some."

After grabbing a soft ice cream at an old roadside stand right around the corner from the facility, we rode back in silence, aside from a small quip here and there. I honestly didn't know what to make of what I'd learned. I wondered if the prosecution had chanced upon any of this. If so, no doubt, they would try to hide it until my court date. I'd bet that they hadn't because they had their suspect. Why waste any more of the taxpayers' money finding out the truth?

When we parted ways, I said. "One thing I can say about you, Ronnie, is you are full of surprises." He gave me a quick hug and headed back to the dock.

Chapter 12

After Ronnie left, I gave Buck a call from the parking lot. "Buck speaking," he answered, sounding as gruff as ever.

"This is Miranda Marquette, Sabine's cousin," I said in my best TV-Weather-Girl voice.

"Yeah," he said, with an air of impatience.

I plunged in and hoped for the best. "I was hoping we could get together and talk."

"Are you gettin' me my job back?" He didn't sound hopeful.

"We can talk about that." I sounded as upbeat as I could.

He growled, "But that ain't what you're calling about, is it?"

I plunged forward, ignoring his question. "I'm talking to all of Sabine's present and ex-employees about Emil's death." He was the only one left, but he didn't need to know that. "We weren't able to connect during my first round, so I thought we could do it now."

"Yeah, sorry I blew y'off, but I had an interview." I had expected as much, but it sounded like more of an excuse than a genuine answer. I was surprised when he offered, "How's about I come down tomorrow morning? We can meet at the boss lady's place so as we ain't disturbed."

I shuddered. There was something about his tone that gave me the creeps. "How about the dock at eight?"

"How's about nine?" he asked. At least he didn't sound angry at the location change.

"Perfect. See you then." I tucked my phone away and hopped on my motorcycle.

I was so ecstatic to see Sabine's car when I pulled into the driveway. I felt like it had been a week since I'd seen her.

I burst through the door with an exuberant, "Honey, I'm home!"

"Welcome home." Sabine ran out of the kitchen to greet me. "I could get used to this."

"I know what you mean. It's so nice to come home to someone." Heather flashed into my mind, and I wondered what she was doing, though a friendly paid assistant living in your house was far different from family. I'd have to call her later. After flopping down on Sabine's comfy couch, I said, "Well, today was interesting."

"Why is that?" Sabine settled in beside me.

"I met Emil's sister." I leaned on her. "She is in a home, a really nice one, which is being funded by Emil's life insurance. Do you know what I also found out? Emil had ALS. He probably had less than a year to live."

Sabine shook her head. "That seems way too convenient." She was thinking the same thing that I was. "Was there an autopsy performed on Emil?"

I had no idea. "Probably not, since it was pretty obvious that he was shot in the head."

Sabine blurted out, "What if it was self-inflicted?"

My shoulders slumped. "No . . . the shot wasn't at that close a range, and the weapon was found in my purse, remember?"

"Too bad. That could've been a lifesaver . . ." Sabine exhaled with disappointment.

"It's a really complicated situation. If Emil had committed suicide, his insurance policy wouldn't have paid out, and Amy would be stuck in that other nursing home." I shook my head. "She was so nice, almost otherworldly. I couldn't do that to her."

"It would be better than a first-degree murder conviction for you or me." Sabine crossed her arms. Then she sighed, "But you're right . . . that'd be terrible. I remember when Grandpapa needed to go into a home. Those places are awful."

I shuddered at the image of my once-proud grandfather laying silently in a nursing home bed. I changed the subject. "Oh, I forgot to tell you. I finally got hold of Buck. He wanted to meet here, but I told him I'd rather meet at the dock."

She looked relieved, "Finally. Why do you think he wanted to meet here?"

I thought for a second. "He was probably just hoping to catch you here and ask for his job back. Based on what I've learned, Emil was likely the one ripping you off, granted it was probably to pay for his sister's care after their parents died. It just seems less and less likely that Buck did anything wrong before he got fired. There was nothing in his personnel file but good reviews."

Sabine rubbed her eyes, "When did you find out all that?"

I smiled, "I put it together today with some help from Ronnie."

She looked tired. "This is getting exhausting. I need a break. Let's eat dinner and retire early."

Dinner was perfect: Cajun catfish, fresh Brussels sprouts, and a spinach salad. She even made crème brûlée from scratch. I wondered if she cooked like this all the time or just when she had company. Sabine was such a mystery to me. After dinner, we both went right to bed. I was exhausted but didn't sleep well with a restless night of disturbing dreams that I couldn't remember in the morning. But when I awoke, I felt like there was a light at the end of the tunnel. I just hoped it's wasn't an oncoming train.

Knowing that I was meeting Buck first thing this morning, I dressed in jeans and a t-shirt. I had gotten the impression back at the Déjà vu that Buck might be easily distracted, and I didn't want to contribute to that in any way.

As usual, Sabine was already up by the time I finally showered. Given Buck's recent separation from employment, she decided that she didn't want to be home while he and I had a discussion across the street on the docks. We had a pleasant breakfast together of bagels, lox, and cream cheese again. Where she got freshly baked bagels and imported smoked salmon out here in the middle of nowhere, I didn't have a clue, and I was pretty sure she would never tell.

Once we finished breakfast, she jumped in her car for destinations unknown. Or unknown to me anyway. I waved out the door to Sabine as she backed out of the driveway. I glanced across the street and could see a woman smoking outside the CrawGator and talking on her cell phone. I guessed it was Becky. Buck should be up at the dock in half an hour, and the closer the time came, the more anxious I got. I was happy Sabine had left since she hadn't witnessed one of my anxiety attacks yet. I sat on the couch and closed my eyes, breathing deeply. In five minutes, my head was clear and I was as ready to face Buck as I was going to be.

I hadn't been this nervous about any of my other meetings, and I had learned over the years to trust my gut, so I decided to give Ronnie a call. It was important that someone else I could trust knew what was going on if things went south with Buck. I didn't want something else pinned on my family, or worse yet, to end up dead on the dock. Sabine was my other option, but she had blown town in a hurry.

My head started throbbing as soon as the call went right to voicemail. I could hear the tension in my voice and feel the tightness in my throat. "Hey, Ronnie, it's Miranda. Thanks again for the eye-opening visit yesterday. I'm just about to interview an ex-employee of Sabine's, and I'm getting spooked. Please call me if you get this. He's supposed to meet me at the docks by nine, so if you get this after nine and before ten, could you give me a call? If I don't answer, I'm in trouble, so call 911 and send them to the marina in Venice. Thanks so much."

I was probably making something of nothing, but at least I felt a little better. It was too early to call Heather, but I figured I would send her a text message to ask how the business was going. I was so unplugged right now, I felt like the worst boss in the world. Granted, I knew I could trust Heather, but it seemed wrong to just turn the business over to her for weeks at a time with no support. I typed on my Blackberry keyboard: "Hey Heather, how's everything? I'm sure you're doing a great job, but I'm feeling guilty about not supporting you as well as I could be, so let me know what's up when you get a chance."

When I looked up from my phone, I saw Buck pulling into the driveway. Wait, what was he doing here? Had he forgotten that we were supposed to meet at the dock? Within seconds, he pounded on the door, and my heart started to pound along with it. When I opened the door, he seemed taller and more menacing than I remembered at the Déjà vu. His eyes were bloodshot. While that could mean several things, I assumed he'd either been drinking, crying, or both. As I approached Sabine's screen door, I could smell booze. A bad sign.

I smiled because it seemed safer than frowning. "Hey, Buck! What are you doing here? We said we were going to meet at the dock." I was trying to cover the nervousness in my voice by being loud and enthusiastic. It wasn't fooling either one of us.

He pushed through the door as if I was an afterthought. "Where's Sabine?"

I had hoped to exchange more pleasantries before admitting to Buck that I was here alone. Lying was probably not a good idea, either. "She had a previous engagement."

He hesitated, choosing his words carefully. "I want my job back. Especially now that Emil's dead. He never had no proof that I did nothin' and you know why?" He paused, waiting for a response.

All I wanted was to get him out of the house without setting him off; he already appeared highly agitated and unstable. "No. Why?" I responded in a smaller voice than I would have chosen.

"It's because I didn't do nothing! Now I'm outta work. No one ain't hiring. I can't even get unemployment. We're gonna lose the house soon if something don't happen now." His voice was getting louder.

I needed to calm him down. I struggled to keep my voice steady. "I did talk to Sabine after we met in the Déjà vu. She was going to address it with Emil, but unfortunately, things got a little crazy, and then Emil was killed. The fleet hasn't even been going out regularly, so nobody is working right now." And she was selling the company, I thought to myself, but that would have to go unsaid.

He wasn't satisfied with that. "Maybe I should jus' stay here 'til she comes back. Then we can have a friendly chat as you women would say." His wide grin belied his intent.

I took a sidestep toward the door, planning on bolting out through it, just as he pulled a .45 pistol out of his pocket and pointed it at my face. The throbbing headache from earlier turned into a tightening vice at my temples. My chest constricted as I struggled to breathe. Buck turned into a blurry image as I sank to my knees, clutching at my throat, gasping for air. The world closed in around me. If he was talking, I couldn't hear him over the ringing in my ears. Sweat ran down my forehead and down my back. I was suddenly freezing. Whatever Buck was up to, gun or no gun, nothing mattered any longer. As I lost consciousness, I was sure I'd taken my last breath.

When I opened my eyes, my heartbeat thumped along at a normal pace and I was breathing freely. I found myself sitting on the floor a couple feet from the table facing the door. My hands were tied behind my back. I assumed Buck had accomplished that sometime during my near-death experience. He sat in a chair staring at me, probably wondering what was wrong with me.

The good news was that I was still alive. The bad news was that he had a gun. On the other hand, if he had planned to shoot me, he would have already done it. He put the Smith and Wesson down on the table and ran his hands through his greasy hair. He didn't look like he knew what to do next any more than I did. Not wanting to get him riled up, I remained silent. I wasn't sure if I could put together an understandable sentence at this point even if I wanted to.

Finally, he looked at me with disgust on his face, apparently ready to move on from my panic attack. "I never liked you, not back in high school when you were Miss Goth or last month at the bar. You always look at me like I'm not good enough. People like you never have to pay for nothin'. When they tagged you for Emil's hit, I figured you'd squirm out of it somehow."

Tears welled up in his eyes, and I almost felt sorry for him. Then he started spilling his guts. "I never should have confided in Becky. When I found out that Emil was selling shrimp out the back door, I started asking her questions about his comings and goings, and she figured it out."

He paced around the kitchen table as he talked. "It was her idea to blackmail him and split the money. Well, with another kid coming along and me unemployed, we sure could use it." On his third trip around the table he lifted me off the floor and set me in the chair I had been sitting in earlier. I had no idea why, but it was way more comfortable than the floor and my legs had been falling asleep.

The longer Buck spoke and paced, the more aggressive he became. "They should have arrested Sabine for the murder. We could have been home free. Becky spoon-fed you the evidence. She was an eyewitness. What else did you need? Now Becky thinks that Teri girl is on to her. That's all we need is her going to the cops." The veins in his neck were popping out.

He continued. "I arranged to meet with Emil at six a.m. I told him I had found some keys to the boats that I hadn't turned in yet. I was surprised when he agreed to meet me. Becky told me to meet her at five forty-five in the parking lot, so we could practice what I was going to say."

He sat back in the kitchen chair and tilted it. "I didn't plan on bringing heat with me to talk to Emil. But then when I came to meet Becky, I saw that Jeep sitting over here in Sabine's driveway, and it hit me. That Mark guy you was with that day up in the Easy, he was going on and on about his right to bear arms and how he kept a pistol in all his cars just in case. I had seen him around home in the Jeep with that lawyer license plate. Bein' a lawyer, I figured he'd probably keep the car locked, I'd jimmied plenty of car locks in my day, and I knew I had an old coat hanger in the truck. Imagine my surprise when the whole damn thing was open. Nice and easy."

Okay. This was not good. The first thing I learned in training was whenever a captor started spilling his guts; it meant that he didn't expect you to live to tell about the ordeal. I couldn't just sit quietly anymore, nor could I afford a repeat of my panic attack. I drew a deep breath. "Hey, Buck?"

"Shut up!" He banged the butt of the gun on the table. "I didn't tell you to talk, did I?"

I tried to stall. "No, but maybe we could get Becky to come over, and I can call Sabine, so we can all talk this out."

He shook his head and stared at me in disbelief. "You think I just fell off a peach truck? You are as good as dead, girly. You know too much. Way too much. Just listen. You can listen, right?"

I nodded solemnly, but my mind was racing.

He closed his eyes and continued. "I didn't think I'd need the gun 'cept for self-defense. Emil could be a hothead. So, I get up to the navigation deck, and he's up there just sitting staring off into nowhere. He looked real sad. He gave me a funny look when I walked in like he didn't recognize me or wasn't expecting me or something."

He was amping up and pacing as he talked. "So, I cut to the chase. I tell him I knew he was stealing from Sabine. I even told him I didn't really like Sabine either, so I didn't blame him, but that I wanted a cut. He didn't say anything, so I talked about us being partners. First, he looks at me like he was confused or that he didn't know what I was sayin'. Then he starts yellin' and screamin' at me like who did I think I was, and he wouldn't be my partner if I was the last person on earth."

Buck started to get really worked up, but at least it was about Emil, and not me, so I figured it would buy me some time to figure out what to do.

He continued. "Then he starts threatening me. Like he's gonna kill me. I was like, 'Okay, man, let's calm down.' He stops for a minute; then he starts screaming at me again. I feel like he is really gonna hurt me. He gets up and comes toward me, and I shot 'em. Yup. I shot 'em. Right in the head." He sat down and started to sob. "What am I gonna do? I'm gonna go to the slammer for life! I'm am so stupid."

This seemed like a good a chance as any to save my butt. "Buck, you didn't murder him. It was self-defense. Actually, it's better than that . . . it was assisted suicide."

He stared at me like he had no idea what I was talking about, and he probably didn't. After all, I was using words higher than the second-grade level. "Buck. Look at me."

He stopped sobbing and just sniffled, so I continued. "Emil was sick."

"Yeah, he was." He almost laughed then realized who he was talking to.

I tried again. "No, I mean, he was dying. He had a sister who needed money and he had a huge life insurance policy. They won't pay if you kill yourself. You did him a big favor. I think he wanted you to kill him. You said yourself that he was baiting you. He was doing whatever it would take to push you over the edge. He knew you had a gun. He wasn't afraid of being killed. He did everything he could do to make you pull the trigger. And when you still didn't shoot, he came after you. Finally, you had no choice. You had to protect yourself."

He looked at me, looked at the gun in front of him, and started to laugh. "You almost had me for a minute. You're good, sister. I'll give ya that!" He picked up the gun and pointed it at me.

Just then, a key turned in the lock. I tried to yell to Sabine not to come in, but he was too fast. He darted across the room, yanked the door open, and pointed the gun at Sabine's head before I could make a sound. I screamed, and he took his eye off Sabine for just a moment. I thought that Sabine was going to turn and run for help, but instead, she rushed at Buck, kicked him in the shin, hit him in the nose with the heel of her hand, disarmed

216

him, and came down on his back with her knee all in one catlike motion. In the end, she had the barrel pointed at his head.

I would honestly have clapped if my hands had been free, but I was more than aware that we were still in a precarious position. Buck was face down on the floor moaning, but that didn't mean he couldn't regain control. Unfortunately, Sabine couldn't risk moving off Buck's back to untie me.

Amid this stand-off, my phone vibrated on the table. I couldn't reach for it, and Sabine was too far away to get to it. I could see that it was Ronnie. I bent my head forward in an attempt to answer it with my face. Miraculously the call connected, but I couldn't possibly pull off the same trick with the speaker button. However, knowing there was some hope of being heard, I yelled as loud as I could, *"Ronnie! Help! We are being held hostage at Sabine's. Call 911!"*

The phone screen went dark, and I was unsure if he had hung up because he didn't hear me or because he did.

The three of us sat quietly for a few minutes. I had no further ideas, and, evidently, neither did Sabine. Every once in a while, Buck would try to move, and Sabine would reinforce her superiority by jamming her knee in his back.

Ten minutes later, we heard a siren in the distance.

I thought I was going to cry when the sheriff and deputy who had arrested me just a few weeks earlier, arrived at the door with guns drawn.

After taking a statement from Sabine and me, they left as quickly as they had come with Buck in the rear seat. It felt good that someone other than me was in the back seat of the police cruiser.

Chapter 13

Mark did everything he could to get my case dismissed after Buck was arrested, but because Buck was charged with illegal trespass and holding a hostage, there was no impact on my murder case. The morning of the trial, Sabine and I rode up together. I was reasonably sure showing up in court dressed in leather was not good form, so I let her drive me. I left Sabine and Mark to whisper in the hallway and entered on my own. They hadn't seen much of one another while Mark was busy preparing for the trial, so they had some catching up to do. He joined me at the table within a few minutes, and before long, the judge entered.

She started the proceedings by addressing the court. "I'd like to welcome all of you back to the State of Louisiana vs. Miranda Marquette. This is the jury trial stage of the case."

She continued. "I met with the prosecution and defense counsel earlier, and it appeared there was some controversy. Some interesting information has arisen during the past few weeks regarding other potential suspects in this case. While I was intrigued, no one else has been charged with this crime, so we will continue with the trial as scheduled. Mr. Prosecutor, do you have witnesses to bring forth for this proceeding?"

The DA stood up. "Yes, your honor, I would like to call Rebecca Fisher."

Who? I thought, but then the waitress I knew only as Becky, made her way from the gallery and up to the witness stand. With everything Buck provided us, Mark should be able to take her apart. I watched her closely as she was sworn in. I wondered if she even knew what the truth was any more.

The DA swaggered up to her. "Please state your full name."

"Rebecca Ann Fisher." She leaned forward and spoke into the mic.

"Are you familiar with the defendant in this case?" The DA asked, barely containing a smirk.

"Yes, Miranda Marquette." She pronounced it 'Market', not Mar-KET. That made me dislike her even more.

"Is she in this courtroom?" he asked.

"Yes, sir." She gave a short nod.

I knew what he'd say next. "Can you point her out for us?"

"Right there." Becky smiled at the prosecutor and pointed a bony nicotine-stained finger in my direction.

"Let the record show the witness indicated the defendant." He sounded so gleeful that I imagined him rubbing his hands together like a leprechaun who'd just tricked a poor sap out of his gold.

Even the judge was getting bored with this, "Mr. Prosecutor, I believe we all know who the defendant is. Please proceed."

Two points for the judge. I applauded in my head.

"My apologies, Your Honor." The DA nodded in the judge's direction and then turned to face Becky again. "I am going to ask you some questions regarding the morning of March thirtieth of this year. Do you remember that day?"

She looked very serious and concerned. "Yes, sir. That was the morning that Emil Abel was murdered."

Mark stood up. "Objection, your honor. It has not been established that Mr. Abel was murdered."

Samantha addressed Mark, "Mr. Peterson, this is the crime your client has been charged with, can we dispense with the bull?"

"Yes, Your Honor." He sat down.

I whispered, "Nice job alienating the judge." I scowled at him.

The judge addressed the DA. "Please continue, Mr. Prosecutor."

He didn't need any encouragement. "Ms. Fisher, can you tell the court what you were doing on that day between six and eight that morning?"

"Yes, sir. I work at the CrawGator, the restaurant located at the marina in Venice. I'm a waitress, and I was helping a co-worker open the restaurant. The restaurant has windows all along the dining room wall, so it's easy to see outside. Around seven, I saw Miranda, er, the defendant," . . . she was so proud of herself for getting the word right . . . "walk up the dock toward the shrimp boats that were docked at the marina." She was such a liar. She was going to tell them the same story about me that she told me about Sabine.

"Did you see her board any of the boats?" he asked.

"Well, not exactly. We don't have that angle from the CrawGator, but I had seen her walk up the dock in the week prior, and the only boat I had seen her board was the *Fergie*. Sabine named all her boats after female singers. I thought that was silly—"

The judge interrupted. "Please stay on task, Ms. Fisher. What you think of Ms. Marquette's cousin's boat-naming habits is not relevant to this case." The gallery chuckled, and Samantha glared at them.

"Yes, Your Honor." She giggled nervously and flipped her dirty hair back over her shoulders. "About ten minutes later, I saw her coming down the dock, and then she headed back to Sabine's shack." She cleared her throat. "I mean house, which was across the street from the marina."

The DA attempted to get back the control he was quickly losing, "Ms. Fisher, did you see anyone else come or go from the dock that morning?"

"No, sir." She shook her head.

He then passed her off to Mark with a flip of his wrist. "Your witness."

Mark strolled up to the witness stand like he was going to have a conversation with his best friend. "Hey, Becky. How are you?"

She smiled. "Fine, and you?"

"Pretty good. Thanks for asking." He returned her smile with an even wider one. "I'm just going to ask you a few questions, is that okay?"

"Sure." She seemed a bit caught off guard by his friendliness.

"Is it okay if I call you Becky? You can call me Mark," he offered. Mark was a genius—breaking her guard down, and then going in for the kill.

"Okay, Mark." She gave a little giggle.

"Let's talk about Miranda. You saw her yesterday, right? Do you remember what she was wearing?" That was a strange question to ask, but I gave him the benefit of the doubt.

"Of course," she answered. "She was wearing jeans with a light blue top and white sandals."

"And how about the last time you saw her in the restaurant?" Mark asked.

"White shorts and a yellow blouse." I was surprised. Even I didn't remember what I wore that day. "I was going to ask her where she got the blouse, but I forgot to."

He smiled in acknowledgement of her response. "And when was that?"

"Oh . . ." She scrunched her face for a moment. "At least a month ago."

"And what was she wearing the day Emil was killed?" I caught on to his plan.

She hesitated. "I don't remember."

Mark swooped in quickly. "So, you are testifying that you remember what Miranda was wearing on those other two occasions, but not the day Emil was killed?"

"Yes," she said, beginning to squirm.

Mark went in a different direction. "Do you know a Buck Walters?" She leaned back in her seat and glared at him. He added, "Remember, you are still under oath."

She leaned toward the microphone again. "Well, yes," she said slowly. "He used to come into the restaurant after work because he worked on the shrimp boats."

He continued in a light conversational tone. "How would you characterize your relationship with Mr. Walters?"

Her lips pinched, and I did a mental fist pump. I'd have high fived Mark too if he were within reach, and we weren't in a court of law. "Um, I'm not sure what you mean."

"Do you have a personal relationship with Mr. Walters?" Mark tried again.

"He was always nice to me when I've waited on him." She was on the defense now.

He paused for effect. "Have you ever spoken with him on the phone?"

The prosecutor stood up. "Objection! How could this possibly be relevant to this case?"

Samantha clearly thought it was. "I'll allow it. Please answer the question, Ms. Fisher, and if you are found to have lied on the stand, you can go to jail for perjury."

"Yes." Obviously, the prosecutor coached her not to expound on answers if she didn't have to, especially if it was damaging.

Mark didn't let it go. "Would you consider him a friend?"

She was noticeably flustered, as evidenced by her reddening face.

Becky finally responded. "Yes, well, no, not exactly. An acquaintance, I guess."

Mark approached the bench. "Your Honor, I would like to submit Exhibit A, Rebecca Fisher's cellular phone records into evidence." He provided a copy to the judge and the DA.

Mark referred to the phone records in his hand. "Rebecca." Suddenly he was more formal because the gloves were off. "According to the information I have here, you have made or received over twenty calls to Mr. Walters over the past three weeks. Can you explain that? I remind you that you are still under oath."

She hesitated, looking at the DA for help.

The judge said, "Ms. Fisher, please answer the question."

Becky chose her words carefully. "Well, okay, I guess we were friends."

Mark continued with his cross-examination. "Did you see Mr. Walters the morning that Emil was killed?"

She sat, staring. It was like she was mesmerized, or maybe she thought that if she sat really still and didn't talk, she'd be okay. Samantha had other ideas. "Rebecca?"

Becky looked at the judge and opened her mouth, but nothing came out. Then she put her face in her hands and started sobbing uncontrollably. The prosecutor finally spoke up, "Your Honor, I'd like to ask for a brief recess while the witness regains her composure."

No, don't fall for it, Samantha. I tried to project my thoughts to the judge. He'll be able to advise her on how to respond. It's is the oldest trick in the book.

As if she had heard me, she responded, "I'm sure Ms. Fisher will regain her composure soon." She smiled at Becky. "Right, Rebecca? If it would help, why don't you talk to me instead of mean Mr. Peterson." That got a chuckle from the gallery. She didn't even glare at them this time.

It didn't take long for Becky to get cried out after that comment. The bailiff handed her some tissues, and she rubbed her red eyes, blew her nose, and was back in business. "Buck came down that morning to talk to Emil. He had come down to the CrawGator a couple of weeks earlier. I hadn't seen him for a while. He told me he had been let go and wanted to talk to Emil to see if he could get his job back. He also asked me some questions about Emil and whether I had ever seen him take any of the boats out after they returned with their catch for the day."

She hesitated, wiping her face and blowing her nose again.

Mark resumed his kinder persona. "Please go on, Becky."

She continued, "The more questions he asked me, the more I realized that he suspected Emil of selling shrimp for his personal gain. The more we talked, the more I realized that this could be a money-making opportunity."

The look on Becky's face was muddled. It was as if she couldn't decide what to say next. She realized, though, that she was in trouble. "So, I convinced Buck that we should kind of, well, partner with Emil and get a cut of his proceeds."

Mark said quietly, "Sort of like blackmail."

Becky raised her voice. "No! I had a lot of friends up-river, and I figured I could find more customers for him."

Mark nodded. "I see. So, what happened next?"

Becky lowered her voice and continued. "Anyway, Buck asked me if I would help him talk to Emil. Buck isn't very good with words, so I said I would. I guess that wasn't a great idea when I think back on it."

"Go on," Mark encouraged her.

Becky gulped and continued. "So, I met Buck in the parking lot. He told me that he broke into the lawyer's—oops—I mean your car and borrowed the gun." My face felt hot, and I didn't want to look at the judge, but I did. She was feverishly taking notes, which didn't seem like a good sign, but she didn't stop the proceedings. I had a bad feeling this would come up later.

Becky was on a roll now. "I got mad and started yelling at him. I couldn't understand why he would need a gun just to talk to Emil. He said that it was for self-defense, just in case. I made him give me the gun. Buck had a bad temper, and I didn't want him just goin' off and shooting somebody."

You could hear a pin drop in the courtroom as she took another pause for breath. I was delighted, but the DA was turning a shade of red that even a ripe tomato couldn't match. His assistant looked mortified and was scrambling around, no doubt looking for her boss's blood pressure medication.

Becky went on. "So, we went up to Emil's navigation room. He was sittin' there at this desk looking really sad or mad or something. I started to talk to him about what we knew about him and our proposal."

I frowned. Becky's story was a bit different than the one Buck blurted out when I was his hostage. I wasn't sure what the truth was, but at this point, I wasn't sure it mattered. Someone other than me was taking the fall for this.

She seemed mesmerized by the judge's lack of reaction and Mark's soothing voice, so she kept going. "After I talked for a minute or two, he got furious and started screaming about how we would never get his money and that he would kill us first. Then he started yelling at Buck, saying he never trusted him and always knew he would end up a 'nothing.' Then he stood up, and I was afraid he'd hurt someone." Becky closed her eyes as if she was trying to picture it. "I pulled the gun out of my pocket, but he didn't seem to see it. He rushed at Buck, so I panicked and shot him in the back of the head," she said very matter-of-factly. I shivered with her lack of remorse.

Samantha kept her cool. "Is there anything else you'd like to tell me, Rebecca?"

"Well, we both got really scared after that and left him there. Buck put the gun back in his car." She shot a nervous glance at Mark as she said it. "And then I went back to work. Miranda found Emil later when she went to meet with him."

Samantha addressed Mark, "Mr. Peterson, do you have my further questions?"

He sat down next to me. "No, your honor."

I tried to hold the serious look on my face, but I couldn't help myself. I beamed at the prosecution table.

Samantha glanced at Becky, who looked shell-shocked. "Well, Rebecca, it appears that this case has taken an odd turn. But your confession on the stand allows the state of Louisiana to place you in immediate custody for the murder of Emil Abel." She motioned to the uniformed officer standing on her right. "Bailiff, please remove this witness from the courtroom. Arraignment will take place tomorrow, same time, same place."

She turned to the DA. "Bill, she confessed in a court of law under oath, do you think you can make this one stick? You know what they say about throwing enough crap at the wall. . ." He looked mortified and mumbled something under his breath. Finally, she turned to me. "Miranda, you have been nothing but cooperative and pleasant to deal with through this process. I am thankful and proud that the justice system occasionally works fairly and equitably. But while I have you, can I give you a piece of unsolicited advice?"

I nodded, still stunned and relieved at the recent revelation. "Yes, Your Honor."

"It is my understanding that, until recently, you have been estranged from your extended family for many years." I nodded. "You are blessed to have a family who cares about you, and I would strongly recommend that you hold them as close as you can. Life is short, and there are only so many years to share with the ones you love and those who love you. Will you promise to do that for you and for me?"

Part of me bristled and I wanted to respond to her imposition into my personal life with a caustic remark, but then, she had just announced my freedom. I nodded, "Yes, Your Honor."

"Case dismissed." She smacked her gavel on the desk, smiled broadly at me and winked. As she headed back to chambers, she motioned for Mark to follow her. I had a feeling this might have to do with the unlocked gun in his car, but I couldn't think about that right now.

The gallery erupted with applause. My mom and Sabine hugged one other then rushed forward to congratulate me. Sabine whispered, "I'm going to take the judge's advice too."

Mom cried as she reached out to both of us. "Me too, Honey. Me too."

I was surprised when my brother Michael came over and gave me a rib-crushing hug. When I finally managed to peel myself out of his grip, he asked, "Do you have a guest room out there in California?"

I laughed with joy. "When can I expect you?"

"I've got some time off coming." He held me at arm's length. "How about the last week of June?"

I was shocked that he came up with a date so soon. I figured it was going to be one of those, "Yeah, we should get together sometime," exchanges that we had had on the phone over the years. I pulled out my phone and put it on my calendar. "It's a date." We hugged again.

After my parents and Michael left, Sabine and I walked down to the front of the courtroom, where Mark was packing up his stuff.

"I know that Mark is going to try to take credit, but we know who did all the work." Sabine laughed and poked me in the ribs to let me know she was teasing.

He stood with his hands on his hips, "Did you witness that cross-examination? Becky folded under my relentless interrogation."

Sabine smiled. "Okay. You weren't bad, either." She kissed him and ran her fingers through his hair. She whispered to him, just loud enough for me to hear, "We'll talk about this later," and gave him a sweet smile. She sauntered back to me and whispered in my ear, "I think maybe he's a keeper this time."

Both Becky and Buck pleaded guilty to reduced charges: Becky to second-degree manslaughter, and Buck as an accomplice. They would both be spending some time in prison.

The judge called Mark into her chambers to register her deep concern regarding the fact that his weapon had not been secured in his vehicle. In a noble gesture, he took sole responsibility and assured her that it would not happen again. When he told me that, I was tempted to give him the kiss I've been dying to plant on him since I arrived, but I gave him a platonic hug in respect for Sabine.

After all was said and done, I hung around Venice and Meraux for a few weeks. It was nice being able to spend some time with Sabine, Mom, and Tom without a trial hanging over our heads. Even Michael was coming around more often, and he had already solidified his travel plans for June. I had travel plans of my own to make. Sabine contacted her parents for me and eased them into the idea of me coming to France to visit my 'new' family. I was surprised to find that they were excited to see me, even my aunt was very gracious and open.

Things were a bit better than average. The sale of Sabine's company finalized six weeks after my trial, and she started muddling over what to do next. She and Mark were seeing a lot of one another, and I was hopeful an engagement might be announced soon.

I was getting ready to leave town when I got a call from Ronnie, saying that he wanted to get together and chat. I hadn't seen or heard from him since he made the 911 call on that fateful day when Buck held me hostage.

I was glad that he called because I had wanted to and thank him for everything he had done for me and for introducing me to Amy. She had made quite an impression on me.

True to form, he was sitting in his tiny office on the dock when I arrived. He smiled when I opened his office door and immediately came to the other side of the counter and hugged me.

"Let's go for a walk." He looked me straight in the eye and sounded like he had something on his mind.

As we walked out on the dock, I was overwhelmed by how great it felt to be free. The sounds and smells of the bayou were like nowhere else on earth. The scent of the muddy water of the Mississippi blending with the saltwater from the Gulf always

229

reminded me of the good times I had as a child before my parents divorced, and my world came crashing down.

I watched a white heron swoop down and scoop up an unsuspecting fish as Ronnie said, "I had to talk to you before you left town. There's something that's been bothering me, and if I don't get it off my chest, I'll probably never tell you after you head back to California."

He hesitated as if he was still deciding whether this conversation was a good idea. I could hardly contain my curiosity, but I thought it best to stay quiet for a little while longer.

He finally continued, "I haven't been candid with you." He took a deep breath and then blurted out. "I killed Emil."

I looked at him like he was from Mars. "No, you didn't! Becky and Buck confessed and are awaiting sentencing."

He nodded, "Yes, that's true, they shot him, but I was behind it."

I stood with my mouth open. How could this kind and gentle man be responsible for everything I went through?

He explained. "I knew that Emil had ALS. However, he had never told me about the accident, and I didn't meet Amy until after I fired him. That's when he told me the whole story, and I thought it was important to meet Amy, especially since she would soon be all alone. After Emil took me to meet her once, I was hooked. First, I just enjoyed her company, but it wasn't long before we fell in love. It was heartbreaking because the conditions in the nursing home were horrible. I would have loved to help her, but I didn't have the kind of money that it would take to get her into a better facility, and I knew I would never be able to take care of her by myself."

At least that part of his story was believable. "I see." I was not happy that he lied to me, but I was willing to listen.

He paced back and forth at the end of the dock. "The whole thing was a catch-twenty-two. Emil was dying and soon wouldn't be able to take care of himself. I knew he was getting increasingly depressed and had nothing in life ahead of him except for a slow, painful death. Then one day, it hit me. He had told Amy about his life insurance policy, and frankly, that wasn't doing either of them any good while he was alive."

He rubbed his eyes as if he hadn't slept in a while. "Buck came to me looking for a job and told me the whole story about how Emil had fired him for no reason. I didn't get the impression that Buck was very stable, so he seemed like a good candidate to do the deed. A couple of weeks after we first spoke, I called him back and made him a proposition to kill Emil, make it look like self-defense, and I would pay him fifty thousand dollars. At that time, I didn't expect him to involve anyone else."

He chuckled. "But after he told Becky everything, she called me and wanted to get together. They both came, but Becky did all the talking. She let me know that she knew all about this plan, and if I didn't cut her in, she would call the police and turn me in. She demanded an equal cut of fifty-thousand, and she and Buck would do it together. I had half a mind to drop the whole thing, but I couldn't stand seeing Amy in that place one more day, so I agreed."

He ran his fingers through what hair he had left. "I guess the only smart thing I did was to pay them ten thousand apiece up-front, with the rest to be paid after the deed was done and after they took the rap for it. I knew they probably would be able to get the charge reduced since there were extenuating circumstances. I was right. They'll be in prison soon, but they won't be in very long, and when they get out, they'll get the rest of their money."

I was stunned by his duplicity. On the other hand, his heart seemed to be in the right place. "How could you have been so sure that Becky and Buck wouldn't rat you out once they were in custody?"

He laughed the rough laugh of a lifetime smoker. "I've been around long enough to know that greed is an amazing thing. They would have lost forty thousand dollars apiece if they turned me in. That's more money than either of them could ever hope to have in one place at one time otherwise."

We sat on a bench on the end of the dock and were quiet for a while. I punched him on the arm. "You lied to me." I tried to frown but couldn't help but laugh.

He smiled, "But you forgive me, don't you?"

I stared out at the river, thinking about it for several minutes. What he did was wrong. Really wrong. On the other hand, he thought he was helping two people he loved. One, Emil, to stop his suffering, and the other, Amy, to improve her life. The two greedy fools in jail would be paid another eighty grand for their time and trouble. I turned to face him. "Yeah, I forgive you. Now just do me a favor and never mention to anyone that we had this conversation." We hugged, and I ambled back to my motorcycle. I yelled, "See you around," and waved as I accelerated the BMW out of the parking lot.

My conversation with Ronnie was a few days before I flew home to LAX and took a limo back to Malibu. It was great to be home; it took a few long bouts in my hot tub to feel normal again.

I enjoyed having Heather there to talk to at the end of a workday, and she was delightful company. Though I did find myself having to follow after her to pick things up and put them in their proper places.

THE END

Acknowledgements

First and foremost, to my loving and beautiful wife Susan. To a large degree, writing can be a solitary activity, but you have always made yourself available to assist in editing or giving me feedback on the story line and just giving me your honest opinion on my writing. The truth be known, I was not a good enough writer to be published when I first started out, but you let me figure that for myself rather than dampening my spirit. Probably had you really given me the tough reality, I would have quit after the first book and never gotten here. I thank you and Love You for that and for all you do and the amazing woman you are.

To Mark Malatesta, you were instrumental in helping me craft a query letter and develop an overall strategy for getting an agent. And even though are you are no longer contractually bound to me, you have continued to support me for years beyond your original commitment.

To Donna Pudick at Parkeast Literary Agency, I am very thankful that you are my agent. I also appreciate that while my initial manuscript need work, that you allowed me to rewrite to the point that it was marketable.

To Mercedes Rothwell, thank you for the editorial work you provided in order to get Relocation into marketable form.

To Mary Custureri and Veronica H. Hart at Taylor and Seale, while we have not had a chance to work together long, I appreciate that you were willing to take me on as a first-time author and hopefully for many books to come.

If you have enjoyed reading this book, please help make an author happy and write a review on Amazon or Goodreads. We appreciate our readers and hope you will feel free to contact us with any thoughts or comments on this or any of our other books.

Taylor and Seale Publishing, LLC

Made in the USA
Coppell, TX
23 January 2020

14919527R10134